AF612169

"SNAFU – Every one of them delivers the goods."
—Tim Miller, director of Deadpool.

"... a great taste of what military horror can achieve."
—Horrortalk.com (SNAFU: Heroes)

"... every single story holds its own and it's damn difficult to pick a standout as they all leave a mark."
—Horrortalk.com (SNAFU 1)

"... Geoff Brown and Amanda J. Spedding deserve immense credit for both the consistent quality and extraordinary variety..."
—This Is Horror (UK) (SNAFU 1)

"... these are books to watch out for, to purchase, and to enjoy thoroughly."
—Hellnotes

"... an entertaining collection of stories... SNAFU-An Anthology of Military Horror is one of the best picks available."
—Albedo 1

Publisher's Note:

This book is a collection of stories from writers all over the world.

For authenticity and voice, we have kept the style of English native to each author's location, so some stories will be in UK English, and others in US English.

We have, however, changed dashes and dialogue marks to our standard format for ease of understanding.

* * *

This book is a work of fiction.

All people, places, events and aliens are purely the product of each author's imagination.

Any resemblance to persons or demons, living or dead, is purely coincidental.

Also From Cohesion Press

SNAFU: An Anthology of Military Horror
– eds Geoff Brown & Amanda J Spedding
SNAFU: Wolves at the Door
– eds Geoff Brown & Amanda J Spedding
SNAFU: Survival of the Fittest
– eds Geoff Brown & Amanda J Spedding
SNAFU: Hunters
– eds Amanda J Spedding & Geoff Brown
SNAFU: Unnatural Selection
– eds Amanda J Spedding & Geoff Brown
SNAFU: Black Ops
– eds Amanda J Spedding, Matthew Summers & Geoff Brown
SNAFU: Resurrection
– eds Amanda J Spedding, Matthew Summers & Geoff Brown
SNAFU: Last Stand
– eds Amanda J Spedding, Matthew Summers & Geoff Brown
SNAFU: Medivac (A Charity Anthology)
– eds Amanda J Spedding & Geoff Brown

COMING 2022
SNAFU: Holy War
– eds Amanda J Spedding & Geoff Brown

Edited by Amanda J Spedding & Geoff Brown

Mayday Hills Asylum
Beechworth , Australia

SNAFU: Future Warfare
Amanda J Spedding & Geoff Brown (eds)

2022 PRINT REISSUE

Anthology © Cohesion Press 2017/22
Stories © Individual Authors 2016
Cover Art by Dean Samed/Neostock 2016
Internal Layout by Geoff Brown

Set in Palatino Linotype
All rights reserved.
No part of this publication may be reproduced, stored in a retrieval system or transmitted in any form by any means without the prior permission of the copyright owner.
Enquiries should be made to the publisher.

Mayday Hills Asylum
Beechworth, Australia
www.cohesionpress.com

Contents

SUITS

Steve Lewis

Graves Farmstead, Tau Ceti IV

It was dark, about midnight, when something woke Henry Graves. He sat upright in his bed and looked around, hearing nothing but the gentle breathing of his wife, Beth. He contemplated getting out of bed to check the security grid in the next room... A few seconds later he had no choice; an alarm screeched out and woke everything within a mile.

He was out of bed and into the farmstead's security room in a heartbeat, the monitors flicking to life in response to whatever threats the remote ground and satellite sensors had picked up. He was hoping it was just cattle from his neighbour's property – Jenkins was renowned for being cheap with his fencing – but by the slowing spreading blooms of light on the screens it was clear this was something much worse.

"Hank, what is it?" Beth asked as she entered the room. "Jenkin's cows again?"

"Afraid not, honey," Graves replied. "Looks we have deebees coming in."

"Crap."

"Crap indeed, honey, crap indeed."

Tau Ceti IV had taken decades to colonise, and it was a few years after the planet had been successfully terraformed that the aliens had shown up. Coming through dimensional gateways on and just above the planet's surface, the 'Dimensionial Beings' – or deebees for short – had initially wreaked havoc amongst the unsuspecting colonists. If it wasn't for an armed cruiser passing through for R&R, with heavy screens, armoured hull and batteries of hot lasers, the planet would have been overrun.

The invasion was finally broken, the gateways closing

quickly and the deebees slaughtered with no line of retreat… now it was only a raid every few years, more a nuisance than anything else.

"Looks like a wide pattern," Beth said, looking over Graves' shoulder at the various screens. "Gates opening up all along the ridge and across most of the farmsteads."

Graves nodded. "They should be easy to mop up, scattered out like that," he said. "I'll go suit up, you get on the horn to Jenkins and the others, make sure they're up and armoured before the gates open completely."

He stood and kissed his wife on the forehead as she slid into the seat.

"Looks like we have about 30 minutes before they open enough to let them through, everyone should be ready and mobile by then," he said.

"Get suited while I make some calls," Beth replied. "Let me know if you need anything."

* * *

Graves's suit was built around the chassis of an old, four-armed agricultural exoskeleton. With an upgraded power plant, some welded armour and batteries of weapons added each year, *Brutiful* was a family heirloom passed down over the generations. Every farmstead had to have one, and the Graves' family took much pride in the effort they'd taken to maintain their deadly, hulking suit.

As *Brutiful* powered up, Graves got into his combat suit – a second-hand, naval-grade skin-suit, it provided a degree of life support, body armour and communications gear that made piloting the heavy exomech far less uncomfortable than it might otherwise have been. Plugged in and zipped up, he checked the ammunition drums and ran last minute diagnostics tests before strapping himself into the suit's cockpit.

"Beth, I'm in," he said as the heavy armoured glass canopy closed around him. "Systems green across the board, heading out now."

"You're showing green across the board here too, honey," Beth replied, coming through clearly over the suit radio. "Jenkins and the others are all suiting up, should be out before the gates open."

"Roger that," Graves said. "Anyone coordinating this?"

"Afraid not. All of them are interested in defending their own property first, and we'll coordinate a clean-up once the gates close and we can see what's left."

"Fair enough... shouldn't take us long, the gates being spread out like they are."

"And we don't want Jenkins trampling down our fences like he did last time he came over to help." They both laughed, though they hadn't been laughing at the weeks they'd had to spend repairing the downed fence-line and retrieve their roaming livestock.

"Where do you want me, honey?' Graves asked as *Brutiful* got underway and stomped out of the barn and into the night.

"It looks like a cluster of gates will open in the eastern quarter first, counting seven gates. After that, the next opening cluster is another five in the south."

"Eastern quarter it is, on my way."

* * *

Graves made good time, the heavy exomech eating up the miles at a rapid pace. With no threat, he set the autopilot and then cycled through his weapon and targeting systems to make sure everything was running smoothly – the diagnostics had indicated everything was green, but he'd long learned the value in checking everything twice, just in case.

By the time he got to the farmstead's eastern fields, some 15 miles away, the gates were beginning to sparkle, the bright inner light of an alien dimension shining through. It was a rare sight, but not one that Graves was overly interested in admiring. Like a lot of things in nature, beautiful also meant dangerous.

He halted his exomech where he could see all seven of the

gates – they were closely bunched – and swung the heavy chain-guns on his right shoulder down, ready for action. The 15mm multi-barrelled autocannons weren't his heaviest weapons, but they were dependable, hard hitting, and could deal with most deebees.

Besides, 15mm ammunition was cheap, and anything he fired came out of the farmstead's operating budget.

"Hank, honey," Beth said," I make the gates opening in three… two… one… now!"

On her mark, a swarm of deebees poured out of each gate, scattering around as they cleared the gate for the aliens following behind, and searching for a target. *Brutiful's* infra-red scanners picked them out in the darkness and automatically counted them. It had reached 80 by the time the gates' sparkle began to fade, and Graves decided he should open fire before they dispersed too much.

With a whir, the autocannon barrels began to spin, and as they reached their maximum rotation, he fired. Over 600 rounds per minute poured out of the 5-barrelled weapon, cutting into the creatures around the nearest gate.

The 15mm rounds were mostly copper-tipped hollow points, with every 5th round a steel-tipped armour-penetrating round, and every 20th round a tracer round that marked its flight in a glowing red arc – at 1,500 metres per second, they streaked across the landscape, lighting the night sky and easily punching through alien hide, flesh and bone.

His first burst cut down the group around the first gate, then he switched to the second. The deebees had reacted now and were spreading out as they charged towards him. He fired the autocannon in short bursts of 25-30 rounds, taking down the leading aliens as they closed, confident he could whittle them down enough before they got to him.

"Hank?" Beth asked. "Got time for an update?"

"Sure, honey," he replied, "but keep it brief, I got incoming."

"Okay. Jenkins, Anderson and Wright have deployed and engaged, they're all dealing with their own first clusters…Peters,

Donaldson and the Singhs are en route, but their gates are all over the place and they might need a hand with clean-up once we've got the main clusters dealt with."

"Okay," Graves said as he triggered off another burst that dropped a clump of half-dozen aliens as they cleared a fence-line 500 metres in front of him. "You sound like you're coordinating with the other wives. "

"I am," Beth replied. "We're trying to keep each other updated on the back channels, just in case there's a breakthrough somewhere."

"Good." Another burst, another clump falling apart under the autocannon fire. "I'm almost done with this group, moving south soon."

"Roger. Be careful, honey, the next group are bigger gates and they'll likely be fully deployed before you get there."

"Will do!" He triggered his last burst, splashing the last of the deebees across his eastern paddock and then turned the exomech south to deal with the next group.

The eastern paddocks were fallow this season, and if nothing else the alien corpses would make good fertiliser when he got around to ploughing them into the soil.

* * *

Wright Farmstead, Tau Ceti IV

Jake Wright hated his exomech and was pretty sure it hated him. *Carnigore* sounded ferocious, but the 'carni' wasn't named after a predator's eating habits – the suit was a built on a mobile amusement park ride, and the old red and white paint job made it look far more 'carnival' than he would have liked.

If maintaining the suit in its original condition hadn't been part of his old man's will, he'd have had it redone and renamed a decade ago.

"Jake," his wife said as he fired his own autocannon into the creatures moving towards him, "you need to get the lead out, that second cluster of gates is opening."

"Helen, I'm doing this as fast as I can," he said, gritting his teeth as he fired another burst. *Carnigore* wasn't a well-padded suit and he swore he felt every jolt of recoil through his bones. "Last group coming up now, I'll head to that second cluster in a moment."

"I hate to nag" she replied, though Jake didn't believe that for an instant, "but Graves and Jenkins have cleared their first gates and are already on route to their second."

"For Christ's sake, Helen, it's not a contest!"

"It never is with you Jake, it never is..."

Wright flicked the mute button on his communication piece and cursed, long and loud, as the last of the deebees died in front of him. He swung *Carnigore* south and headed towards the river, where the second cluster of gates was already opening. He threw in a few curses towards his exomech for good measure, bracing himself for every bump and jolt the insanely grinning suit was going to pass on to him.

* * *

Anderson Farmstead, Tau Ceti IV

'Crazy Bill' Anderson was the old man of the colony, a silver-haired widower in his 70s. He'd built his suit himself, turning an obsolete agricultural exomech into a formidable fighting machine. It was a blocky, hulking brute that lacked the sleek lines of newer suits, but he and his *Grampage* had weathered decade after decade of deebee raids without showing any signs of slowing down.

He'd dealt with the first cluster of gates easily enough and was perched on a low hill overlooking the slowing blooming forms of his second cluster. The three gates were very tightly bunched, much tighter than he'd ever seen before, and he waited patiently as they grew. Close-packed like that, the deebees would run out into a withering hail of fire, and he certainly had no problem with that.

Still, the sight bugged him. Gates were always spaced apart, likely to stop them interfering with each other. The energy required to cross the dimensional barrier was stupendous, even if the colonists didn't have a clue as to how it all worked. Anything might happen if the gates actually overlapped.

* * *

Graves Farmstead, Tau Ceti IV

"Hank, we have a problem."

"Talk to me Beth."

"The wormholes on the ridges, they're getting stronger."

"How strong?"

"Off-the-chart strong. The satellite view shows them growing every minute."

Brutiful was nearing the second cluster of gates, and in the distance Graves could see them spiralling closed. Whatever deebees had been using the gates had already been dropped off and were spreading out across his property.

"Keep an eye on them, honey, while I deal with this second group, and then I'll go take a look," he said. "And keep the others in the loop; I don't want any surprises coming our way when we get around to mopping up."

"Roger that," Beth replied. "I've got one of the crop-duster drones headed that way, should give us some eyes on the ridge in about ten minutes."

There was a sharp 'ping' as *Brutiful's* sensors picked up something moving his way – fast – and Graves zoomed his suit's cameras towards the motion.

A dozen deebees were headed right for him, and they were close.

"Okay Beth, I have some unwanted guests heading my way, need to focus a little," he said. "I'll let you know when I'm done here, but let me know if anything super-important happens."

"Will do, honey," Beth said. "Be careful."

The deebees swarming towards *Brutiful* were closing from a wide arc, too far spread for his autocannon to sweep them all.

He fired a few bursts at those on his right side anyway though, dropping three of them while he got himself ready.

His left-shoulder weapon was a heavy-barrelled, semi-automatic shotgun, if you could call a weapon with a 4″ bore a shotgun. Twin ammunition belts fed the beast, allowing Graves to fire either fin-stabilised slugs or heavy loads of 8-ounce buckshot. He thumbed the selector for buckshot and put away the autocannon as the aliens closed.

It always disturbed Graves that the deebees looked nothing alike. They were mostly four legged, or six, or occasionally eight; their heads were usually long-snouted, like dogs, though many were round-faced like great cats or sharp-beaked like birds; and their skin was typically thick hide, though many had feathers like soft down, or slabs of chitin that provided some slight armour protection. Some of them had combinations of all of these things, and Graves had long given up wondering how and why the deebees had evolved the way they had.

One thing they all did have in common though was a serious hatred of humans, and every deebee they'd ever seen wanted to do nothing but kill anything human within its reach.

Brutiful's shotgun aligned briefly on a deebee closing fast on the left, and coughed a swarm of tungsten balls…the creature was fast, dodging aside as the weapon spoke, but the spreading cloud of balls covered too large an area. Struck by three balls the creature went down, chest and head ruptured completely, the deebee's equivalent of blood gushing into the dirt.

The creatures continued to close, and Graves backed his exomech away slowly, sending out a cloud of tungsten every six seconds or so – it took that long for the belt to feed the next round, chamber it and align the heavy barrel onto the target. At a kill every six seconds, that was ten dead deebees a minute, but it was going to take them a bit less than that to get to him, and there were more than ten of them out there.

The first of the deebees launched itself at him, a four-legged beast that shimmered with the residual energy of the alien dimension. Its mouth opened wide, showing row after row of gleaming, serrated teeth, and Graves swung his suit's right arm to block it. More by luck than design, he managed to catch it in mid-air, and squeezed the creature as hard as his exomech could.

Trapped in the metal grip, the creature swung its hind legs down and began to rake, long claws gouging chunks of armour of *Brutiful's* thick torso. For a moment Graves thought the creature might get through, but then the suit's grip tightened and the creature exploded into a multi-coloured burst of flesh.

He didn't even see the other one coming. It was big, strong, and travelling at speed, and barrelled the heavy suit over like a man pushing over a child. *Brutiful's* gyro-stabilises shrieked in protest as they tried to correct the unexpected fall, but to no avail. With a loud thud, the exomech went down, the fall stunning Graves for a moment.

When he came to, the creature was on top of him, clawing and biting away at the glass canopy, only a foot or so from his face. The heavy glass was holding for now, but wouldn't for long...Graves needed to end this one quickly and get *Brutiful* back on its feet.

The creature was inside his reach, so his two heavy weapons would be useless. I Instead, he activated the cutting torch on the exomech's smaller right arm. With variable settings for welding or cutting through thick steel, the torch was a legacy of the suit's original purpose, and one he'd never gotten around to replacing.

Pushing the flame against the creatures hide brought a shriek of pain, which did nothing to reduce the creatures frenzied clawing on the glass canopy; in fact, it only seemed to make it worse. He couldn't quite bring the torch to bear on something that might prove vital, and he had to endure the creature's attacks for another 30 seconds before he finally managed to find something important. The creature gave one enormous spasm and then died.

Flicking off the torch, he pushed the creature off him and slowly struggled to rise. The exomech wasn't designed for agility, and it took him a good five minutes to finally get back on his feet. If there'd been any more aliens around, he'd have been dead for sure.

Sweating – the suit generated a lot of heat – he checked his scanners and toggled the radio.

"Honey?"

"Here Hank," Beth replied. "You okay?"

"Scratched up, a little bruised but otherwise okay. How's everything else look?"

"Honey, I think we might have a problem..."

* * *

Singh Farmstead, Tau Ceti IV

Unlike the other colonists that ran one small family unit per farmstead, the Singh family were a polygamous family collective that ran a farmstead twice the size of the others. Graves and the others figured there to be three distinct 'marriage arrangements' amongst the Singh farmstead, which gave them a requirement for three exomechs in accordance with the colony's laws.

Crescent Moon was piloted by Jaswant Singh, the elder of the family. Based on the chassis of an old construction suit, it was well suited for the slabs of thick armour and heavy weapons the Singh family had added to it over the years.

The other two suits were *Hawk* and *Eagle,* two much smaller exomechs based on warehousing droids. Fast and nimble, the two light units were built for close-quarters combat only, and spent most of their time keeping *Crescent Moon* clear of deebees so it could do all the long-range killing.

The three suits had cleared their first two clusters of gates, and were advancing on their third, *Hawk* and *Eagle* scouting ahead as *Crescent Moon* followed slowly along. Putting his suit on autopilot gave Jaswant time to update his tactical display from the various sensors around their property and from the satellite above. His update was showing some unusual activity, something he felt warranted caution.

"*Hawk, Eagle,*" he said into the radio, "hold on the next hill... something is amiss here."

"*Hawk* acknowledging," replied Agun, Jaswant's eldest son.

"Hill clear, covering left flank."

"*Eagle* acknowledges," replied Kubai, his daughter's husband. "Will clear the peak in fifteen seconds, will cover the right flank."

The two smaller suits took up covering positions atop the hill as *Crescent Moon* trundled slowly up behind them.

"There's nothing here, brother," Agun said. "Should we push on to the next hill?"

"No," Jaswant said. "I need to assess the situation before we get too far from home."

"The place is barren," Kubai replied. "There's nothing to assess."

"Exactly… but there should be."

Jaswant's exomech drew level with the smaller units and looked over the flat, ploughed field below. The next hill was a mile away, and beyond that was the next cluster of gates, which should be opening any minute.

"Our initial reading showed six gates opening beyond that next hill… readings now show only four."

"Fewer gates are a good thing, isn't it?" Kubai asked.

"Gates never just disappear," Jaswant replied. "They open then they close. These ones haven't opened, yet two are missing."

"I don't understand," Agun said.

"Neither do I," Jaswant said, "But now sensors are showing only two."

* * *

Graves Farmstead, Tau Ceti IV

"Hank, the gates on top of the ridge are disappearing," Beth said. "Not opening, just disappearing, a few every minute or so."

"Do we have a visual on the ridgeline yet?" Graves replied. "Something might be messing up the sensors."

"I'm sorry, honey, something knocked the drone out." Beth said. "I've powered up another three and having them fitted with cameras now, should be airborne in a few minutes."

"Good thinking, honey. Anything else to report?"

"A little. Jenkins is shutting down his gates, but taking his time about it, and Crazy Bill Anderson wants to know if anyone needs his help…he seems to still have gates open on his property though."

"Jenkins is just taking his time so he won't have to help clear the ridgeline," Graves said with a chuckle, "and Crazy Bill wants to be able to claim ammunition and fuel from the Colony account for helping others."

"Other than that, the Singhs look like they have their area under control, as always, and the others are mopping up as they advance towards the ridge. Oh, and the drones are on their way."

Moments later, *Brutiful's* sensors picked up the flight of crop-dusting drones as they sped towards the ridgeline. As they passed, Beth switched the video feed over directly to the suit and Graves toggled between the three camera views.

At first there was nothing but the well-ploughed fields he expected to see. As the drones moved beyond his property the vegetation grew wilder, mostly tall trees. As the passed over the first growth of forest beyond his fence line, one of the cameras went out.

"Beth, what was that?"

"No idea, honey," Beth replied. "I'll go back over the video feed and check."

The drones were approaching the ridgeline now, and Graves toggled the controls to make them move in a more erratic manner. Even as he did, a second camera went out.

"Honey!"

"Working on it, Hank, working on it!"

The remaining camera made it to the ridgeline, Graves piloting this one manually now to be as erratic as he could make it. The sight wasn't a good one.

The gates *were* disappearing, in a manner of speaking. As Graves watched, two gates slowly expanded until their edges touched, and then they merged into one larger gate. All along the ridgeline, gates were coalescing, and at the rate they were merging they'd be one giant gate before too long.

"Beth, drop whatever you're doing and take a look at this!" he said, urgently. "Take in as much of it as you can, just in case I lose this drone."

There was a moment's silence and Graves could hear Beth's breathing quicken over the radio.

"Oh. My. God!"

"Patch this through to the others, and make sure Crazy Bill and the Singhs acknowledge...if anyone knows what this is about, it'll be one of them."

"Will do, honey!"

"And Beth?"

"Yes, dear?"

"It might be a good time to start powering up the Bunker."

* * *

Wright Farmstead, Tau Ceti IV

Carnigore had taken some scratches dealing with the first two gate clusters, but nothing significant. Jake was sure he'd been knocked around more than his exomech, and could feel bruises already forming where his skin had come into contact with hard metal. Not for the first time, he made a promise to himself to get a better combat suit and to put some padding around the cockpit.

He was approaching his third gate cluster, *Carnigore* set on autopilot as he transferred chain-gun ammunition from the bins on the suit's lower back to the internal hoppers.

"Jake?"

"What do you want, Helen?" he asked, annoyed at the interruption. "I'm kinda busy here."

"You'll be busy dodging deebees if you don't pay attention," Helen replied. "I have some video feed from the Graves'."

"Are Hank and Beth in trouble?"

Jake punched the autopilot's 'Off' button, bringing *Carnigore* to a lurching halt. Jake had a lot of time for the Graves family, despite Graves setting some impossibly high standards for Jake to live up to. If the two of them needed his help, things were very bad.

"I think we all might be," Helen replied, some real concern in her voice now. "Patching some video through to you now."

Jake watched the video feed, recognising the ridgeline that marked the southernmost boundary of the colony area. Deebees often had gates up there, giving them time to spread out and consolidate their numbers, but this was looking weird.

There were only three gates now, each enormous and slowly growing. The middle and left gates touched and merged, and then there were only two. Minutes later, the remaining gate was absorbed, leaving one giant gate that covered the entire ridgeline.

"What the hell is that?" he asked.

"I don't know, Jake," Helen replied, "but I'm sure it's not good."

"Any word from the others?"

"Jenkins says he's got gates of his own to worry about, but he'll help out when he deals with those. The Singhs are finishing up their final cluster and are sending some drones to keep an eye on things until they can get over here, and Crazy Bill is on his way to the Graves' farmstead right now."

"He's cleared his clusters already?"

"No, but he thinks this is more important. He's sending his kids over to the Graves' place now, Beth has their bunker powered up and plenty of room."

"You might want to join them."

"I'll be fine," Helen said. "Besides, you need me here to keep an eye on things while you wander around in your giant clown suit."

Jake bit back a curse; his wife always knew how to needle him.

"Suit yourself," he said, after a moment's pause to regain some control. "But if things get out of hand I want you to out of there and on your way to somewhere safe."

"Why Jake Wright, that's the sweetest thing you've said to me in years!"

* * *

Graves Farmstead, Tau Ceti IV

Beth ran quickly from the farmhouse control room to the metal and concrete monstrosity standing in the yard behind the house. Affectionately known as 'The Bunker', it was built to military specifications as a fortified command and control facility, a legacy of Graves' grandparents who had the foresight to see that the war with the deebees would last generations.

With its own internal fission pile, water tanks and food supplies, it could easily house a headquarter staff for three months. Add the communication links and self-defence turrets, it was looking like a good place to be right now.

The screens inside had already powered up, showing clearly the video feed from the last remaining drone, plus *Brutiful's* cameras, satellite imagery and live feeds from the various security cameras around the farmstead. She hit the safety switch as she ran inside, dropping the armoured concrete slab that passed for a door into position, and slipped into her own combat suit and command helmet.

"Hank? You reading me, honey?"

"Loud and clear, Beth, loud and clear," Graves replied. "How's it looking?"

"Not good at all. That one giant gate is giving off some ferocious readings, completely off the charts for even the Bunker's sensors."

"I don't have much fine detail on the drone camera," Graves said. "Anything I need to know?"

"I'm getting plenty of flicker, all along the gate, looks like it's ready to open."

"I'm not feeling too particularly happy about this one, Beth—"

The gate opened, and deebees poured out. The overhead satellite tracked their heat sources, counting them automatically, and Beth watched open-mouthed as the counter climbed rapidly. 100. 200. 400. 700. 1000… she tore her eyes from it when it reached four figures.

"Beth?"

"Hank, honey? *Get the hell out of there!*"

She could see from *Brutiful's* video feed that it was now moving, walking backwards on autopilot. Graves was too good a pilot to just turn and run, he'd want to keep his guns between him and the enemy.

"Moving now," Graves said, quite calmly. "Where do you need me?"

"Anywhere but there, honey," Beth said. "The sensors are showing 3000 deebees and counting."

There was a moment of silence as that figure registered on Graves…the biggest raid in a generation had been less than 500, and that had stretched the colony to the limit. Many families died that day, and the colony still hadn't recovered.

"Beth, I need you to patch this through to the others, right now…we're going to need all of the exomechs together."

"All right, honey, I'm on it."

* * *

Jenkins farmstead, Tau Ceti IV

Keith Jenkins was having a bad day. He hated deebees with a passion…or rather, he hated that they made him have to do things he didn't want to do. He didn't want to be out of the farmhouse today, and certainly didn't want to be in his exomech having to fight.

The only saving grace was that *Shepherd,* once a medium-sized agricultural exomech, was refitted over the years to be big on comfort and big on speed, so he could wander around his farmstead and avoid fighting if he could. Any fool can fight, why be uncomfortable about it?

Shepherd's main armament was a long-ranged, three-barrelled autocannon, firing high-velocity 35mm slugs in three-round bursts. The long barrels severely affected the exomech's centre of gravity, so he had to stand still to fire, but the long range meant that he could deal with deebees from ranges well beyond anything his fellow farmsteaders could match.

Right now he was in a standing in a clump of trees on a hill, taking pot shots at a group of deebees milling around his second cluster of gates a mile and a half away. At this range accuracy wasn't great, but he was getting hits every third burst or so, and the deebees still hadn't worked out where the shots were coming from.

The crackling of his suit's video-comm interrupted as his wife, Jessie, came on-screen.

"Keith, I have an update from the Graves'," she said. "Things are going pear-shaped on the ridgeline, they need you to get down there right now."

"Tell them I'm busy, got problems of my own," he replied, firing another burst. He fist-pumped as he saw at least one of the heavy tungsten rounds strike one of the aliens, splashing it across the soil.

"I think they're serious, Keith," Jessie said. "Most of the others have acknowledged and are already on their way."

"They've dealt with all their clusters already?"

"Nope, leaving them as they are," Jessie replied. "That's what makes me think this is serious."

"Any word from Crazy Bill?"

"Oh, plenty of words from him…mostly to tell you what he's going to do to you if you don't get your arse into gear and join up with the others. Assuming you survive of course."

Jenkins sighed. Crazy Bill was just that. Crazy. And he hated to have to listen to him. Everything 'back then' was bigger, tougher and harder than it was now, and he traded on his age to influence the others. Since when was being old a substitute for being right?

"Tell them I'm engaged right now, will head over as soon as possible," he said. "I've got some suit trouble, don't think I can disengage safely, so I'll have to fight my way clear."

"You have suit trouble? I'm not seeing anything on *Shepherd's* feed."

"No, the suits fine… though they don't need to know that."

He fired another burst, missing completely.

"Keith," Jessie said with a sigh, "this looks serious. You might want to consider doing the right thing, just this once."

"You're right," he replied. "I'll consider it."

* * *

Peters Farmstead, Tau Ceti IV

Carl Peters hardly knew what hit him. He'd had three clusters of gates on his property, and had cleared them out with minimal bother. His exomech, *Hamfisted,* was a dependable suit with solid armour and reliable weapons, and the deebees hadn't posed much of a threat. The smallest of the farmsteads, squeezed between the southern ridgeline and the Toolong River, his clusters were relatively close, so it didn't take him much time to find and destroy the deebees coming out of his gates.

One minute the screens were clear, then suddenly there was a wall of deebees headed his way. *Hamfisted's* sensors counted what they saw, and Peters stood in shock for valuable seconds as the numbers registered, but it was too late for him to have done anything with those seconds.

He brought *Hamfisted's* chainguns down, firing bursts on his maximum rate of fire, carving swaths through the creatures as they closed. High-speed tungsten carved through alien bodies, but still they came.

So swift was the deebee assault that he didn't have time to get a shot off from any of his other weapons… the wall crashed over him, knocking *Hamfisted* to the ground, stunning him for a moment. Something in the swarm was strong enough to drive an armour-piercing claw all the way through his armoured glass canopy and into his chest, and he died without even a scream.

Or a chance to say goodbye to his wife, who watched the whole thing through *Hamfisted's* video feed.

* * *

Donaldson Farmstead, Tau Ceti IV

'Angry' Andy Donaldson was the second to die. His exomech, *Mariner*, was an old combat droid his grandfather had bought and refitted fifty years ago, heavily built with military-grade weapons, it was the family pride and joy.

It was also expensive, and building it and keeping it running had almost bankrupted the family. The other farmsteaders had long forgotten where he'd picked up his nickname, but they all assumed he was still angry at his grandfather for lumbering him with a white elephant of exomechs.

The Donaldson farmstead was also south, much bigger than the adjacent Peters' property, and he'd had two clusters to deal with. His primary weapon was a ridiculously expensive battle laser, firing 3" diameter beams that vaporised almost anything they struck. Designed to fight other heavily armoured units, it was a massive overkill against anything unarmoured, and Donaldson hated it.

The wave of deebees that swept over Peters now came for him, and he knew he'd never make it to anywhere safe. He planted himself on top of a low ridge, giving himself a good field of fire, readied his weapons and began firing.

His laser took time to recharge, and spat a beam of death every four seconds, with enough energy to punch right through the first deebee it struck and go on to the next. From his elevated position, a good shot could kill three or four of them before it dug into the ground. It was effective, but not against a swarm that size.

He wasn't going to make it, and he knew it… time to call his wife.

"Sarah, you there?"

"Yes, Andy, I'm here," Sarah replied.

"I need you to grab your things and get over the Graves' place, get yourself into their bunker."

"Okay," she said, "swing by and pick me up."

"Not this time, Sarah, not this time."

He knew she could see his video feed, could see the wide

wall of aliens bearing down on him rapidly, and knew that she knew how this was going to end.

"Andy?"

"Just go!"

"I can't just leave you…"

"Yes you can! Don't make me do this for nothing." He lowered his secondary weapons now, a 4" cannon firing high-explosive rounds, and began targeting tight clumps of aliens with it. He could hardly miss.

Sarah was crying openly now.

"Sarah… say goodbye now, while we still can, then get out."

"Andy… I love you."

"And I love you too." He had the luxury of the battle to keep his emotions in check, but it was all he could do to keep from crying himself.

"Goodbye, Sarah."

He cut the video feed, knowing that she'd stay there as long as she could while he was alive. He knew he was going to die, but wanted her to have as much time as possible to get to the Graves' bunker.

Both weapons were firing now, as fast as they could, and he cut the safety overrides on both to keep their rate up. He knew he was burning out his laser and would soon warp the cannon barrel, but didn't expect it to be a problem for much longer.

At 100 meters, the laser stopped firing, overheated.

At 50 meters, the warped cannon barrel caused a misfeed and jammed.

At 20 meters, he managed to get his close range weapons into action, a pair of 10mm machine guns and a small flame-thrower. The machine guns cut a handful down as they closed, but without the instant-kill of the bigger weapons, the ones he hit just provided mobile armour for the ones behind for a few seconds, which was all it took.

Something from his left struck *Mariner* and knocked him down, and then a swarm of deebees was over him, gouging his armour and looking to get at the human inside. His armour was solid, very solid in fact, but he knew it was a matter of time before something gave.

He had the machine guns on automatic now, but they weren't protected by armour and lasted a few seconds before a deebee claw cut through the metal and put them out of action.

The flamethrower lasted longer, burning anything on his right side to a cinder. It was well protected, housed within *Mariner's* left arm, but a deebee must have sliced deep enough to cut the fuel intake… the flame sputtered and then went out as flamer fuel gushed all around him.

Weaponless now, he could do nothing but thrash around with his armoured fists and feet. They took a toll as well, crushing alien bodies with each solid blow, but the press of creatures above him made it harder and harder to get a decent strike in.

Suddenly, a warning light flickered on. He barely had time to recognise it – something had carved deep into his right arm, striking the laser housing and shorting the small fusion pile – when a spark ignited the flamer fuel pooling around the prone exomech. The explosion was small, but that detonated the unspent high explosive rounds still in his ammunition drums, and that in turn breached the fusion containment cell.

The resulting explosion killed hundreds of deebees, scattering them around the farmstead in shattered chunks. But in a swarm of thousands, it mattered very little indeed.

* * *

Graves Farmstead, Tau Ceti IV

Graves stood on a low, wide hill, and looked around.

Brutiful was in the centre of a line of exomechs, with *Carnigore* on his right and *Grampage* on his left. It wasn't much against a horde of killer aliens, but it was the best they could do.

"Hank, honey?" Beth said over the combined command net.

"Here, Beth."

"The Singhs are on their way in, but they'll be a while, and Jenkins is reporting suit damage, not sure when or even if he can get here."

"Suit damage my arse," Crazy Bill said. "He's either chicken-shit lazy or chicken-shit scared."

"Either way, we can't rely on him, so it's just the three of us for now," Graves said. "If we can hold out until the Singhs get here, we might have a chance."

"We could always hole up in your bunker," Wright said. "Plenty of room down there for everyone."

"We'd have to come out eventually," Crazy Bill replied. "Our best chance for the colony is for the exomechs to deal with them now, while we've got them in a bunch."

"I agree," Graves said. "We kill what we can here then fight as we fall back to the Bunker. That should slow them down a little at least."

"The command and control suite has some suggestions for fall-back routes, honey," Beth said. "I'm sending data now for your autopilots."

Brutiful beeped as the data came in, and Graves quickly looked over it before setting it up as his autopilot program.

"Got it, Beth, thanks," he said, as both Wright and Crazy Bill acknowledged receipt of their information packets.

"I have all our drones fitted with cameras now, and Helen Wright has sent hers in as well," Beth continued. "We should have plenty of real-time video coming in, and I'll punch it through as you need it."

"What's the satellite showing?" Wright asked.

"Nothing good," Beth replied. "There's a wall of deebees coming your way, should be in sight in a few minutes, and there are some gates still yet to open."

"Any sight of Peters or Donaldson?" Graves asked. There was a long pause before Beth replied.

"Nothing on the sensors, nothing on satellite, and I can't raise anyone on the radio."

"That's not good."

"No it's not," Beth continued. "And that swarm headed your way would have swept right over their farmsteads."

There was silence as the three men made last minute preparations for the onslaught to come.

* * *

Singh Farmstead, Tau Ceti IV

Jaswant Singh stood atop a steep cliff, his *Crescent Moon* raining death into the valley below him. His exomech's main armaments were a pair of long-range 3" cannon on the right arm and a heavy rocket launcher on the left. The cannons each spat out high-explosive shells every six seconds, giving him one round every three, and amidst the swarm of deebees headed his way the bursting charges and their tungsten shrapnel were leaving great gaps in the alien ranks.

The rocket launcher was a box-shaped, 6-tube weapon, capable of firing single rockets or volleys of six. It wasn't as accurate as the cannon, but didn't need to be – a volley of six rockets had enough scatter and burst to fill quite a large area with shrapnel, and close enough was good enough when it came to big explosions.

Its only problem was that it was slow to reload, and he was getting a volley away every five minutes.

Below him, midway up the hill, *Eagle* and *Hawk* waited, both pilots nervous as they watched the swarm approach. Their weapons lacked the long range of *Crescent Moon*, but were lethal at close range… how lethal, and how quickly they could kill swarming deebees in these numbers, was about to be tested.

The aliens were now 50 metres from the base of the hill, and *Crescent Moon* had time for one last volley of rockets before the creatures were too close for Jaswant to use his heavy weapons. All he could do now was pick off the creatures following behind, and hope the other exomechs could handle the rest.

As the deebees closed, *Hawk* and *Eagle* opened fire. Both arms mounted a pair of linked 15mm machines guns, capable of firing over 800 rounds per minute each and loaded with a mix of solid tungsten slugs and hollowpoint rounds. Each arm could fire independently, and the wall of tungsten that they spread before them stopped the first ranks of the swarm dead in their tracks.

The next waves met the same fate, but as each creature fell it created a small wall for the ones behind. Both exomechs walked slowly backwards up the hill as the wall grew, hoping to maintain some elevation so they could shoot at the creatures massing behind it.

From around both edges of the wall, however, more creatures swarmed, and *Eagle* and *Hawk* turned to face the new threat.

Hawk's heavy weapon was a pair of semi-automatic mortars that fired over the exomech's shoulder. They only had a range of 50 metres, but were able to empty their 5-round clips in a matter of seconds, generating enough firepower to devastate a large target almost instantly.

Agun Singh stomped the foot pedal for his mortars, emptying the clip at the approaching swarm. The mortars were set to target 40 metres away initially, then increase a few metres for each successive shot... the first three rounds from each mortar, all high-explosive, flattened the incoming wave, while the fourth rounds airburst and scattered shards of white phosphorous around.

The creatures beneath the white-hot halo burned as the hot phosphorous dug into the skin. Some collapsed instantly, the shards deep enough to cook them from the inside, but the rest kept coming, despite their horrible wounds.

The fifth rounds were napalm, splashing across the side of the hill and covering anything it touched with intense flame. Very few creatures made it through, and Agun dispatched those that did with tightly controlled burst from *Eagle's* twin machine guns.

Behind him, Kubai deployed *Eagle's* own heavy weapons, a pair of flamethrowers, one over each shoulder. Unlike the smaller flamethrowers on other exomechs, these were military grade, emitting white-hot jets of plasma that incinerated anything they touched. His approach was to let the creatures approach to within 20 metres and then spray them all with gouts of plasma.

They died by the dozens, the dead providing no cover at all as they turned to ash under the incredible heat. *Eagle's* canopy darkened to protect him from the intense glare, which made Kubai blind to what was happening in front of him.

He toggled the camera feed, tapping into *Crescent Moon's* video to get a third-party view of the battle, and adjusted his flame jets to deal with a group that were trying to flank him. They never made it, though the last of them was a charred corpse only a metre or so away.

Jaswant had reloaded his rocket pack now and looked for a target worth expending the high-explosive six-pack on…there was nothing as yet, so he used his time to fire cannon shells into small groups of deebees that were trying to push their way through or over the wall of corpses *Hawk* and *Eagle* had made with their machine guns.

Using his command suite, he checked the ammunition states of his small force. Everything was getting low, and he knew it was going to be close. Soon, the plasma jets would be out of fuel and the machine gun hoppers would be empty, and then they'd be in serious trouble.

Suddenly, it was over. The flank attacks proving futile, the remaining deebees swarmed directly up the hill, clumping together to push through the wall of their dead. It took Jaswant a second to align his rocket pack and fire, and the swarm disappeared as the volley of six rockets detonated amongst them.

The three men sat in their exomechs for a moment, happy to be still alive after the onslaught, and then it was back to the business at hand.

"*Hawk*, *Eagle*, report," Jaswant said quietly.

"*Hawk* intact," Agun replied. "Heavy weapons empty, gun ammunition at five percent."

"*Eagle* intact," Kubai added. "Plasma gone, gun ammunition at nine percent."

"And *Crescent Moon* intact," Jaswant said. "Rockets gone, six rounds of cannon left."

"We're in no state to fight, father," Agun said. "We don't have enough ammunition to fight through to the Graves' farmstead."

"I concur," Jaswant replied. "Let's head for home."

* * *

Toolong River/Donaldson Farmstead, Tau Ceti IV

Sarah Donaldson was still in tears as she left the farmhouse she and her dead husband had turned into a home. She wanted to race to the battle, hoping beyond all hope that Andy was somehow still alive, but she knew it was less than futile…it would be suicide. Andy hadn't been able to stay alive in *Mariner*, she'd have no chance in anything less than a fully-armed exomech.

Racing into the shed, she wheeled out a powerful motorcycle, one of the pair that was always kept fully charged for emergencies. Stuffing her overnight bags into the vehicle's panniers, she climbed aboard and thumbed the starter switch, kicking the electric motor into life.

She had visited the Graves' place regularly, and swung the rapidly accelerating bike onto the dirt road that ran towards the neighbouring farmstead, paralleling the Toolong River. She and Andy had always joked about the name, inherited from the initial survey report a century ago, and this time it really did seem 'too long'.

Ahead was the concrete bridge that Andy's grandfather had built, the old Donaldson crest on all four of the concrete support pillars. As she approached the bridge her eyes misted over again, thinking about grandchildren of her own that she and Andy would never have.

Lost in her thoughts, she didn't notice the rippling surface of the water or the sparkling gleam of alien bodies as they rose from the depths.

Three deebees leapt out of the river just as she pulled onto the bridge, knocking her from the bike and sending her sprawling into one of the concrete pillars. Even if she'd been wearing a helmet, the impact would still have knocked her out and it would have done her no good at all as a swarm of deebees burst out of the river and tore her body to pieces.

She died not even knowing that she was pregnant with Andy's child.

* * *

Graves Farmstead, Tau Ceti IV

The three exomechs held the line as best they could, using their long-range guns to slow down the advancing horde as they slowly retreated along the line of hills. Ammunition was quickly becoming an issue though, and they all knew they had fewer rounds than there were deebees.

"Hank, honey?" Beth cut in over the radio.

"Kinda busy, Beth," Graves replied. "Unless you got news worth hearing, I don't have much time to chat."

"I got news, some good, some bad."

"Start with the good," Crazy Bill cut in, "I think we could all use some cheering up right now."

"Okay," Beth said. "Helen has re-routed some of her drones your way, carrying ammunition drums. "

"That *is* good news, honey," Graves said. "I'll be throwing rocks at them if this lasts much longer."

"The drones can't reload for you, only drop the drums close by."

"That's fine, honey, drop them close, we'll do the rest."

The three pilots switched to manual control and drew closer together as their sensors picked up the incoming drones. There were six, two each, and they were coming in slow and low… clearly, Helen had loaded them with as much as they could bear.

Which was good, they were going to need it all.

"Jake, how's your ammo state?" Graves asked.

"Almost out of everything that matters," Wright replied. "I got some close-in stuff left, but was really hoping not to need it."

"Okay, you reload first, Crazy Bill and I will cover you."

"Roger that!"

"And get the lead out," Crazy Bill added. "I'm down to my last rounds as well."

Carnigore fell out of the line, leaving *Brutiful* and *Grampage* to face the horde. Two drones passed over him, dropping heavy drum canisters into the soft ground within a few metres…one struck a rock and burst open, scattering autocannon ammunition everywhere, but the other canisters stayed intact.

One of *Carnigore's* saving graces, as he was just learning, was that it had much nimbler hands than your typical exomech. It was relatively easy to pick up a canister, eject an empty one, and reload the canister directly into the waiting drum feeder. 'Relatively' still meant that it took him minutes however, and he was out of battle during a time when mere seconds were critical.

Graves was very aware of his rapidly diminishing ammunition supply, and was firing controlled burst of 2-3 rounds each. It was never going to make a dint in the oncoming horde, but killing those in the lead would buy them some time… no idea what for, but maybe the Singh's would get there in time to rescue the wives and children locked into the Bunker.

Crazy Bill was firing constantly, preferring his own heavy cannon over his lighter autocannon. The high explosive rounds tore clumps out of the enemy and caused some confusion, which helped slow them down a little. Not enough, but everything helped.

"Hank," he said over the firing, "something just occurred to me."

"What's that Bill?" Graves replied, simultaneously firing a burst from his over-sized shotgun into a clump that was just begging to have a spray of tungsten sent its way. "You leave the gas on?"

"No," Crazy Bill said, chuckling loudly. "That wife of yours, she never gave us the bad news."

"You're right," Graves said. "Beth, honey? You got something else for us?"

"The bad news? You want it now?"

"Sure! What could possibly make anything worse?"

There was a pause, and Graves could hear his wife's sharp intake of breath.

"It's the giant gate on the ridgeline… it's still open."

The three men in the exomechs paused a moment as that sunk in. Gates always closed after they'd dropped off their load of deebees. *Always.*

"Well, shit!" Wright said, trying to push the last of his reload canisters into place.

"And then some," Crazy Bill added.

* * *

Singh Farmstead, Tau Ceti IV

The three exomechs stood open, family members working quickly to repair and reload them as best as they could, while the three pilots stood around the tactical display in the farmhouse's security room. The picture looked grim, and they doubted that Graves and the others would last much longer.

"If we move quickly," Agun said, "*Hawk* and *Eagle* might get there in time to be of some help."

Jaswant shook his head. "You'd need *Crescent Moon* to support you, you don't have the firepower to make much of a difference."

"We could give them close defence like we do for you, keep the deebees clear while they clean them out."

"Good idea, brother," Kubai said, "but that would leave *Crescent Moon* without support."

"Someone needs to stay here and guard the families."

That brought a frown from Jaswant, one that silenced his son. "If Graves and the others fall, there's no point guarding anything else." He pointed to the satellite images of deebees pouring towards the distant farmstead. "The colony lives or dies at the Graves farmstead."

"What do we do, father?" Agun asked.

"The best we can my son, the best we can."

* * *

Graves Farmstead, Tau Ceti IV

Brutiful's autocannon whirred and clicked as they finally ran out of ammunition. He was down to his last three shotgun rounds and then he'd be useless until the deebees got into close range, and by then it would be all over.

"Hank!" Wright's voice cut over the radio. "I'm reloaded, you're up!"

Carnigore stepped beside him, its clown-face a garish red grin as it opened fire on the aliens. Wright had no concerns at all about ammunition now and was firing it as fast as he could – there were certainly plenty of targets for everything he had to throw at them.

Graves stepped back out of the line and moved quickly to the clump of ammunition canisters the drones had dropped off for him. *Brutiful* was a large exomech, with lots of ammunition storage and he knew it was going to take him a while to get completely reloaded.

"Crap," Crazy Bill cut in, "I'm out too, nothing but close-in guns and my fists!"

"I can hold them," Wright replied, "But you'll need to be quick!"

"Bill, grab your canisters, make for the next hill," Graves said. "We'll cover you, you reload up there and cover us as we move back."

"Roger that!" Crazy Bill picked up his ammunition drums and ran for the next hilltop as fast as *Grampage's* servo-motors would go.

Graves could hear the sounds of firing behind him as he reloaded.

"Hank!" Wright yelled over the radio, "I need you real bad!"

Graves picked up the remaining canisters on *Brutiful's* lower arms and turned back to the line, his heavy shoulder-weapons coming back down, as reloaded as they were going to be.

The swarm was only a few hundred yards away now, and the exomech sensors still showed thousands of creatures out there. True, they could see the swarm was smaller than it was before, but they both knew it wasn't going to be enough.

Graves started firing, autocannon on maximum rate, shotgun blasting out a spread of tungsten as soon it chambered another round. Beside him, *Carnigore* matched him round for round, and the slaughter amongst the deebees was incredible.

But not enough.

"Hank," Wright's voice came through on a private direct channel. "I don't think we're going to make it."

Graves knew he wasn't wrong, but really didn't want to admit it.

"I know," he said softly, "but we'll go down swinging, give the Singhs and the others as best chance we can."

"I guess we will," Wright said, triggering another burst. "I just hope it counts for something."

The two men were silent for a long time, firing rapidly and switching fire to deal with the targets that presented the greatest threat.

"Hank, honey!" Beth's voice cut through urgently, "I need you to both get off the hill, and now!"

"What?"

"Don't argue, just get the hell off there!"

Graves shrugged and powered *Brutiful* off the hill as fast as he could, and a moment later he saw *Carnigore* do the same, with the front ranks of deebees only a dozen or so metres behind and closing.

His suit sensors pinged as they picked up a flight of something coming in fast and low, and he instinctively ducked as something flew overhead. He'd barely made it half-way down the slope when there was an explosion on the other side of the hill, powerful enough to knock both *Carnigore* and *Brutiful* off their feet and send them tumbling down the hill.

* * *

Southern Ridgeline/Jenkins Farmstead, Tau Ceti IV

Jenkins day just wasn't getting any better. Jessie was sending him the video and satellite feeds and he knew the colony was well and truly screwed over. There was a small chance Graves and the others could hold the deebees back, and he wanted to still be alive when the battle was over, but sitting back and watching wasn't going to help anybody, including him.

"Keith, I'm picking up movement on the ridgeline," Jessie said. "Big biomass, headed towards Graves' place."

"Well, that's them screwed then," he replied. "Might be best if you start packing some things Jessie and we take our chances in the wild until the next ship arrives."

"Might not be so bad, Keith… that big swarm of deebees isn't showing up on the satellite at all!"

"What now? That son of a bitch Graves took out an entire swarm by himself?"

"No idea," Jessie replied. "Might be worthwhile getting over there though, just in case."

"Good idea, Jessie," Jenkins said. "There should be plenty to claim from the colony account after this."

Turning *Shepherd* southward, he started mentally calculating the claims he was going to be putting in for his defence of the colony… and very, very inflated claims they would be.

* * *

Graves Farmstead, Tau Ceti IV

Shaken, Graves struggled to get his exomech back on its feet, but whatever had knocked him down must have had enough force to throw *Brutiful's* gyros out of alignment.

He noticed the ringing in his ears only when he started to get his hearing back, and only when that died down did he hear Beth calling out for him over the radio.

"Hank! Hank! Do you read me?" Her voice was frantic, and Graves had no idea how long he'd been out.

"I'm here, honey," he replied. "Quit yelling and tell me what the hell just happened."

"Oh, Hank, honey!" she said, the relief evident in her voice. "I thought I'd lost you!"

"Nope, still here… what did I miss?"

"You missed a lot! The Singhs came through, the smaller gates are all closed and the two Singh boys are on their way over, should be at the bunker within twenty."

"Just the boys?" Graves asked. "Jaswant didn't make it?"

"Jaswant's fine!" Beth replied. "They stripped the fusion cell out of *Crescent Moon* and sent it in on a drone, rigged to detonate on command."

Graves paused as that sank in… fusion cells were expensive and temperamental , and it would have been fast and risky work to take one out of an exomech and rig it to a crop-dusting drone.

No wonder Beth had wanted him off that hill in a hurry!

"Wait… the Singh's just nuked my back yard?"

"Honey!"

"We'll talk about it later, Beth," he said. "Right now, I need an update on everything else."

"I can't give it to you, honey," Beth replied. "The blast's EMP took out our sensors and all the drones, and our satellite link is going to be down until you get back and fix it."

"Okay… I'll look around here and let you know what's going on."

"Roger that… I'll get this place sorted out and see to the families I have here."

He had to shut down and then reboot the gyros before he could stand up, and then he turned and went back to the top of the hill. The place was a mess.

On the fields below, the deebee swarm was now ash, turned to scorched dust by the force and heat of a fusion explosion. It would take him years to deal with the radiation, and he might have to move to maintain enough land to make a viable homestead, but he was glad to be alive.

He was saddened, however, at the sight of *Carnigore,* lying shattered and twisted at the base of the hill. The blast must have picked the exomech up and hurled it down the slope, and looking at the torn armour the following wave of radiation must have cooked Wright inside his suit.

Hopefully, he'd have been unconscious when the wave hit and he'd died quickly.

There was movement behind him, and he turned to see *Grampage* moving towards him. The exomech waved at him, then the right arm carefully tapped the suit's head, indicating radio failure. *Grampage* would have been well protected from the explosion, but high up on the next hill it would have been quite vulnerable to the EMP.

Crazy Bill came closer, and Graves could see through the armoured glass canopy that he was waving a hand-held radio at him. The hand-helds were standard equipment for all colonists, and it took Graves only a moment to unclip his.

"You okay old-timer?" he asked, smiling to take the sting out of his words.

"Never been better," Crazy Bill replied. "You got a lot of dead deebees on your land, Hank, going to be good fertiliser come next summer."

"Summer in about 300 years you mean," Graves said, "after the radiation dies down."

He could see Crazy Bill laughing at him.

"Don't be foolish, Hank, the deebees will absorb that radiation as they break down."

"Really?"

Crazy Bill was nodding now.

Suddenly, there was an almighty roar, loud enough to shake them both through their armoured exomechs. Looking around, Graves saw a creature that even his worst nightmares wouldn't have thrown at him.

It was a deebee, but like nothing of them had ever seen before. His visual sensors were out, but it towered over the trees it was brushing easily aside, and must have stood at least 30 metres tall at the shoulder. Graves counted six clawed legs, could see from the sheen that it was chitin armoured, and the snout was fanged like a hungry cat.

"What... on... earth... is ... that?" was all he could mutter.

"That," Crazy Bill replied, "is as good a reason as you'll ever need to run the hell back to your bunker."

Nodding, Graves turned his exomech and moved as fast as he could back to his farmstead.

* * *

Graves Farmstead, the Bunker, Tau Ceti IV

By the time Graves and Crazy Bill got back to the Bunker, the two light Singh exomechs had arrived, and Beth and Helen were out chatting to the two men. Beth waved happily when Graves arrived, but stopped waving when she saw the state of *Brutiful* and the urgency on her husband's face.

"Hank, honey, what is it?"

"Deebee coming, get back in the Bunker!"

"How many?" Agun asked, strapping himself back into his harness.

"Just one, son," Crazy Bill replied, "just one."

Agun and Kubai frowned as they sealed their exomechs and powered up their sensors – they'd known when the fusion cell was due to detonate and had shut down their systems to avoid the worst of the EMP – but they weren't making much sense of the readings.

"My sensors must be fried," Kubai said.

"Mine too," Agun added. "I'm picking up one signature, of enormous mass."

"There's nothing wrong with your sensors," Graves said. "Just the one, and it's the size of a deep-space shuttle."

The creature appeared at that moment, towering over the trees, and Beth and Helen both ran for the safety of the Bunker. Moving at great speed, the deebee headed towards them and Graves barely had enough time to reload the last of his ammunition canisters before the thing broke through the electric fence surrounding the farmstead. Built to keep out cattle, it barely registered on the behemoth above them.

The Bunker was equipped with a pair of 200mm cannon, capable of firing both high-explosive and anti-armour rounds. The ammunition hoppers were always filled with high-explosive, and Beth was firing them at the rapid rate, hoping to bring the creature down under a hail of fire. Against the thick chitin armour, however, the rounds did nothing.

Brutiful's autocannon had much the same effect, bouncing harmlessly off or exploding on impact without troubling the creature at all. He didn't even bother firing the shotgun, knowing the lower-velocity rounds would do nothing.

The Singhs charged in, *Hawk* and *Eagle* moving swiftly around the creature, firing their machine guns hoping to find a weak spot. The creature didn't appear to have any, and the rounds did little more than distract it.

Kubai's flamethrowers did little better, managing to infuriate it, and the creature reared up on its four hind legs and brought its fore-paws crashing down…

Both of the lighter exomechs managed to dodge, though only just.

The Bunker's twin cannon were still firing, and still having no effect at all.

"Beth," Graves said as he moved *Brutiful* around to the giant deebee's right side, "quit wasting the hi-ex. I need you to unload as fast as you can and reload with the anti-armour rounds."

"Hank, honey," Beth replied, "what do you think I'm doing?"

Graves conceded that she had a point… unloading manually would have taken much longer than just firing it all off.

"Okay," he said. "Let me know when you've got a few anti-armour rounds loaded, we'll try to keep the thing off the bunker until you do."

"Roger that!"

Eagle and *Hawk* were running between the creature's legs now, still firing, and it didn't seem to like it much. It reared up again, this time on its rearmost pair of legs, and brought its whole body down.

This time *Eagle* wasn't so lucky, and a descending claw caught it and pressed it to the ground. The giant head came around, jaws open, and then the creature's teeth crushed and tore into the exomech and the pilot within. Graves winced as he heard Agun's screams, and then there was silence.

"Brother!" Kubai yelled, and darted forward to avenge his

fallen kinsman. The creature was grinding the suit between its teeth, shredding the armour and Agun's remains. Ignoring his other weapons, Kubai slammed *Hawk* directly into the deebee's head, using the suit's armoured shoulders as a battering ram.

The impact was incredible, and Graves saw teeth fly out of the mouth as the creature sagged for a moment, and Kubai took the opportunity to slam *Hawk's* fists into the creature's head, massive roundhouse blows with power and weight behind them that only an exomech could generate.

The creature's exoskeletal armour began to break apart, and Kubai dug his suit's hands deep into a crack and heaved… Armour pulled away, revealing bright pink and yellow flesh beneath. He shoved his right arm into the hole and fired a burst from his twin machine guns, digging deep as the rounds finally punched into something vital.

The creature roared in agony and lifted its body, dragging *Hawk* with it. Kubai used his left arm to hang on and continued firing as the creature shook his head frantically in an effort to dislodge him.

"Hank, honey!" Beth cut in. "I have six anti-armour rounds loaded, ready to fire!"

"Roger that," Graves replied. "Kubai, drop clear!"

"Negative, Henry Graves," Kubai said. "You know the saying about riding the tiger."

Graves did indeed – there was no getting off once you started.

"Beth, Kubai can't get clear… I'll try to turn it so you can get a clean shot."

"Negative again," Kubai said. "Beth Graves, take your shot now, while I have it distracted."

"Hank, honey?"

"He's right, Beth, take the shot. Try to aim low, and be sure not to miss."

Graves watched as the twin cannon slewed around and then dropped, aiming right for the creature's chest, and fired three rounds from each barrel. At that range, they couldn't miss.

The anti-tank rounds were a tungsten slug with a hollow charge, that turned into a shaped charge on impact…striking the creature, they formed and detonated, with enough heat to melt the tungsten and fire it at supersonic speeds into the target. The six rounds struck in quick succession, each a metre or so apart, and the resultant explosions turned the creature's torso to pulp.

It rose up in its death throes and thrashed around uncontrollably… Kubai couldn't maintain his grip and *Hawk* fell, landing heavily on its back, only to have the creature fall on top of him, its sheer weight crushing the exomech and cracking open plates of armour.

And then it died.

* * *

Graves Farmstead, Tau Ceti, IV, Aftermath

Graves, Jaswant Singh, Crazy Bill and Keith Jenkins stood outside the Bunker as the other colonists cleaned up the mess, which included cutting up and dragging away the corpse of the giant deebee.

With a lot of families dead, there'd be room for more colonists. The Donaldsons were gone, so their farmstead was vacant land, and Peters' wife and family had decided to leave Tau Ceti and head home to Earth, which freed up that land as well.

They managed to drag Kubai Singh out of his exomech's wreckage… he was still alive, but had lost both legs and an arm, and would require expensive prosthetics, which the Colony account would happily pay. Likewise, replacement exomechs for the Singhs, who had lost all three of their suits, would come from the Colony account.

Jenkins had put in claims for damages and repairs that they all knew were ridiculous, but no-one had the energy to argue – he'd survived, that counted for something, and they needed everyone to move forward together. Jaswant Singh had suggested giving Jenkins the deeds to the Donaldson and Peters farmsteads, in exchange for his own, as payment for his efforts, and the others had reluctantly agreed – the Singhs had lost too much for them to deny any reasonable requests right now. Graves could see Jenkins mentally rubbing his hands together in glee, and it sickened him.

The really good news was that Jake Wright had survived after all. Despite his complaints about his exomech, *Carnigore* had one feature no-one had counted on – it had more radiation shielding than any of them had ever seen, likely as a measure to protect patrons from radiation leaks from when it was still an amusement ride droid. It was a wreck and would need replacing, but Jake was okay.

And that left the giant gate on the ridgeline. It lacked the sparkle that indicated an open gateway back the deebee's home dimension, but it was still there. None of them had any idea what to do about it, other than to arm up, stay vigilant, and invest heavily in defences. It was going to be expensive and hard work, and it dawned on Graves that Jenkins new farmstead would be right in the path of any further attacks… Jaswant Singh was much wilier than he'd given him credit.

With the creature dragged away and the other colonists gone, Graves and his wife surveyed the land they'd fought hard to defend. It never occurred to them to pack up and leave, to head to somewhere safer. This was home, and alien invasion or no, this was where they were going to stay.

UNDER CALLIOPE'S SKIN

Alan Baxter

Andy Collins flicked his eyes to operate his virtual HUD. An adrenaline suppressant dumped into his bloodstream along with a tweak of endorphin as the Alliance Battlecruiser Belvedere fell out of jump with a bone-deep whine. He hated the inertia of re-entering real space.

"Take a moment to message your loved ones," Capstan barked. "We drop in three minutes."

The massive Lieutenant stomped from one end of the dropship to the other, enhanced musculature rippling under his form-fitting battlesuit. He paused at each team member to stare hard into their eyes, his virtual HUD relaying reams of data – pulse rate, blood pressure, serotonin levels, a hundred other markers. You couldn't hide a thing from a party Lieutenant. When he reached Collins, Capstan stared a moment longer.

"You okay, buttercup?" he asked, almost a whisper. His eyes were mean and his mouth pressed into a flat line as he waited for a response.

Collins watched the golden flicker across Capstan's eyeballs, wondered just what data he was reading. "Fine," he said, pleased his voice was strong. "You know I hate interstellar."

Capstan nodded once, paused to read another roll of information. His deep forehead relaxed under a mat of salt and pepper hair shaved close. "Just as well you're such a good soldier. Makes up for your flaws."

He stalked away before Collins could respond, but Collins allowed himself a smile. Capstan always acted the hardass, but he was a father to the whole squad. Though no one would ever say so to his face. He might love them all, but he'd kick seven shades out of anyone who suggested he had emotions.

"We green, Daisy?" Capstan called out.

"Across the board." The dropship AI's voice was a soft, velvety feminine.

Capstan turned at the head of the bay and scanned the two rows of marines facing each other, four along one side, three the other.

"We are eight of the best," he said, smiling to reveal the chromed shine of replacement teeth. He could bite through steel with those and his jaw augments. "In fact, we are *the best* eight and that's why we get sent out to these asshole shitheaps on the edge to do things no other fool would do. But this one is pretty routine, right?"

Laughter rippled around the bay and Capstan grinned wider.

"Fuck yeah, ain't no such thing as routine if we're involved. So here's what we know, and it ain't much." He tapped at his wrist pad and a holographic cube sprang into life between the two rows of warriors. A small moon swelled into view, orbiting a massive gas giant. "This is Calliope," Capstan said. "Fourth moon of the third planet in the Arteeria system. Distant scans revealed huge deposits of allerinium beneath the crust, and you don't need me to tell you what lengths the Alliance will go to for interstellar jump fuel. So a remote unit was sent to build a habitat. Once the robots had finished, a scientific team of twenty specialists was sent in to survey. Results were good for about two months and then all communications ceased. This is the last transmission."

He tapped his pad again and the three-dimensional map switched to a recorded video. A face leaned close to the camera, sweat running down the brow from soaked hair. The man's mouth was stretched in a wide grimace and his teeth were stained.

"That blood in his mouth?" Aiko Hayashi asked, her eyes narrowed.

"Looks like it," Tanveer Malik said. He glanced at Hayashi with a smile. "But is it his or someone else's?"

She flicked him a sour look, shook her head. Collins smirked. Those two were about due their occasional hook-up. It was a good tension diffuser that otherwise saw them fighting.

The man continued to stare and grin at the camera.

"He gonna say anything?" Collins asked.

Capstan shut off the image. "Nope. He stands there like that, not moving, not even fucking blinking, for three hours and fourteen minutes."

"The fuck?" Kirsten Watts said quietly.

"The transmission ends with a power drop," the Lieutenant continued. "Remote connections confirm the power was only out for a few minutes. As far as anyone can tell, the whole operation is still green. Except now there's no response to hails and no cameras anywhere inside the station are working."

"So they're sending us in," Charlie Finlay said.

Capstan pointed one finger at the tall, burly marine. "That's right."

Finlay grinned, his teeth like Capstan's, even brighter against sun-tanned skin. Wisps of blond hair poked from under the front edge of his helmet, an affectation that never failed to annoy Collins. "Cool," Finlay said in a low growl.

Collins scanned his squad mates, all buzzing with the excitement of a job about to start. He buzzed along with them, always keen for action, though the image of that sweating, staring guy with blood on his teeth gave him pause. But what threat were scientists to this team?

Red lights flashed and a siren wailed. "Ten seconds," Daisy said calmly.

"Here we go, my flowers!" Capstan shouted as he jogged to his rack and strapped in.

The dropship detached and fell for Calliope. The display up front showed the battlecruiser disappearing away from them, then space folded around it as it jumped away to sit far from the gravitational pull of the system and await the hail to pick them up again. Collins dumped a little pick-me-up into his blood as Daisy guided them in.

* * *

"Locked and docked," Daisy said. "Pressures equalised. You're good to go."

"Keep the engines ticking," Capstan said. "In case we need to facilitate a quick exit."

"I'll be ready," the dropship replied.

The Lieutenant moved to the hatch. "Form up."

The squad unbuckled and arranged themselves. Capstan took the lead, flanked by Hayashi and Finlay. Behind them were Alex Lau and Malik, followed by Henna Sterns and Collins. Watts, the medic, brought up the rear.

"All comms to closed group," Capstan said. "Inter-squad hails only, and keep those to a minimum. Rebreathers on."

Full face masks slipped from their helmets and joined seamlessly to their battlesuits. As soon as the toughened flexiglass was down, Collins felt the familiar tightening of his fatigues, every tiny gap closing, contained tight against even the hint of microbial attack. The flex-armour plates in the super-tough fabric swelled and shifted into place, a form-fitting carapace with micro-gyro strength and movement assistance. He felt safe in the body-hugging outfit, the familiar weight of his pack, ammo and weapons pressing down on him, the air in his helmet lightly scented with ocean salt as it passed through the suit's filtration system.

"Move out!" Capstan barked.

The hatch irised open and they jogged into the docking corridor of the scientific station. Lights were on, everything appeared normal at first glance.

"Check the map," Capstan said, and floor plans of the station appeared to each of them at a virtual distance of about thirty centimetres along with the rest of their HUD data. Each squad member was marked by name and a glowing icon. "I'm taking Hayashi and Finlay to the location of the last transmission, which is the engineering and mech bay. At the end is a vehicle bay for EVAC, so we'll account for assets there too." He highlighted the area off to one side of the sprawling habitat.

"Big fucking place for twenty scientists," Lau said.

"They intended it to house a lot more once mining commenced," Capstan said. "So it's going to take a while to cover everything." He zoomed out. "Malik, Lau, you two head north and start checking each of the sleeping quarters and lounges." He blipped a collection of about two dozen rooms along the northern edge of the centre. "Report as you go. Then work your way back towards the Command and Control centre, where we'll all regroup." A central room blinked.

"*Hai,*" Lau said and peeled off, Malik jogging alongside.

"Sterns, Collins and Watts, you three need to go west and search the labs." A collection of six large rooms flashed three times.

Without waiting for a reply, Capstan hustled away to the right, with Hayashi and Finlay on his heels. Collins turned to his companions. "Ladies, after you." He gestured to his left.

Watts laughed. "Fuck you, soldier."

"I'll take point," Sterns said. "You two can enjoy my ass as we go."

Collins grinned. He most certainly would. And so would Watts for that matter. Though bonds throughout their squad were tighter than family, it was Henna who touched him most deeply, and he knew he was not alone. Sterns was a little bit mother and a little bit lover to most of them. And probably the most deadly when shit went down.

Watts nudged him with her rifle butt. "Wipe the grin off and focus, dickwad."

Collins winked at her. "I'll bring up the rear."

"Sure you will."

They moved forward, heavy assault rifles cradled ready, scanning as they went.

"It's too quiet," Sterns said.

"We know they're here somewhere," Collins said.

The corridor led to a large double door that hissed open as they approached. A lab lay beyond, all manner of survey equipment and data stations. Lights flashed, information rolled through holo-displays, everything looked normal. Except for the lack of surveyors. Collins approached one desk and leaned over to look at a coffee mug, still half full with black liquid. He blinked up his helmet scanner and it confirmed filter coffee, now long cold.

Watts gestured to a series of large tanks along one side. "What the fuck are they doing in a mining survey station?"

"What are they?" Collins asked. Pale blue liquid rippled in each one, shimmering under bright lights embedded in the top. Each could easily fit three large men.

"Uterotanks," Watts said, eyebrows knitted. When the others gave her blank looks, she said, "Breeding tanks."

"For what?"

The medic shrugged. "No idea. But I've never seen them that big before."

"Well, doesn't that just bode all kinds of good," Sterns said. "Let's spread out, search the room."

They moved apart, helmet scanners processing reams of data as they let their eyes rove for anything that might be a clue.

"Here," Watts said. She pointed with the barrel of her weapon.

A chair was pushed out from under a desk, the seat and the floor around it smeared with blood. Scarlet drops sprayed across the desk and holo emitters. Watts stood back, hands raised as though framing up a photograph. They waited while she used her scans, then she said, "Best guess is a heavy blow to the back of the head, then another across the face." She mimed the actions, indicating the direction of blood spatter. "The victim fell here and was dragged a short way." The smears ended only a metre or so from the desk.

"Then what?" Sterns asked.

Watts shrugged.

"Picked up and carried off?" Collins suggested, his stomach tight.

"Maybe," Watts said. "But there's no more blood. Someone doesn't just stop bleeding when they're carried."

"Maybe they got wrapped up."

"Again here," Sterns said from across the room.

A similar pattern covered more equipment.

"When I was growing up," Sterns said, "my father used to tell this story about the draugen. It was an old-fashioned monster story, you know, a kind of Norwegian ghost or bogeyman. Bullshit designed to scare us. He used to say, 'Henna, if you don't behave, the draugen will come to get you!' I always thought that was an asshole way to make your kids do the right thing."

Collins had seen Henna take out an enemy squad single-handed while he was close to bleeding out. Then she had carried him back in. But in that moment he felt strangely protective of her.

"That's fucked up," Watts agreed. "But what's your point."

Sterns turned to face them with a grin. "I'm thinking maybe the bogeyman lives on Calliope, not Norway."

Collins was about to suggest they move on to the next lab when Sterns suddenly arched forward. A hole twenty centimetres across appeared in her chest, blood spraying forward as her ribs angled out like reaching bony fingers. She looked down in surprise, uttering a quiet, "Oh." The desk behind her was clearly visible through the hole, then she collapsed.

"The fuck?" Watts screamed, rushing over.

"Scan the fucking room!" Collins shouted. *Not Henna. No, no, no, not Henna!*

He crouched, moved in a circle looking for the source of the attack, but the lab was unchanged. There had been no muzzle flash, no sound. He quickly rewound the footage recorded in his HUD and watched again, playing close attention to Sterns. Nothing anywhere around her, then she launched forward, her chest exploded. *Oh*. She dropped.

Watts crouched beside the fallen marine shaking her head. "Dead before she hit the ground. Fuck. Henna!" As she rose to face Collins, she staggered to one side, then screamed as her left arm fell, sheared off at the shoulder. She sat down hard, blood arcing from the gaping wound. She scrambled for a patch can and frantically sprayed fast-expanding foam across the injury.

Collins began cycling through light bands. He swept his gaze left and right, looking through infra-red, microwave, gamma, ultraviolet, around and around, his vision a kaleidoscope of changing images, looking for anything that might be a source of the attack. Then movement. Subtle, almost immediately ceased. Without giving himself away, moving only his eyes, he looked back into the corner of the lab. Under the arm of some strange mechanism like a giant dentist's light, something stood stock still. Visible only in ultraviolet, it was a shape made of mirrors, quicksilver. No discernible features or details.

Collins raised his weapon and it came directly for him. Bigger than a man, it seemed to project itself forward on four pounding legs that thrust vertically up and down against the floor without a sound. Four more upper limbs stretched out, reaching for him, each ending in a long hand of three blade-like fingers. Its head was a flat wedge, arrowing forward.

Collins fired, his finger grinding against the trigger on full auto. The weapon barked deafening projectile death and gouts of fire, ripping into the creature. It staggered back, the wedge head splitting open as though it were screaming in agony, but still it made no sound. With less than five meters between them, Collins thumbed a mini-grenade from the barrel-mounted launcher and it exploded against the thing's torso, threw it back into the corner where it lay still. Collins staggered under the shockwave, but kept his feet.

"Lieutenant, everyone, we have aliens here!" he yelled over a squad-wide waveband. "Use ultraviolet!"

There was no reply. No blips marked their positions on HUD. He realised he hadn't seen their blips for a while. How long?

"Lieutenant?" Nothing. "Daisy?" Nothing. "Fuck." Collins hurried over to Watts, turning slow circles as he went, scanning everywhere.

"Make sure it's dead!" Watts said, waving him towards the creature he'd shot. Her face was pale and sweaty behind her visor, the slash of freckles across her nose standing out clearer than ever, but her shoulder was sealed up in med-foam. "I'm dumping painkillers like a junkie," she said. "I'm okay for now."

Collins nodded once. His eye fell on Sterns and he tore his gaze away, stifling a sob of grief and fury equally combined. Weapon trained on the inert thing in the corner, he approached cautiously. It seemed to flicker slightly, the mirrored body switching between invisibility and a dark, shining greenblack shell. "Cloaking device?" Collins whispered, as much to himself as to Watts. "And a sound suppressor?"

The thing's chitinous exoskeleton was revealed in the flickers to be split in several places by his bullets, a wider rent in the centre of its torso where the mini-grenade had exploded. Thick, black fluid leaked everywhere, presumably its equivalent of blood. The bladed fingers were extensions of its carapace, one or two of them spastically extending and retracting, a smaller many-tentacled hand-like appendage quivered under the shifting knives. It twitched and shivered, seeming to swell and collapse, its form fluid. It had no face to recognise, but a wide mouth in its wedge of a head and a thin, glistening line around the upper ridge that might have been some kind of visual organ.

It reached up weakly, blades flicking forward. Collins skipped back. Those things had gone right through Watts' armour and her shoulder. Right through Henna's body. He stepped back in, pressed the muzzle of his rifle to the band of maybe-eye, and fired a burst into its head. It danced and writhed under his attack and fell still. The flickering ceased and it lay there, a dark, ugly, armoured thing.

"Fuck you," he said and went back to Watts. He helped her up and she leaned on him heavily. "We can't leave Henna."

"We'll come back for her," Watts said. "The drugs are kicking in but I'll need your help for a minute. We gotta regroup."

"Stay on ultraviolet and be extra eyes for me."

She threw her arm over his shoulder and brandished her weapon. "I can still fire one-handed."

Collins glanced at the rifle so close to his head, nodded. "Just keep the muzzle up."

"Took my fucking arm," she said, voice low with incredulity. "Took Henna!"

"They'll build you a new arm once we get out. And everything here will die in Henna's name!"

He looked over at Sterns laying in a widening pool of blood as he led Watts away. "We'll avenge her," he said through gritted teeth, pushing away the emotion of the loss. He loved Sterns. They all did. She was the best of them.

"Three o'clock!" Watts yelled. She grunted as she swung her rifle up one-handed and triggered short, controlled bursts.

Collins winced against the volume of her rounds, kept his left arm around her waist to keep them moving, and matched her method with his right, as three mirror-bright shapes raced into the room from the lab next door. He pumped mini-grenades, drove them back. One broke right and tried to get behind them so he swung Watts and they danced a pirouetting retreat, raking fire and grenades as they went, ears ringing with the ordnance in the confined space. Smoke and light filled the room, equipment shards rained down. Lights blew out and sparks fell like bright orange snow.

They stumbled into the corridor and Collins spotted an emergency lock down beside the door and kicked it. His heel smashed through the glass covering and drove into the large button. Red lights flashed around the doorframe and a thick blast shield dropped as the double doors whooshed shut. Metallic thuds rang out as several masses hit the other side. The same three, unstopped by their bullets and grenades, or a new wave he couldn't know. And he didn't have time to care.

"Let's hope that holds them for now."

"There are other ways around," Watts said breathlessly.

"Let's just get to the C and C."

They ran for the Command and Control Centre, Collins calling for Capstan and Daisy the whole way, but comms remained dead. As the C and C drew within about fifty metres on their HUD map Capstan's voice boomed out. "...asses in here now, we're locking down in thirty seconds."

"We're ten seconds away," Collins yelled.

Something smashed and clattered behind them, then a symphonic rain of shattered glass. Watts tipped her weapon upside down on her right shoulder, let loose random short bursts, strafing left and right. Collins glanced back to see two glimmering masses, wider and lower than before, galloping up behind them, less than ten metres away.

The command centre came up on their left and he threw Watts forward. "Run!"

Spinning in place, he plucked a concussion shield from his belt and slammed it into the ground only a couple of metres from his feet, way too close for safety. As it pulsed into life, filling the corridor, he was lifted and thrown back, vision crossing like he'd been punched in the jaw. The creatures bounced back the other way.

Collins crashed hard against the C and C doorframe and fell inside. Capstan was at a control desk and punched a console. Heavy blast doors slammed closed and Collins lay face down on the hard floor, gasping. He looked up to see Capstan spare one narrow-eyed second for Watts' foamed shoulder stump, then return his attention to the console.

Hayashi stood beside the Lieutenant, Finlay nowhere to be seen. Of the four doorways leading into the C and C, only one remained open.

"Hey Aiko," Collins said, knowing better than to talk to Capstan at this point. "Finlay?"

She sniffed, shook her head almost imperceptibly. "He's in about six pieces back there. He just fucking split apart right in front of us. Henna?"

"Same thing."

"Fuck me, man." Hayashi looked back towards Watts. "Looks like you got too close as well."

"Looks like I got lucky," Watts said. "Finlay and Sterns! Shit. We've all been through too much together to lose two in a day. This ain't fair."

"When is it ever fair?" Capstan said. "And brace yourselves, because we're still two more down. Get over here and cover this door."

The four of them stood in a line in front of the only opening, weapons levelled. A corridor led away for about thirty metres before ending in another closed double door. Several rooms to either side were also shut. Watts insisted she was fine but Collins scanned her vitals, saw that she was surviving on drugs and grim determination. She badly needed to go under and set reknitters to work.

"Malik, Lau, respond!" Capstan said. The only answer was static hiss. "Seems like all comms are suppressed beyond about fifty metres. I can't tell how. Internal interference."

"They have to be coming, right?" Collins said.

Capstan gestured with his weapon. "Speculating is for fucking stock brokers. Watch and respond."

"Did you see them?" Collins asked.

Hayashi nodded. "Powerful cloaks, light and sound. Only UV works."

"You think the cloaks are tech or biological."

"Who knows."

"What do you think they are?"

She turned cold eyes to him for a moment. "Death."

Collins swallowed. He'd seen fear in Aiko's eyes and that made his stomach icy. He'd never seen her afraid of anything, didn't think she could be afraid. He dialled a cocktail into his bloodstream to calm his nerves, sharpen his senses, boost his muscles. Limits and safe doses be damned, he needed every advantage he could get.

"...incoming, Lieutenant! Fucking loads of them!" Lau's voice burst into their comms. "Can you fucking hear me?"

"Roger, Lau, we hear you. Please repeat."

"I said there are invisible bastards coming after us, can only see 'em on UV. We'll need some heavy cover fire!"

"Keep coming," Capstan said calmly. "I've tagged the door on your map. You both run straight for it and do not veer left or right. We'll fire around you. Collins, Hayashi, either side of the corridor, halfway up."

"Right."

Collins ran, Hayashi right beside him, and they dropped into alcoves for cover. Bursts of gunfire and explosions echoed along with Lau's voice screaming obscenities and promises of death and dismemberment, muffled by the double doors ahead. Lau and Malik's blips pinged onto the HUDs, closing rapidly.

"Here we go," Capstan said, and triggered the far doors to open.

Sound burst into full volume, Lau pumping bullets and mini-grenades blindly back over his shoulder as he ran, dragging the inert form of Malik with one hand. Blood smeared the floor where Malik passed.

Collins and Hayashi began setting blasts of cover fire. They both pulled larger explosives from their webbing and lobbed bombs over Lau's head. The corridor behind exploded into fire and smoke and resonating metallic screeches, and then Lau was through. Capstan slammed the far doors shut.

As booming reverberated from the other side, Collins and Hayashi dragged Lau and Malik into the C and C and Capstan sealed those doors too.

"Locking down!" he yelled.

A siren bleated, red lights flashed and blast shields slammed over the last portal. The siren stopped and everything sank into a submarine silence, even the compressors fell quiet as air recyc shut off. After a second or two, a new hum arose as the C and C went into defence mode, recycling its own air, providing all life support from inside the room, sealing itself off completely from the rest of the habitat.

Watts hurried over to Malik's prone form and crouched, wincing in pain, close to unconsciousness. She sat immediately back on her heels, deflated. Collins knew the others were seeing what he saw in his HUD. Malik's life signs were flat.

Lau put both hands on his head and turned in a slow circle. "Fuck, fuck, fuck!" He stopped suddenly, looked around. "Henna? Charlie?"

Watts shook her head.

"Fuuuuck!"

Watts tipped Malik half over to reveal his back open from right shoulder to left buttock. Stark white knobs of spine and a glistening half-orb of kidney showed through the blood and sliced flesh. With a grunt, almost a sob, she let him fall back.

Capstan crouched beside her. "How bad is it?"

She glanced at the mass of hardened foam covering her left shoulder. "Took it clean off. Got it covered pretty quick and I'm up to the eyeballs with antibiotics and painkillers."

"Okay. I want you to lie over there, put yourself under to reknit. We're gonna need to fight our way back to Daisy and I need you fit if not whole."

"If I go under, I'm out for half an hour."

"I know how it fucking works, soldier. We're safe in here. Go!" He turned to gaze at each of the survivors. "This room is in full bio-chem lock down and shielded. Let's take stock."

They let their masks up and removed helmets, stretched stiff necks. Capstan turned back to Watts. "Go!"

She ran her remaining hand through her short red hair and nodded, moved to lay down under a desk unit. Collins went with her, made sure she was comfortable.

"I'll monitor," he said.

She smiled. "Hold the fort. I'll be back in thirty."

"No problem. We got this." He put a hand against her cheek, his dark skin a shadow against her paler than ever alabaster. "Fix up."

He watched his HUD as she dialled in anaesthetic and her breathing settled to become deep and even. Nano reknitters in her blood, triggered awake by the anaesthetic release, immediately swarmed to any areas of hurt, rebuilding the flesh, sealing off wounds. Similar microscopics in her fatigues would already be doing the same to reseal her in where the sleeve had been sliced away.

Collins stroked a hand over her sweat-soaked hair once, then stood. "She's under," he said.

Lau was crouched over Malik, his forehead pressed to the

dead man's brow. "I'm sorry, my brother," he whispered. As he rose, his eyes were wet, but murder lived in them.

Capstan flicked the map to front and centre of their HUDs. "Here's our way back to the dropship. Once Watts comes around, we go. Then we call in the cruiser, and flatten this shithole from orbit. Whatever those things are, they die here. We don't."

"Were there really loads of them?" Hayashi asked Lau.

He shrugged, mouth twisted in contrition. "Felt like it, but I don't know. I took out two, saw at least three more."

"You?" Capstan asked Collins.

"Took out one, and there were three after that. Hard to tell. Maybe two more. I think they were breeding the fuckers here."

"What?"

"The labs. It's not a mining operation."

Capstan nodded, lips pursed. "So what? Not our concern now. There's at least six to eight of the fuckers out there. Or maybe hundreds. And five of us. Doesn't matter. One door, three corridors, and we're back on the dropship and away, but we have to assume it's going to be a hell of fight to get there. You got thirty minutes. Check your gear and ammo."

Collins glanced at Watts, checked her vitals. They were already improving. Nano-reknit listed twenty six minutes to go. He reloaded his assault rifle and hers, double-checked his remaining grenades and other armaments. They were still well-equipped for a fight. To while away the time, he keyed up one of the consoles and started scanning through base logs.

"Incoming," Hayashi said quietly.

Their HUDs showed five lifesigns moving towards the C and C.

"Those things never showed up on our sensors before," Collins said. "Why now?"

"They're not life as our gear knows it," Hayashi said. "These must be something else."

"Cameras across the base are still out," Capstan said. "Sabotaged beyond repair. We'd need new circuit boards and bio-processors. Same with all the vehicles and base shuttles."

The lifesigns reached the western blast doors and there were three quick, sharp bangs. Pause. Three more.

"They fucking knocking now?" Lau asked.

"We assumed the scientists were all dead," Collins said. "But are they?"

Hayashi moved to the door. "What's the code for the view pane?" she asked.

Collins keyed up internal security and a moment later said, "Eight seven one hash D."

Hayashi tapped the code into a small pad on the door and a thirty centimetre square panel slid aside revealing a thick glass pane with a speaker grill below it. A small crowd of people outside slumped with relief.

"Please, let us in!" the front one said. His eyes were dark and haunted, his face blood-stained.

"How do we know you're safe?" Hayashi asked.

The scientists kept looking frantically behind themselves. "Please!" the front man repeated. "Some of our people went mad, homicidal, but we managed to hide. We're starving! We heard gunfire, knew rescue had finally arrived. Quickly, those monsters could be here even now. We can't see them!"

"And the ones who went mad?"

The scientist shrugged. "No idea!"

Hayashi turned to Capstan who returned her gaze with hard eyes. He ran his tongue along his top lip.

He lifted his chin to Hayashi. "Weapons up," he said quietly. Keeping his rifle level in one hand, he keyed the override with the other.

The door hissed open and five people fell inside, faces almost melting with relief. The door whooshed shut quickly behind them and Hayashi closed the view pane. The lead man strode towards Capstan with both hands out as though he were coming in for a hug. Two more men followed close behind and two women hung back.

"You're in charge?" the first asked. "Thank you! Thank you so much."

Capstan backed up, took a two-handed grip on his weapon. "Stay back!"

The front scientist shot forward, preternaturally fast, and fell on Capstan like a rabid dog. The Lieutenant squeezed a quick burst of fire, but the scientist wrapped him up like an octopus even as exit wounds exploded from his back. The following two joined the first, inhumanly quick and strong, slamming the Lieutenant to the ground. Capstan's weapon barked from inside the scrum and chunks of flesh and bone few out of the attackers, along with sprays of blood, but they continued their assault. Growling and hissing, snapping their teeth, hands rending in a blur.

Collins stepped forward and took line of sight to shoot without hitting Capstan and squeezed off three quick headshots. As each skull exploded, that body fell still.

Collins dragged the corpses off the Lieutenant, but the man stayed down, blood-stained and twitching. His throat was a ragged mess, blood pulsing out across the floor. One eye was gone, his left cheek torn away from lips to ear, bite marks all over his face, head and shoulders, right through bone, exposing muscle and brains.

He'd given as good as he'd got with his enhanced teeth. The attackers lay around him with chunks missing. Silica filaments striated their exposed bones, glistened in their wet, red tissue. It glittered in their spilled blood.

Collins pulled a med-foam can from his webbing and stood numb, staring. Where the hell did he even start? There was more injury than flesh across Capstan's head, neck and shoulders. The Lieutenant gargled on his own blood, his remaining eye swivelled hectically in the socket. Collins sighed as Capstan's signs all flickered to a flat line.

The C and C was strangely quiet. He turned to see Hayashi and Lau, each with a weapon levelled at the two remaining scientists.

"Look in UV," Hayashi said.

The scientists stood as if frozen, not even blinking. Glass-like webbing criss-crossed their bodies like veins.

"Remember that last transmission?" Lau whispered.

"Poor bastards were already just puppets of those fuckers out there," Hayashi said. "We should have looked with UV before we let them in. Stupid."

Collins moved a little closer, weapon ready. Their eyes were as still as their bodies. "Fuck 'em," he said.

Hayashi and Lau fired simultaneously and the women slumped to the ground as their heads disintegrated.

"And then there were four," Hayashi said quietly.

Collins checked the medic's signs and was glad to see improvement rather than degradation. "Nineteen minutes until Watts is done."

Lau sat and triggered a holo-display, began working through comms diagnostics, trying to raise Daisy. "We need her hardware!" he said to no one in particular.

Collins returned to the console he'd been studying and continued to read. Eventually he found some encrypted logs and set about cracking them. It didn't take long with the military software on board his neural boost. "Motherfuckers."

"What?" Lau asked.

"This breeding program has been active for over nine years," Collins said, anger starting a hot flood in his gut. "According to this, surveys discovered previously unknown silicon-based lifeforms on this moon, most likely introduced hundreds of years ago."

"How long? By who?"

"It doesn't say. They live in warren-like structures in the first few metres of crust. Small, eight-limbed creatures that can reshape themselves and remould their exoskeleton. They naturally generate a tight energy field that interrupts light and sound waves, renders them silent and almost invisible.

"They were about the size of domestic cats, baseline intelligence roughly equivalent to a smart dog, no respiratory system to speak of, virtually no body heat, able to exist in vacuum and any temperature. They reshape their shells to carve through pretty much anything, including rock to make their homes, and consume silicate deposits in the crust to survive."

Lau shook his head, stared at the floor. "Fuck me. But those things are bigger than cats!"

Collins read on silently for a few moments, flicked between reports. "The fucking idiots started genetically manipulating them. They codenamed it Project: Future Warfare, began enhancing size and strength. They wanted to breed these things into trained warriors, invisible fucking killing machines under Alliance control."

"Shitheads!" Lau hissed.

"According to the most recent reports, they didn't understand the brain biology properly and the creatures' intelligence was exponentially enhanced along with size. They first began escaping confinement, then quickly developed a method to infect the humans and came back to gain control of the scientists. The last entry is from a Doctor Alice Orszulok. She planned to go and sabotage all the vehicles so the things couldn't escape and then blow the place after transmitting this full report."

"She was successful in the vehicle sabotage," Lau said.

"They must have caught her before she did any more."

"But her message got through," Hayashi said.

They turned to her.

"What?" Collins asked.

"It's why we're here."

"Why didn't they warn us?" Collins asked. "Send more of us. We've got sentry cannons on the fucking dropship we could have deployed from the outset."

"Future warfare, remember." Hayashi shook her head, sighed.

"What?" Collins asked again.

"They wanted to watch us, see how their new soldiers perform. We're fucking fodder. But I don't think they realised the bastards had compromised all comms, base-wide and what we're carrying. We can't send a signal fifty metres, let alone back up to the Belvedere."

Silence fell over the room like a cold fog.

Lau punched a console. "Motherfuckers."

"When have we ever been anything but dispensable?" Hayashi said.

Collins caught a blip on another console and moved to check. It took him a moment to figure out what he was seeing. Then, "Hatches are opening and closing along the maintenance conduits. Several different locations, all leading towards the docking bay."

"Those things would never fit," Lau said. "People can barely squeeze along those fucking tubes."

Hayashi laughed derisively. "Reshape themselves and remould their exoskeleton."

"They're heading for the dropship!" Collins shouted. "We think we're hiding in here safe to regroup and they don't give a fuck. They're escaping."

"What do we do?" Lau asked.

"We have to stop them," Collins said.

Hayashi leaned back in her chair. "Why?"

"What?" Collins was starting to feel like an idiot, repeating the same word.

"They threw us to the fucking wolves. Or silicon shape-changers or whatever. So why do we care?"

"Two reasons," Collins said, anger rising again. "One, we're soldiers and we defend. Two, if they take our dropship, how the hell do we get home? You think Alliance will rescue us now we know this bullshit?"

Hayashi scowled.

Lau nodded. "He's right."

"Why are they in the conduits?" Collins asked.

Hayashi stood. "Because the only way to the docking bay is through here and we've sealed them out. They're bypassing. Let's go." She tapped at the console Capstan had been using and the southern door hissed open.

"What about Watts?"

"She's dead weight right now. We'll stop those fuckers first, then come back for her."

Collins downloaded the command codes to his neural implant. "Let's go."

The three of them resealed their suits and helmets and ran from the C and C, Collins remotely dropping the blast door behind them. *Hang tight, Watts,* he thought, then focussed all his attention on the imminent fight. Three corridors, two hundred metres, was all that stood between them and the dropship. He called out to the AI over comms. "Daisy, you hearing me?"

No response.

They ran on. Collins hailed Daisy again, still no response. They turned into the last corridor, maybe forty metres and one corner between them and the docking seal. "Daisy, you there?" Collins said.

"I'm here. I'm reading something in the conduits."

"Prepare to defend yourself," Collins said. "Deploy the sentry cann…"

The ground between them and the dock exploded upwards. UV clearly showed three glassy serpent-like creatures, three metres long, erupt up from the maintenance lines, tiny legs scrabbling at the broken floor. The squad skidded to a halt and backed up, firing controlled bursts, deafening in the confined space. As they pumped mini grenades, the creatures twisted and writhed like sentient smoke to evade the attacks. Bullets and explosions that did hit their targets had less effect than before.

"Their shells are flexible, must be thicker now!" Hayashi yelled. "They're adapting to our abilities."

"Marines, hit the deck," Daisy said over comms.

The three of them didn't pause, fell to their bellies. Three sentry cannons rolled around the corner and barked fifty-calibre destruction into the corridor. The sweeping fire ripped through the aliens and howled by just over the marine's heads, tearing the walls to shreds. The creatures fell in several pieces to the ground and silence sank over them.

Lau whooped and rose to his knees. "Way to go, Daisy!"

"I'm compromised," Daisy said in her calm, soft voice. "Get back to the C and C and lock down."

Lau frowned. "What?"

The sentry cannons roared again and Lau burst into a spray of blood and body parts.

"They've accessed my overrides from outside," Daisy said. "They're on the moon surface and gaining entry to me. I have no..." She fell silent.

"This was all a fucking distraction," Hayashi yelled. "Move!" She used elbows and knees to furiously snake her way back up the corridor.

Collins matched her as the sentry cannons swivelled towards them. He lobbed a concussion grenade behind as they went, the explosion knocking the cannons back. Their deadly stream of ordnance tore open the corridor ceiling and sparks flew as the lights went out. The cannons quickly reasserted their equilibrium and rolled on rubber tracks in pursuit.

Hayashi and Collins made the corner as more fifty cal fire ripped up the walls and floor behind them, and they bolted for the C and C. They fell inside, Collins triggered the blast doors which rang with cannon fire as they slammed down.

Laying on their backs, gasping, Collins and Hayashi listened as the dropship powered up and launched.

Hayashi sighed. "Then there were three."

"With no hope of escape," Collins said.

He got up and checked Watts. Eleven minutes to go. He moved to the console and tried to key up a view, any view, to see what might be happening. None of the internal cameras were working, but an external array, watching the skies, was still operational. He tracked the dropship as it made orbit.

Space folded and the battlecruiser dropped out of jump, only a few hundred clicks from Daisy. Collins and Hayashi watched in silence. The dropship veered, heading straight for it.

"They recalled the Belvedere," Collins said. "You think they can gain control of a ship that size?"

Hayashi snorted. "Why not? They owned us since before we fucking landed."

"Reckon Alliance has any idea what's coming on board?" He sent repeated hails to the battlecruiser, knowing there would be no response. "I wonder how many of those bastards are on Daisy?" he said.

Hayashi shrugged. "Could be dozens. How many are still here? How big an army did those idiot scientists breed?"

Collins zoomed in on Daisy as she entered the Belvedere's docking bay. There were several moments of silence that seemed to drag into hours, then fire belched and billowed out into space as several hull panels around the bay split and buckled.

"Fuck," Collins whispered.

Nothing happened for several more minutes, Collins and Hayashi watched in silence.

Watts groaned and sat up, shifted her wounded shoulder. "We ready? Where's Capstan? And Lau?"

Shuttles began launching from the Belvedere, headed for the surface a couple of hundred clicks from the science station. Weapons ports opened along one flank of the battlecruiser and a wave of missiles launched, arcing down towards the habitat.

"Motherfuckers," Collins said.

THE ASH AT FT PRESTON

Case C. Capehart

By the time Max realized men were in his apartment, it was too late to go for the antique Mossberg 12-gauge under his bed. The WASPs breached the door of his bedroom before the men in suits did. Their automated 30-caliber guns focused on him immediately, but the green LEDs on their bee-like faces were encouraging. At least he did not qualify as a threat. They might have been red had he reached his shotgun in time.

"Lieutenant Maximus Ishikawa?" The man in the suit barely glanced at him, but grimaced at the name he read off the tablet in his hand.

Max slid his legs off the side of the bed, easy not to move suddenly enough to turn the green lights on the front of the WASPs to yellow. "Former Lieutenant. Why?"

"Do you still have a Go Bag, former Lieutenant?"

Max nodded.

"Dust it off and come with us. We'll explain on the way."

Max expected the usual pokiness of military bureaucracy once they arrived at Central Command: the intake protocols, waiting for all the leaders to come in, hours of dress-right-dress bullshit.

However, he underestimated the gravity of the disaster that brought him there.

Without even issuing a temporary uniform, Max was rushed directly into the War Room with nothing more thorough than a single retina scan. Ten minutes after arriving, Max found himself at a long table with several men he only recognized from their pictures on the Chain of Command wall in the Mess Hall. General Edgers sat near the front, but he did not lead the meeting as Max had assumed.

Command General Einhart stood at the head of the table

looking out over the men. The screen behind him queued up a recorded video for playback. "Gentlemen, less than ninety minutes ago an unidentified threat attacked Fort Preston – a munitions disposal base on Ishtar 4. The attack was unforeseen and unprovoked; civilian casualties have been high. The remaining forces have locked down the lower levels, but it's simply a matter of time before there is a breach."

A black and gold-trimmed drone hovering over one of the chairs extended a foldout vid-screen from the front console. A few clicks signaled an interstellar connection, and a man with golden hair swept back in a fashionable haircut appeared on the screen. "General, how in the hell did these attackers overwhelm our defensive drones? My WASPs have taken down Hedge Tanks in seconds. What does this invasion force have that stood up to that kind of power?"

Terry Dawn was the Minister of Defense, the civilian leadership for the Galactic Expansion Force and the CEO for DRAGO, the largest military drone manufacturer in the solar system never travelled anywhere in person.

"The WASPs ignored the enemy, sir."

* * *

Nikki awoke and rolled off her cot and into a crouch. The flames of the industrial smelters glinted menacingly along the Aerolite blade of her combat knife, reflecting her mood.

It was another dream; a byproduct of being disconnected for so long. They served as a reminder of her intended purpose. She hated them.

She glanced at her wrist and the faint, blue-green digits appeared beneath her skin. It was just before three in the morning, well before her upcoming shift. Relaxing from her crouch, she cast about for the source of her sudden wakefulness. The flames of the smelters put everything through a red filter and enveloped the entire room in heat that only she could handle without gear.

Nothing stirred in her current home, far-removed from the

soldiers and civilians above her. The fortified combat dummy she kept in the corner, its grey poly-alloy skin – decimated with thousands of nicks and gashes from a bladed weapon – stood alone in resembling anything human in that industrial volcano.

Still, something itched in the back of her mind.

She walked to the intercom on the wall and punched the button. "Beast to Overwatch, come in."

The speaker squawked back after a moment. "You know how I can tell you woke up in a panic with your knife out in front of you, Nikki? You always forget how much that call-sign bullshit bugs me when you're still groggy."

Nikki flexed her jaw, a habit she'd formed in order to hold her tongue. Sergeant Kaminski was not exactly her superior, but he was the Non-commissioned Officer on Post for the night. She could not back-talk him. "Sergeant, is there anything going on up top?"

"Don't worry about up top, Nikki. You don't go up there anyway. Get back in your rack. Or here's an idea, why don't you go to your actual dorm? You're off duty for another four hours and you probably need a shower anyway."

"Sergeant, can you please just check in with someone up top?" Seventeen years of the most intense combat training devised by humans had prepared her for hell, but nothing had prepared her for undisciplined and sarcastic leadership.

She heard him sigh, and he most likely did it loud enough to come through the intercom on purpose. After a few moments, she heard the intercom click on again and his voice came through. "Nikki, can you come up here for a moment?"

Nikki ascended the stairs and entered the security office of the Materials Recycling Bay. Sergeant Kaminski laced up loosened boots as she snapped into parade rest before him. The office WASP hovered near, its green LED staring at her. He was leaving his post and venturing up to the surface. In past days, soldiers would strap a carbine to their web gear before investigating suspicious activity. Now they simply ordered the closest WASP to escort them.

The sergeant looked up at her and then to the WASP. "No

one is answering my damn comm checks. I'm heading up top to find the night post and kick their asses. I'm taking the WASP, per procedure... assuming you don't mind being on your own."

Nikki glared at the green light on the flying death bot. She wondered if, within its super-advanced robot brain, it understood her loathing for it and why. Did it look at her and laugh inside? Did it know what its birth had taken from her, or was it coldly indifferent? Which answer would be worse?

"I'll be fine, Sergeant," she replied, fingering the hilt of the knife resting on her hip.

"Yeah, just don't start doing pull-ups on the rafter and forget to—"

The elevator doors opened and a dull-grey, metallic spike ripped through Sergeant Kaminski's chest. The segmented spike writhed like a tentacle, whipping the shocked NCO to the side. He crashed into the bay door and slumped, blinking in stunned confusion.

A metallic, insectoid creature burst into the room. Nikki froze as the thing turned its flat, carapace-like head and looked at her with a set of eight eyes that glowed green like the threat indicators on the WASP. She expected the drone to open fire on the monster any second, but it hovered to Sergeant Kaminski and scanned him for vital signs.

Nikki recovered and got her arms in front of her as the swipe from the creature's clawed hand sent her crashing through the office window and plummeting thirty feet to the cold concrete floor below. Just before she hit, she saw the WASP zoom out of the window to follow her down, ignoring the demon inside.

* * *

"A malfunction? What are we looking at, sir?" General Edgers asked.

The Commander General shook his head. "There is no malfunction with the drones. All remote scans continue to show perfect working order. We think it's something with the unidentified force; our initial hypothesis is that the WASPs' AI is having difficulty reconciling the threat posed by them. Basically, the drones do not know what the aliens are and will not engage until they figure it out."

"Can we fix them?" another general asked.

A pallid man in a technician's uniform straightened and cleared his throat. "The base is too far away to force a data link without someone on site reciprocating, and no one has done so since the attack. We have no information on the enemy and without knowing what's blocking them we can't know how to fix the error."

General Stinson leaned forward, resting his elbows on the table. "We still have a few human units, mostly Spec Ops, as Quick-Reaction Forces for this scenario. We have absolutely no info on this enemy's capabilities. Our boys would be going in blind."

"What about the soldiers inside? They have a whole base at their disposal for Christ's sake."

General Edgers laughed and shook his head, motioning toward the screen. "Engineers and technicians. Hell, we barely combat train them in Basic anymore."

"General Einhart, do we have a more immediate plan?" The drone carrying the minister's face hovered in place as the front-mounted cameras panned the room, likely using advanced facial-recognition software to gauge the room. No one in the room flinched, such was their comfort with the perverse mockery of human behavior by the robotic sentinels. "If not, we need to think about… we need to consider the possibility of writing this one off."

General Einhart shook his head. "Sir, you don't understand. When we say we have nothing on this enemy, we mean it. We cannot destroy them with no data collection. What if this is not an isolated event?"

"I need to contact the President. We need to call an emergency conference to consider our options." At the other end of the video feed, Minister Dawn stood, preparing to end transmission. "But the only options I see are sending in men or sending in ordinance."

"I see one other option." General Edgers turned his eyes on Max.

* * *

Nikki shook off the impact and got to her feet. She had not taken a hit like that since her first day in the Recycling Bay when she got confused and let a crane slam a steel beam into her from behind. The pretense of being a normal human was impossible for her to maintain after that.

The creature scurried down the side of the bay wall and dropped to the floor like a cockroach. It did not hesitate or act confused by her survival. It sensed only prey and did not overanalyze the situation.

Nikki reciprocated.

It moved like a bullet, closing the distance in a heartbeat. Nikki dove out of the way as razor-like claws sliced the air above her. The tail came next, following up the attack with a stab meant to impale her like Sergeant Kaminski. She parried the blow, but the force was enough to stagger her. She dropped to her ass and scrambled back, sliding out of the creature's reach.

Nikki halted right next to the closed-arch plasma saw, a high-grade steel cutting tool that resembled a flaming chainsaw on a lever arm attached to an 800-pound, mobile surface that she used to cut through old tank barrels.

As the creature charged, she ripped the saw from its hinges and fired it up. She took the enemy's fingers with the first swipe. As it retreated, the tail came at her again. It did not learn quickly; Nikki did. She dodged the strike, and her left hand shot out, grabbing the tail as it passed. The blade blazed through the steel-like armor of the monster's tail like a dry twig.

Nikki over-extended and the creature's reflexes rivaled her own. The swipe caught her from behind, slicing into her back and sending her tumbling across the floor. She still gripped the saw, but the creature bore down on her with the frantic haste of an imminent kill.

Instead of getting to her feet, Nikki pushed herself backward and swung the saw above her head. The tool cut halfway into the sturdy pylon, but it was enough considering the weight atop it. With a loud groan, the metal gave way to drop the front end of the shelf.

The monster paid no heed to the shelf above; its focus fixed on taking her while she was still prone. At the last second it looked up and tried to reverse its momentum, but the rack of saw-cut artillery barrels rained down on it like a volley of quarter-ton arrows.

Nikki climbed atop the pile of steel tubes and looked down at the insectoid head of the creature. It focused on her and tried to move, but the wreckage had mangled its body. Nikki flared the plasma arch on the saw and bent to her task.

* * *

"I'm sorry, but… what on earth is an ASH Soldier?" General Stinson glanced around the room, flummoxed.

"Advanced Synthetic Humanoid." Max pulled out a data card and plugged it into the table, throwing a general outline of the project up on the screen. "Genetically engineered and trained from birth to be more human than a human. Then, before seeing her first battle, we replaced her with the WASP and sent her to an outdated munitions surplus to be a glorified janitor."

"The WASP has saved countless human lives, including those of your obsolete abominations." Minister Dawn had taken offense to Max's statement, as expected.

Max did not back down from the argument. "68 dead, Minister, all by suicide. Seven remain. Is that what you mean when you say you saved them? We nurtured them into warriors from conception. When we took that job away from them we took away their reason for living."

The minister smirked, the drone camera focusing on Max

even as the image on the screen remained facing forward. "Then I guess they weren't as tough as you say."

Max clenched his fist. "If any of my girls were on Ishtar 4, you can bet your damn company they would be fighting these attackers, not hovering overhead in indecision."

"Actually, Mr Ishikawa, your statement is about to be put to the test," General Einhart said. "There is a single ASH soldier stationed at Fort Preston. She works deep under the surface, away from the public."

Einhart slid a photo of a pale, athletic woman with short, crimson hair onto the screen and Minister Dawn scoffed. "That Amazonian stripper is supposed to be some sort of super soldier? She belongs on a stage at a porn club that caters to freak fetishists, not in the field."

"Nikki... the Beast," Max whispered as he stood and stared at the girl on the screen.

"Was she yours, son?" the Commander General asked.

"Lieutenant Ishikawa piloted Ryoko, the Death Angel; the only ASH to see real combat." General Edgers slid a dossier cover sheet into the lower corner of the screen. The picture was of a black-haired, East-Asian woman with a scar over her nose. The letters MIA were stamped over her face.

Max flinched at the sight of his ASH soldier. "Sir, I can pilot Nikki... if there's still an operational Chair and we can form a connection. With a Pilot guiding her, we might turn this from disaster. If she's there, in that hell-hole, I guarantee she's already fighting."

* * *

Nikki ripped her bed from the brackets that anchored it to the ground then slammed the forty-pound sledge into the wall behind it. With her adrenaline still spiking from the battle, it only took a few seconds for her to smash through the concrete. She reached into the hole and pulled the sturdy cargo chest free from where it slumbered. What remained of her combat gear was still serviceable. She wished she still had her tech or some of her weapons, but at least they'd allowed her to keep the Aerolite knife she was issued upon maturity.

She stripped out of her maintenance overalls and stretched the snug, polymer combat suit over her legs. The green and slate material reminded her of training and her skin tingled as she zipped the front over her breasts and up to her neck.

Without warning, Nikki's body locked up and an intense pain washed over her with dim familiarity. She could barely remember what it felt like to experience a forced link. The neural connection was no longer strong; a muscle she could not exercise to keep it operational. She fought her brain's reaction to the foreign Pilot and tried to relax.

Nikki? Nikki, are we linked up?

The voice was in her head. For a moment she thought it might be Gavin and elation filled her. But the voice held a different accent, sounded older. It was not her Pilot.

"Connection is green. Nikki, call sign: Beast, awaiting orders."

Maximus Ishikawa, call sign: Shogun, assuming Pilot Chair. What is your status, Beast?

She recognized her Pilot as soon as he stated his name. Lieutenant Ishikawa had piloted Ryoko throughout the training. "I am five-by-five, sir. I encountered an unidentified Tango seventeen minutes earlier. Tango was threat level red; it killed Sergeant on Post and came at me."

Where is the Tango now, Beast?

"Tango neutralized, sir. I subdued it with an improvised trap of old artillery barrels and then decapitated it with an industrial plasma saw. As the Tango was unknown, I quartered it and inspected its internal structure to ensure death."

You cut it into pieces?

"I had to be sure, sir."

She could feel his laughter in her head.

Beast, I will upload all the intel we have. The higher-ups are still crafting your mission parameters, but here's the situation: as far as we know, the base is overrun. We have little intel on the attackers, and that's the problem. However, the drones keep all recorded info and reports on a shared data cloud. If you can make it to the hangar bay on the top level, there should be ships with AI on board who have access to this data. That's your way out, Beast.

Nikki finished gearing up and returned to the recycling bay. No other creatures had entered yet. "Sir, all I can tell you is that the enemy is incredibly dangerous and its internal makeup is biotechnological. Sending you images now."

Nikki looked through what remained of the creature. Through the Neural link, her Pilot uploaded the feed from her eyes into the computers at Central Command.

Beast, right now we must assume the WASPs will never break free from this glitch that keeps them from recognizing the Tangos. If there are any survivors up top, they are not equipped to defend against something like this. I will upload the mission parameters as soon as I have them. For now, I want you to locate weapons – anything you think will be effective against these things, and button up. You're going into combat.

* * *

Sergeant Lancell checked on what remained of his staff as a few of the heartier engineers worked on the barricade at the only entrance to the Human Resources office. His secretary, Private Fialto, lay across a cot, her left leg shredded from the ankle halfway up her thigh. The painkillers helped, but every time Fialto glanced at what was left of her leg, Lancell could see the havoc it wreaked on the private's mind.

"Why aren't the WASPs firing?" Lancell looked up into his subordinate's frenzied eyes. Though numbed to the pain, she gripped the side of her cot until her knuckles whitened. "They just floated there, Sergeant. That thing sliced Renfro right in half then came straight at me and tried to filet me like a damn halibut... the WASPs didn't do a damn thing. I thought they were supposed to protect us."

Sergeant Lancell gripped her shoulder but he had no answers.

He stood and looked around at the others. When he spoke, he kept his voice just loud enough to be heard. "I need someone to take inventory – anything and everything we have available. Prioritize tech and communications… we need to find out who else is out there."

"Sergeant, uh… shouldn't the Colonel be giving the orders?" Private Holiday had been in his office for sporting a non-regulation Mohawk when the invaders hit.

Lancell straightened and took another look around. A female in an officer's uniform sat along the wall, staring off into the distance. On her collar was a subdued black bird with spread wings. Amid all the chaos, he had not immediately noticed her.

He walked over to where she sat and stood at attention. "Ma'am, it appears you are in line for command—"

"I'm not, Sergeant." The woman cut him off and broke out of her stare to look up at him. Her eyes held as much fright as Private Fialto, if not more. "I… can't. You, Sergeant… you're doing well. Please, whatever you need to do… you're in command."

Sergeant Lancell nodded. He did not bother with a salute and, considering the combat zone they found themselves in, figured he could argue his decision if needed.

He turned from her and made his way back through the cramped office. "I need some kind of communication, soldiers. Get me something I can reach out with."

As if on command, a voice drifted from near the back of the office, near Private Holiday. "Beast to Home Station, calling anyone up top."

Sergeant Lancell snapped his gaze to where the voice emanated. "What is that, the intercom? Private, find it and drop the volume, now."

Any of the survivors who could still walk crowded around as Sergeant Lancell took control of the comm link and answered. "This is Sergeant Lancell; I copy. Who am I speaking to?"

"Call sign: Beast, Sergeant. I am currently in the Recycling Bay. Give me your coordinates and I will make my way to you. Over."

"Someone's still alive in the Recycling Bay?" Sergeant Lancell looked over at the green Private. "That's deep below us; at least a thousand feet."

Sergeant Lancell depressed the comm button. "Negative, Beast… whoever you are. Topside is overrun. I say again, topside is overrun. For your own safety, stay put and do not rely on the WASPs; they are on the fritz."

The voice came back, cold enough to match the attitude of the invaders. "Sergeant, if you want to live, you will tell me where you're at and then keep radio silence until I reach you. Do you copy?"

Sergeant Lancell glanced at the other soldiers gathered around the comm link. They all wore puzzled expressions. If this were a drill, they would laugh their asses off at the jack-ass who had watched too many action movies during R&R. Whomever spoke on the other end of the link seemed to know they were under siege and by something sinister, yet they still insisted on emerging from what had to be the safest place on base.

He depressed the link once more. "Soldier… who are you?"

* * *

"It doesn't make any sense. Why females?" Max could hear Minister Dawn's drone hovering behind him as he fine-tuned the synaptic calibrations to strengthen his link to Nikki. They had wasted too much time talking already, but the Minister still worried about his corporate interests and would not let his skepticism rest. "You make men for combat; anyone knows that."

"We tried males first," Max said. "The genetic treatment kept causing them to process protein incorrectly. They naturally bulked up too much in training, which caused their mobility to plummet." Max finished his work and launched himself into the Chair. "The females did not have this issue. Since we were, at the time, warring with Fundamentalists, we also speculated the enemy would underestimate female soldiers… as you just did."

"Well, it doesn't appear this enemy goes easy on either gender." Minister Dawn's drone glided over to the uploaded photos of the alien creature and the man on the screen shuddered. "She's a hell of a killer, I'll give you that much, Lieutenant. But if she had a time with just one of those things, what can she be expected to do against a dozen?"

Max fitted the cranial controls into place and stared forward, bracing himself for the link. "Find a good seat, Minister. I'm about to show you what an ASH Soldier is capable of."

* * *

A sword?

Nikki lifted the blade and then slapped it to the electromagnet on the back of her harness; it snapped into place and held. "I needed a hobby. It's antiquated… like me."

But you have a gun, too… right?

Nikki buckled the prototype 30mm, cylinder-fed shotgun to her harness and holstered a 50-caliber Harkama Juggernaut to her thigh. "Of course."

She started the GravLift on the manual cart and pushed it into the elevator.

Is that what I think it is? Where did you even find that?

"In the back," Nikki replied with a smile. "Let's hope there's ammunition left for it in the ordinance bay on level two."

Why is it still in the protective case?

Two Tangos entered the elevator as the doors opened, searching for the occupants. When they noticed the opening in the ceiling, it was too late. Nikki cooked off her improvised incineration grenade and dropped it into the carriage, kicking the hatch shut after it.

The aliens screeched and thrashed below her and the soles of her boots smoked against the metal roof. After a few minutes, when the thrashing stopped, she opened the hatch and dropped down into hell. One Tango still scratched at the walls of the elevator, its metallic exoskeleton blackened and warped. Her knife penetrated its bulky skull and shut down its brain with ease. The other Tango took the brunt of the initial flare and lay in the corner, resembling the remnants of tunnel rats that had strayed too close to the recycling pit.

The protective case of her big gun, designed to endure the extreme heat of the lower levels, was slightly compromised, but still operable. She grabbed the cart and pushed it out of the flaming carriage, turning her head and blowing out a small flame that had caught on her shoulder.

* * *

Sergeant Lancell leveled the carbine at the door alongside five other men. They had found an old cache of emergency weapons and ammunition; a throwback to the days when the drones were new and untested. The log registry on the cache showed a name he did not recognize, and he had worked this area of the base for over five years.

Sergeant Lancell placed Holiday in charge of servicing the weapons and making sure they were in operation. The man still had his mosquito wings and his full combat training amounted to two weeks of voluntary training in Fort Kyle, Texas, on Earth –learning how to fire and clear jams on old bull pups. That made the private the most experienced weapon specialist among the group.

"Sergeant, I can't do this," Private Holiday wheezed. His knuckles glowed white as he gripped his weapon to his shoulder. "I shot at fragging holograms on Earth. I wasn't even a squad leader in Basic."

Sergeant Lancell grabbed the skinny kid by the lapel and yanked him close. Outside the door, the creatures tore at the metal, clawing their way in through reinforced steel like plywood. "Lock it up, Private. Fate doesn't give a shit about your readiness; it calls you up regardless. You are the most experienced among us; I don't need you to be a squad leader; I need you to remember how to clear a jam and to shoot straighter than you've ever shot in your short life. That is the extent of your responsibilities *at this moment*. Now can you do that, Private?"

A metallic claw punched through the steel of the door and tore a diagonal line across it. Alien hands pulled on the weakened steel, widening the breach. Green, drone-like eyes peered in at them, taking in their numbers and resistance force.

Sergeant Lancell lined up the quick-sight apertures on the hole in the door. "On my command! Select your target. Alternate your fire. Ready?"

The sergeant's finger slipped over the edge of the trigger and he wiped the sweat off against the side of his uniform before replacing it. He might have worried about normal things like recoil or ricochet if it were not for the face of death glaring at him from behind the six-inch gorge in the top half of the door.

A loud boom resounded outside the door, followed by another and then a third. The alien looked to the right and screeched an unearthly scream just before the fourth boom obliterated its skull and half its torso.

A deathly silence settled over the room as all inside froze in confusion. Sergeant Lancell concentrated so hard on the door that he forgot the challenge word the mysterious 'Beast' had given him.

"Frisky! Frisky!" His voice cracked under the anxiety, but he kept calling out the challenge, simultaneously hopeful and fearful of hearing the return password.

"Dingo."

Sergeant Lancell reached out and grabbed Private Holiday before he hit the ground and nearly dropped his weapon. Someone was outside the door; someone who had given them an old military verification technique they knew the aliens could not compromise and who had just cut through four alien creatures that hours ago had seemed invincible. It seemed almost too much for the boy to handle.

"Pull the barricade back, Sergeant, and rally your men. We're moving out." The voice came from around the corner, but no one peered through the hole the aliens had cut into the door.

Sergeant Lancell gave the order and every able-bodied soldier in the room scrambled to pull the makeshift barricade from the door. Once the exit was clear, the door opened and Sergeant Lancell stepped out into the hall, weapon raised.

Gore coated the ground and hall. Something had torn into the aliens with such force it splattered them like warm paint-balls. The next thing he saw took him completely off guard.

Leaning against the wall, just to the left of the doorway, stood the tallest woman he had ever seen. She wore a skin-tight, grey and green suit with heavy-looking web-gear. Her short hair was blood red and her cold blue eyes reminded him of Neptunian glaciers as they cut into him. In her right hand she gripped a weapon straight out of a history program.

The colonel pushed past him. "Is that a Milkor? Wait, no, it has too many barrels on the cylinder." She stared right at the bulky, old-world weapon the soldier had slung to her front. "That's a shotgun… with 30mm slugs. You've also got shrapnel and incendiary rounds. It must be a prototype. A weapon that big is too impractical for regular troops."

"Are you in command here, ma'am?" The soldier ignored the Colonel's peculiar interest in her firearm and studied the hall as she addressed the officer.

Sergeant Lancell winced at the breach of decorum then grimaced when the colonel deferred to him. "I am in operational command at the moment, soldier."

She continued scanning the hall as she spoke. "What is the status of your men, Sergeant? How many can move in five minutes?"

Sergeant Lancell glanced back in to the room. "I have twelve who can move now, but three are wounded and need help getting along. One of my privates is shredded below her left knee. Two of my men are badly wounded and need immediate EVAC if they're to make it."

The soldier leaned close enough to whisper, which scared him. "We are moving to the hangar bay in five and we will be moving at double time the entire way. Anyone who cannot hobble on a shoulder or be carried stays."

"Stays?" Sergeant Lancell eked out a nervous laugh. "They

cannot stay here; they'll die. We need to evacuate them to the med bay and stabilize them—"

"We're not going to the med bay, Sergeant." Her blue eyes were tiny icicles as they bore into him, freezing him to the bone. "A molecular induction device has been activated on level 3 with a medium fuse. It will sink this base into the planet and anything still inside. My mission is to get as many survivors as possible off world before detonation. If you stay here or if you slow down the group… I will leave you. Four minutes, Sergeant."

* * *

Sergeant Lancell stared at the ground as he carried Private Fialto on his back. He could not believe what he had just done. Not only had he left behind two dying men, but his conscience had also deprived the group of two carbines and a grenade. It was the least he could do for them after the choice he had to make.

Fourteen survivors followed the impossibly-tall female soldier through the halls. Every few minutes they would come to a stop and the soldier would stare to the side, as if listening to something, then she would nod slightly and press on, confident in her direction. He wondered where she'd come from and whether she had arrived after the attack or had always been here. He could not remember ever noting someone like her in the logs.

A scream pulled his head up and Sergeant Lancell noticed a dark, metallic shadow down the hall.

They were discovered.

More shadows appeared and charged. He cursed the soldier for insisting the last two carbines be kept at the back. That was the most foolish thing he had ever heard. He commanded his two armed men to assist the soldier, but they both froze. Private Fialto screamed at him to turn and run, but he passed her off to the man next to him and grabbed a weapon, pushing to the front as the shotgun boomed.

The Beast pushed forward into the charging monsters, her weapon spitting fire and obliterating everything it hit. Grey torsos blasted into chunks, helmet-like heads fragmented and the bio-goo inside the creatures painted the once-sanitized walls. In seconds she'd downed six aliens, but on the seventh shot, her mighty shotgun clicked. A misfire.

She dropped the gun without hesitation and pulled the mammoth pistol from her thigh, slamming two rounds into a creature inches from the end of her barrel. The pistol reports rivalled the shotgun in sound, but the loads did not pack as mighty of a punch.

"Clear the jam on that weapon," the soldier yelled as she closed with the wounded creature and rammed a combat knife up through its jaw and into the brain.

The Sergeant raised his carbine at the three remaining aliens. "I'll cover you."

Beast yanked the carbine from his grip and shoved him behind her. "Clear my weapon, dammit!"

His carbine's fire sounded meek compared to her other weapons, but by the time he reached her shotgun, she had already unloaded the clip into the first invader. The shotgun had to have weighed fifty pounds and he just stared in confusion at it in his hands.

The colonel was beside him, pointing and yelling. "Pull back the hammer and rotate the cylinder. The hammer… that thing on the back."

He cocked the lever on the weapon and rotated the cylinder in the middle of the gun until it clicked over to the next barrel. He looked up and yelped, seeing the soldier backpedaling right at him as she unloaded her pistol into the last two attackers.

"Here! Here! Here!" he cried, holding out the gun and wishing she would stop before the creatures reached him.

Beast slammed a round into the second alien's head and dropped her pistol as the last one lunged for her. She spun on the ball of her foot and kicked backward into the alien's chest, stopping it mid-lunge and snatching the gun from Sergeant Lancell in one motion. She completed the spin and swung the shotgun barrel right into the enemy's face, pulling the trigger at the moment of impact. The last round fired and blew bits of the alien everywhere.

The soldier swung the cylinder of the shotgun out, dumped the spent rounds and slipped eight new shells into the barrels. With a flick of her wrist, she spun the cylinder and then slammed it home. Swapping out the magazine on her pistol took her a second and then they were moving.

She dropped the magazine out of the discarded carbine and gave it back to Sergeant Lancell. "Reload and keep this thing at the rear. You fire only at anything coming behind us. Leave the front to me."

Sergeant Lancell stood there, stunned. He nodded slowly. "Yeah… understood."

Beast pushed forward and Sergeant Lancell waited where he was for the rear to catch up to him. Most of the men stared at the back of the soldier in similar states of awe.

Private Holiday had a grin on his face as he passed. "I think I'm in love."

* * *

The colonel audibly yelped when she saw what waited for them in the elevator. "That's an M-2. And you found ammunition! It's operational?"

Nikki ignored the exuberant officer and waved the survivors inside. She closed the gate and sent the carrier up to the top floor.

"How many of them are up there?" The NCO in charge, Sergeant Lancell, hid his fear poorly in front of the others, but he acted under fire instead of freezing or fleeing, and that was more useful than a brave face.

"Unknown." Nikki didn't like conversation and feared any conservative speculation on her part would panic the others. She knew what would be waiting on the other side of the doors when they opened. As the carrier reached the floor, she racked the slide and hugged the butterfly grips to her chest.

"Plug your ears and take cover."

A flurry of chrome claws and gun-metal teeth lashed out as soon as the doors parted. Nikki opened fire and turned the beasts to pulp. She barely noticed the expanding pressure inside the elevator carrier, but the others likely thought they had been transported to the bottom of the ocean. In seconds she had cleared the first wave of the attackers at the door. She looked around at the others. Those that still stood wobbled on legs of jelly, but most hunkered in the corners. Blood trickled from a few ear canals. Nikki had not been ordered to deliver them in perfect health; simply alive.

She kicked on the hover drive and pushed the cart and 50-caliber machine gun down the ramp and out into the hangar. The two ships to the left appeared in good condition. By divine fortune the aliens seemed uninterested in destroying technology as demonstrated by all the still-active drones circling above the carnage.

The path to the closest ship was clear of enemies, but as Nikki gave the command for the survivors to move, an alien exploded from cover to her right. She tried to swing the barrel of the M-2 around, but the beast cleared the short distance too swiftly.

The cart, the gun, the ammunition and Nikki flew in different directions. Nikki got her right forearm in front of her throat and the metallic talon skewered it instead. The bay spun around her as she tumbled across the concrete with the creature. She heard the survivors screaming and hoped their fright did not indicate more aliens.

The shotgun still clung to the strap on her harness and she found the grip while ignoring the dozen razor appendages digging into her flesh. She swept the barrel up and bisected the alien with a loud blast. The top half of it lashed out in a frantic death throe, catching the weapon with a claw and flinging it. She shoved the thing off in time to see a second tango looming over an injured soldier.

It lifted the impaled man off his feet with its spear-like tail and chomped down on his head and the top half of his torso in one bite. The others sprinted for the ship, but the alien discarded the dead soldier and quickly turned its attention to the fleeing humans.

Nikki noticed the spasm in her stomach more than the pain when she put her feet under her, and the amount of blood already soaking her suit foreshadowed the information Shogun fed her.

Beast, you're mangled inside. Mobility is at sixty-three percent and dropping. You won't regenerate quickly enough in combat. Proceed to the second ship immediately!

"The survivors are boarding the first ship already; it's too late to switch ships." Nikki gave chase, drawing her pistol, but she could not unleash and sprint without hitting those in her line of fire; not with being fifteen years out of practice.

Leave them, Beast, or you won't make it and they'll be dead either way. We need that drone data. We need you alive, soldier!

Nikki had no room to stop and hesitate. Her mind comprehended the order and worked through the logic of it, but her body did not react quickly enough. She slammed into the alien from behind as it slowed to pick off a straggling soldier and the injured man hanging on his shoulder.

There was no backing out now; no Plan B. Nikki rammed the barrel of her 50-caliber pistol into its side and fired off two rounds. She wounded it, but the pistol rounds did not create the same magnitude of damage as the shotgun.

The alien turned on her.

The claw cut across her chest, from the side of her neck to her deltoids and nearly cleaved her right breast clean off. Dark blood sprayed the creature and Shogun screamed obscenities in her head. She cried out inside her mind, commanding him to tell her how long she had before expiration with that wound.

His voice came soft and from a distance, drowned out by the sound of an inferno somewhere deep within her. Her vision blurred and heat flooded her body. She heard a scream, but it may have come from her. She felt armored skin in her grasp and she yanked upward, lifting the monster over her head and then brought it down hard, slamming it into the solid concrete. A swift kick sent the beast spiraling into a stack of crates and her vision returned in a red hue.

The creature rose to its feet, but it moved slower. Everything moved slower.

There's no room to reach the ship now, Beast. You have to kill it or it will not allow any of you to leave.

"Understood."

Nikki rushed forward, closing the gap between her and the creature in an instant. Her firearms were gone, but her synthetic muscle tissue generated more than ten times the capabilities of a normal human. Her right cross was like a hydraulic piston firing into the side of the creature's skull. She followed with her left while reaching for her combat knife with the right.

She never saw the tail darting out from under its right arm. It shot through her chest, just to the right of her left shoulder and stopped her attack. The monster lifted her off the ground to take away her leverage. Shogun's voice tore through her mind.

You have no reserve, Beast! It's you or it! Right now!

Nikki had nothing left. Wounded and unarmed, she braced herself for the cold embrace of defeat. The alien lifted its left claw for the swipe, its line of glowing, LED green eyes forming a robotic grin.

Sword!

Nikki's eyes snapped open and she reached over her right shoulder as the monster swiped. Her hand closed around the hilt and she twisted, breaking the blade away from the magnetic clip that held it in place. Her arm responded automatically and the alien waved a bloody stump past her face as its massive paw thudded against the concrete.

The creature glanced at its amputated limb and Nikki swung again. The forged steel blade stabbed through the alien's neck with a crunch and its head turned slightly to look her in the eyes.

Nikki roared in its insectoid face, a primal scream uttered only by those few who had stolen victory in mortal combat by a razor's-edge margin. With a jerk of her shoulder, Nikki wrenched the blade aside and the monster's head flopped to the floor.

She hit the ground as the alien crumpled and the darkness threatened to take her. Shogun was in her head, begging her to get up and get to the ship. She was bleeding out faster than she could heal and by his estimate she was at less than fifteen percent mobility, but she pushed against the cold ground.

She looked up to see a dozen more aliens pour out of a hall at the other end of the bay.

She could hear the sergeant yelling for her back at the ship. Could she reach the ship in time? Those foolish technicians had not even fired the engines, yet. How long would it take for the ship to boot up?

"Move out, Sergeant! I've got you covered." Nikki got to her knee, gripping the hilt of her sword in one hand and looping her index finger through the 'last resort' grenade on her harness.

Fifteen percent mobility.

* * *

Sergeant Lancell stood on the loading ramp of the EVAC ship. Inside, several of the techs scrambled to get the ship's AI booted up. Private Fialto prayed aloud, strapped into the corner seat along the wall.

The colonel leaned on his shoulder to peer out with him. "She's telling us to go, Sergeant."

"She means to stay here and hold all of them off by herself?" Sergeant Lancell groaned with frustration. "She can't even stand."

"She will give us enough of a window to lift off and head for orbit," the colonel replied. "I believe she can pull it off, but if we do not go now her sacrifice will be meaningless."

The ship shook as the plasma engines fired up and raged. Inside a few shouts from the crew signaled success. "We're up and running, Sergeant!"

He stood and looked onward as the aliens got closer to the soldier that had come out of nowhere and saved them from a grisly death. Not an hour before he had left two men behind with two carbines and a grenade to allow them to go out on their own terms instead of in the razor-lined maw of a monster. He had abandoned them because there was no choice; because he was not powerful enough to stand against the attackers like the Beast. He did not have her bravery. He did not have her weaponry.

Sergeant Lancell jerked away from the railing on the ramp as if burned by it. He hopped down from the ship and looked toward the elevator ramp.

"Sergeant?" the colonel yelled over the engines.

"I'm not leaving anyone else behind!" Sergeant Lancell sprinted across the hangar pad, back the way they'd come.

He scooped up the ammo can on the fly and skidded to a halt over the downed 50-cal. With a grunt, he heaved the weapon turret upright and slapped the first, enormous round of the old-school ammunition belt into the cradle. It took him a moment to align it correctly and he slammed the top down and traversed the barrel to where the enemy advanced on Beast.

Remembering how she had tucked the grips to her chest, he mimicked her and sighted in his first target. "Not today, assholes!"

Click.

The sergeant jerked in anticipation of the recoil from the powerful weapon, but there was nothing; only the hollow, soul-shattering click of a misfire. Sergeant Lancell pushed the thumb trigger harder and when that did not work, he frantically pounded on the top of the gun and pressed the trigger over and over. He had no idea how to clear a jam on something so ancient.

He jumped as quick footsteps clopped behind him. The colonel nearly bowled him over in her rush to reach the weapon. She thrust her hips against the butterfly grips and grabbed the charging handle on the right side. With a terrified groan, she hauled back with all the weight her tiny frame could muster and racked the weapon.

She immediately leapt away, dropping to her ass. "Now, Sergeant!"

Sergeant Lancell dropped behind the weapon, jerked the grips to his chest and depressed the button.

Gouts of grey dust kicked up in a straight line to the alien's side and a second later its midsection exploded as the armor-piercing rounds cut it in half. Sergeant Lancell's adrenaline turned the powerful kicks into a gentle vibration against his torso as he walked the concrete eruptions forward, into the next alien. Several of them stopped and turned, confused by the new threat. He took advantage of their hesitancy and turned his death-spitting flesh-pulper on them.

"Get her! Someone get her now!" Sergeant Lancell screamed in between bursts.

Private Holiday, jumped from the ship's ramp, his short Mohawk bouncing as he hauled ass across the hangar, carbine in hand. He slid to Beast's side on his knees like some kind of action movie hero and unloaded his rifle at the aliens. Dropping the magazine, he threw her arm over his shoulder and stood.

It took more effort than Holiday had assumed, gauging by the slow squat-thrust he used to lift her. Two more men raced to him, helping share the load as they carried her toward the ship.

Sergeant Lancell noticed the red glow of the barrel just as he watched the aliens take cover for the first time since their attack. A smile crept across his face and he yelled.

"Have a taste, you sons'a bitches!"

There was a flash of brown beside him and he turned his head to see the colonel booking it back across the bay to the ship.

"Shit." Sergeant Lancell fired off another burst at a brave invader that stuck its bug-like head out from behind a crate and then he bolted after the officer.

"Lift off! Lift off!" he yelled, vaulting over the rail and up the loading ramp.

The ship lifted into the air and the roof opened to allow their exit. The ramp in back closed and after a few minutes the on-board AI appeared on a screen. In a surreal moment, the digitized human bust politely advised them of the safety protocols in the same manner as the AI flight attendants in commercial crafts and announced that they would be breaking orbit in five minutes. The advanced, self-learning operating system that precisely guided them off-world and toward the nearest transit station urged them to remain strapped in and cautioned them on tomfoolery while in the gravity-free environment of space minutes after they escaped from deadly, metallic alien abominations. The safety briefing ended with some forgettable AI-inspired wise-crack as the ship broke free of the planet's gravity and entered space.

The crew exhaled for what felt like the first time.

"Sergeant Lancell."

The sergeant looked over to the voice. The red-haired soldier's face peeked out from inside a Zero-G medical containment suit that kept her blood from floating about the interior of the ship. She nodded at him. "Thank you."

"Hey, I'm the one who ran out and grabbed you." Private Holiday was strapped in beside her and looking the soldier over. "Also, please don't bleed to death inside that giant condom, because I would really love to take you out for a beer for saving all of our asses back there."

The soldier looked over at the private and gave him an awkward half-smile. "My wounds have already closed up, so the danger of bleeding out is slim at this point. However, I *have* sustained tremendous injury. If you do not mind, Sergeant, I am going to drop consciousness for a while to let my body recuperate faster. Don't be alarmed by my deathly appearance, my Pilot is monitoring my vitals. I will be fine."

Sergeant Lancell stared at her for a moment, trying to comprehend her words. He glanced at the colonel, who shrugged. "Uh… carry on, soldier."

She gave him another nod and then closed her eyes, quickly drifting to sleep and growing pale.

Private Holiday looked on in horror. "Oh my god, is she a robot?" He scanned her up and down and then turned away with a smile. "Nope, don't even care if she's a robot. We're dating."

* * *

Max scanned the room and the surrounding eighty yards five times before pulling out his bed and activating the wall safe behind his headboard. He shut off all power to his apartment appliances and routed it to the headset that plugged into the wall port. A glass of whiskey and 400 milligrams of Polycodone relaxed him enough to endure the thin, shaky neural link his home-engineered Chair would establish for him.

Max breathed through clenched teeth as the connection linked. "Where are you?"

Outskirts of the Corthax region. I've whipped these metal buggers into a frenzy; they're ready to go on Warpath with humanity. They just need a ride. How did our Beast do?

"She's still alive, thankfully. With everything we've been through; all those men and women that died at Preston… losing Nikki would have made it so much worse."

The fallen at Fort Preston did not die in vain, Shogun. We showed humanity they cannot rely on AI technology as their sole defense… and we sent a message to Central Command that the ASH soldiers cannot be discarded and thrown in the ashes of the old world. We did this for the sixty-seven that died ingloriously, with no memorial. With this new war, we will finally have a purpose.

Max's smile was all teeth. "Command is already pulling in all the others from whatever outskirt posting they've been stuck at for the last fifteen years. The stored embryos are being thawed; I've already been placed in charge of overseeing training of the second generation of ASH Soldiers. Even Minister Dawn was forced into a concession after Nikki's successful evacuation on Preston… saving so many in that hellhole. By the time your new friends start invading populated locations, we'll have enough ASH Soldiers to push them back and secure our future in the eyes of the public. Then, when we're on every civilized planet, we'll bring you back, to take command of your sisters, my dear Ryoko."

HUMAN STRAIN

Benjamin Cheah

As the hunters fell upon him, Sergeant Major Abel Santiago prayed his instincts were right.

They appeared so swiftly, so silently, it was as though they had grown from the shadows at the end of the tunnel. Their skins colored in midnight hues, Santiago saw them only as moving blurs. Pressed against the wall, he counted the outlines. Two, three, four, eight, *twelve*. This wasn't an ordinary patrol. It was a reconnaissance in force.

Santiago breathed as deeply as he dared. If they were going to pass over him, it wouldn't do if he passed out. If they were going to attack him, he needed oxygen to fight. To flee.

"Boss, what's the call?" a voice whispered in his head. It was Staff Sergeant Sera Meyers, his second-in-command.

Santiago swallowed, mind-keyed his quantum communicator, let his suit translate his thoughts into words. "Stay put. Let them pass, but prepare for the worst."

"Acknowledged."

The rest of his team were spread out behind him. They had cover. Little nooks and debris to hide behind or under. All Santiago had was the wall. If anyone was going to be detected, it was him. But if they passed over him, they were safe.

Santiago adjusted his position just so, pressing his chest against the wall, turning his head to watch the hunters. His suit's active camouflage layer shifted, mimicking the colour and texture of the wall. Every fibre of his being screamed that he was giving his back to them. But as so many people had learned the hard way, hunters were likelier to recognize the front profile of a human under active camouflage than the back. Not that his animal brain was convinced.

They came.

Half of their number crawled along the floor on all fours. The other half traversed the ceiling, inverted. This close, he heard the sound of their passage. Claws going *click-click-click*, tails swishing softly, the almost inaudible *thuk* as their adhesion pads engaged and disengaged. They were closer, closer, closer.

One of them broke off, taking to the wall. Right in front of Santiago. It approached him, beheld him. Its skull was a smooth dome interrupted by a line of dark unblinking eyes. Massive jaws jutted out under its head. The hunter growled, raising a paw lined with sharp claws. Mounted under its wrist was a personal laser. Lifting its tail, Santiago saw it terminate in a fine, almost invisible, stinger.

Nothing to see here, all you are seeing are bits of circuitry and wires, go away.

The hunter stared at him, perhaps running through its sensor suite, trying to reconcile multiple anomalous data sets. Santiago kept still. He had to keep still. Hunters roamed in packs, and they would not, could not, stray from their packs. He just had to hold on.

The hunter cocked its head and noticed its pack-mates scampering off. It took to the floor and raced to catch up.

Santiago remembered to breathe. Softly. The last of the hunters had passed. And if they passed over him...

"FUUUUUUUUUUUUUAAAAAAARRRRRRRRRRGHH!"

"Hold position!" Santiago q-commed. "Do not engage!"

The men held position.

Crunching, chewing sounds bounced off the walls.

Santiago waited.

Breathed.

Ten minutes later, he stepped away and looked around. The hunters were gone.

"All clear," Santiago said. "Who was it?"

"Lenny," Meyers replied.

"You saw what happened?"

"A hunter poked him. He moved."

Santiago sighed. *Goddammit*. Before the Hivers came Lenislaw was a civilian. He had made his bones in the Resistance but he had no place among the Rangers. Lenislaw hadn't been conditioned to iron discipline the way Santiago was. This was supposed to be an all-Ranger operation, but Central said there were too few Rangers left.

"Distribute his load. Five minutes."

"Roger."

Santiago knelt, bringing his M592 gravitic accelerator carbine to his shoulder, and kept watch. Five and a half minutes later, Meyers spoke.

"We're done."

"Form up. Move out."

"And the remains?"

"Mark them on your map. We'll come back for him later."

It was a polite fiction and they knew it. If the Hivers wouldn't take the corpse the rats would. But Santiago, Meyer, and the rest of the team were only human, and they needed that last inch of faith in their fellow humans.

The tunnel ended in a metal door recessed into the wall. They stacked up, weapons at the ready. Meyers inspected the frame for traps and alarms. Grabbing the doorknob, she turned. Pulled.

Beyond was once a bustling concourse. Now there was simply darkness. Santiago lowered his enhanced vision monocular over his left eye and the world filled with false colour. The shops were shuttered forever. Glowing mould and alien roots covered the ceiling and walls. Water dripped and gathered in dank corners. Santiago gently swept debris away with his boots, ears primed for errant noise.

At the end of the concourse was another door to another tunnel. It led to a staircase that spiralled down to darker depths. A gentle hum filled Santiago's ears. He peeked over the railing, aiming his M592 down.

All clear.

Keeping to the outer edge of the stairs, they descended the creaking steps. Santiago kept his eyes open for lasers, motion detectors, ultrasonics, magnetics, even simple tripwires. There was no telling how the Hivers would secure this route.

At the bottom of the stairs, a door awaited. Its hinges had rusted, the frame welded shut. The third man on the team, Rook, aimed his forearm-mounted nanospray and squirted, generously slathering the frame. He stepped clear.

"Breaching," he called.

Blinding light banished the dark. The metal melted, and the door fell. A gentler light flooded through the doorway. Santiago stepped through, the monocular automatically reverting to real-sight.

The corridor beyond was white. Clean. Sterile. Santiago pulled up his maps on the monocular and picked a waypoint. In his augmented vision, a thick green line grew at his feet and snaked down the passageway.

Navigating a labyrinth of white corridors, he followed the line to a pair of unmarked doors. Santiago and Rook took one door; Meyers and the last Resistor took the other.

Santiago held up three fingers. Dropped one. Another. The last.

Meyers nodded.

Santiago dropped his fist, shouldered his carbine, and opened the door.

A man wearing spotless blue overalls spun around. His hands were empty, his face slack, his eyes set. His pupils were unnaturally dilated, the sclera an empty white.

Santiago shot him in the face.

The thrall's head caved in. Santiago fired again and again until it dropped. Turning his back to the nearest wall, he scanned the room. This was a target-rich environment, full of blue-uniformed thralls. Santiago aimed at the closest and cut loose. The M592 whined, the *clack-clack* of the moving bolt louder than the bullet in flight.

Caught in the crossfire, the thralls dropped, twitching. Santiago checked for more targets, saw Rook on the ground grappling with a thrall. The Hiver flipped Rook onto his back, mounting him. Rook's dagger flashed in his hand, stitching into the target again and again and again, to no effect. The thrall brought a fist crashing down. Rook rolled, guiding the fist into the floor. The tile powdered. The Hiver reared up and Santiago drilled it twice in the face.

"Clear!" Santiago called.

"Clear!" Meyers agreed.

Rook coughed. "Shit. There went the element of surprise."

Santiago nodded. Shattered circuits and snapped wires flowed out of the broken heads, carried by pseudo-blood and whatever was left of their organic brains. Like all Hivers, the thralls were networked to every other Hiver in the area. The rest of the swarm would come. Soon.

The corpses smoked and hissed. Santiago stepped back as their skin blackened and crisped, their limbs curled, tendons snapped. Then in a flash of blue light they disintegrated, leaving smoking puddles on the floor.

Meyers extracted a scanner from a pouch, running it over Rook. "You've been tagged," she said.

Hivers sprayed targets with pheromones in close proximity, marking them for other Hivers. Some variants mixed in different chemicals, with less pleasant effects.

"Meyers, Rook, exterior security," Santiago said. "Clean up as best as you can. Ismail, you're up."

Meyers and Rook left the room. Ismail set down and opened his heavy haversack.

Santiago surveyed the room. The walls were lined with computers, most of which he had no idea how to use. He did, however, recognize a dataport. He removed a memory stick from a utility pouch and plugged it in. The tip of the stick glowed red.

Windows lined the control room. Beyond, Santiago saw a sprawling assembly line. Assemblers digested raw materials and alchemized them into feedstock. The fabricator turned the feedstock into goods, rolling them out for collection and storage. Robots scurried around the assembly lines, performing a thousand different tasks. Before the War, this was the largest, most sophisticated underground fabricator on the planet, capable of producing almost anything the programmers could dream of. Santiago pressed his hands against the glass, allowing himself to believe that one day *true* humans would possess such a fabricator again, that in some not-too-distant future it could produce the goods they needed to reclaim the land and sky.

Ismail hauled the Special Demolition Munition from his bag and dashed Santiago's hopes forever.

"SDM ready," Ismail said. "Just give me the word."

"Roger."

Santiago watched the memstick. It contained a limited artificial intelligence, closer to a search engine than a true AI. The AI scoured the fabricator's databanks, copying a treasure trove of Old World knowledge. Most of it would be useless. But the Hivers were running the fabricators now, producing the cybernetics and biomechatronics that defined them. If there was any hope of understanding the enemy's strengths and weaknesses, it lay in the stick.

The memstick turned green.

Santiago pulled it. "We're done. Ismail, set the timer for thirty minutes."

It pained him to give the command. But the Hivers had to believe this was a demolition, not a data extraction.

CLUNK

"What was that?" Ismail asked, closing the SDM's control panel.

"Came from above us."

CLUNK-CLUNK.

Not a hunter. They weren't that clumsy. But it was coming closer. Santiago plugged the stick into a suitport and powered up his q-com. Tuning it to a channel reserved for the mission, he began uploading the contents of the stick. Now they just needed to survive long enough for Central to receive its contents.

"Coming out," Santiago called.

"Come out," Meyers replied.

The team regrouped outside.

CLUNK

"That came from the ceiling," Meyers said.

"We have to—"

Five feet away a ceiling vent opened. A large cube dropped down, slowing into a mid-air hover . Klaxons screeched. The cube pulsed multi-coloured lights in rapid patterns. As Santiago shut his eyes and turned away, the walls and floor around the cube cracked, buckled, and exploded.

Chunks of ferromagnetic material gathered around the cube, twisting and separating and re-forming into springs, cogs, legs, arms, claws. It rolled, crawled, walked towards them.

"Golem!" Meyers yelled.

Rook hosed the construct with full auto fire. The intense gravity fields around the golem assembler snatched the rounds out of the air and repurposed them as mass.

"Run!" Santiago shouted.

They fled, retracing their route. The golem graduated to long, loping bounds, each step a heavy thud. Santiago rounded a bend…

The corridor was filled with thralls. All were armed with improvised weapons: clubs, knives, engineering tools.

Santiago turned up his GAC to full power and fired. His first round blew a hole clean through the nearest thrall, and into two more behind. He worked the crowd with short bursts in full auto. The team took his cue, mincing up the thralls as they surged forward. The wall of flesh fell before them.

Revealing a floating golem assembly. Its energy fields ripped out metal and bone from the corpses, assembling a twisted facsimile of a skeletal giant.

Behind them, the other golem advanced.

"Run!" Santiago again ordered.

Santiago pulled down his map, solving the maze that lay before him. He raced down a corridor, turned right, blew through another thrall, another right turn, and the exit was before them.

Running up the stairs two and three at a time, Santiago didn't dare look back, tracking the golems by their heavy crashing footfalls. They were getting louder. Closer.

At the top of the stairs, he brought up his wrist-mounted nanospray. He doused the steps in front of him, keying the nano for command detonation. Meyers slipped on the liquid. Santiago caught her and hauled her past him. Ismail was right behind, huffing and puffing.

Rook was the last. Half a storey to go. But the golems were gaining on him,

"Come on!" Santiago yelled.

Rook scrambled. Thirty steps to safety. Twenty-five. The golems ate up the stairs behind them, lengthening their legs and arms, widening their gait. Rook glanced over his shoulder, and cursed.

"Look at me, damn you!" Santiago shouted. "Fucking run!"

Rook ran.

Fifteen steps.

The golems nipped at his heels.

Ten steps.

Rook jumped, clearing several steps at once.

Five steps.

A golem reared up and extruded a pair of metal-encrusted bone scythes above him. The curved blades hooked into his torso, piercing his armour and reeling him in.

"Shit!" Rook yelled.

Santiago fired. The rounds *halted* in mid-air, then whipped around and meshed itself with the golem.

"Go!" Rook screamed. "Fucking go!"

Cursing, Santiago jumped clear and detonated the nano. The blast consumed Rook and collapsed the stairwell. The golems fell into the darkness below. Santiago staggered away. The survivors grabbed him, pulling him away from the rising dust cloud.

"Rook?" Ismail asked.

"Didn't make it."

Meyers shook her head. "Damn. Did you deny him?"

"Yeah."

Meyers patted his shoulder. "You did good. At least they can't turn him against us."

"No time to rest guys," Santiago said. "The SDM is still active."

They ran back the way they came. Out the door, back through the tunnel, out into the concourse—

The ground rumbled.

"Initiation!" Ismail called.

The earth trembled. Crumbled. Hardened concrete broke and fell. The Rangers sprinted. Dust fell from the ceiling. An extended roar reverberated behind them. Santiago didn't dare stop. A Hiver must have triggered the SDM's anti-tampering mechanism. The two-kiloton fusion weapon was a 'clean' bomb, but it still released prodigious amounts of neutrons, which would punch through all but the thickest shielding material. Run, or die.

They ran.

* * *

They sprinted down the length of the concourse before Santiago called for a halt. They leaned against walls and benches, panting and gasping. Santiago's eyes were blurry. His gorge rose, and he swallowed it down. He was fine, he had to be fine, it was just fatigue, but his dosimeter was crackling through his earpieces. He unhooked the device from his suit and examined the screen.

Six grays.

"Fuck me."

"You're not my type, boss," Ismail said.

"Check your dosimeters. Now."

"Fuck... " Ismail muttered.

"What'd you get?" Santiago asked.

"Six grays."

"Meyers?"

She stepped aside and emptied her guts onto the floor. Santiago's will broke. He took a deep breath, ripped off his mask, stepped back and turned away as his stomach rebelled. A stream of yellow-green exploded from his mouth. As he blew his nose, expelling more waste, he heard Ismail retch.

"Meyers," Santiago gasped, massaging his belly. "Dosage?"

"Six grays," she whispered.

"Antirads. Now."

Santiago fished a small orange case his thigh pocket. Inside was an autoinjector and four spare cartridges. He pressed the needle into his neck and hit the plunger. Cool liquid invaded his blood. Sighing, he discarded the used cartridge and replaced it with a fresh one.

The medicine circulated rapidly through him. The nausea faded. His eyes focused. He spat out the last drops of bile, kept the case, donned his mask and took a deep breath.

"Good news, bad news," Santiago said. "Bad news is, six grays is a lethal dose. Good news is, a medbox can still reverse the damage. Antirads will buy us time to get to one."

"And where's the nearest?" Ismail said.

A soft buzzing filled the air.

"Wasps," Meyers hissed. "We have to go."

Ismail sprayed the puddles with nanospray. "Burning. Stand clear."

They couldn't leave any trace behind. Who knew what Hivers could do with DNA.

They ducked into a corner. "Burn," Santiago said.

A flash of light. The wasps buzzed, swooping in on the fire. Soft *thud-thud-thuds* rose above the beating of a thousand wings. Dark shapes slinked across the ground. Hunters.

Using touch and squeezes, Santiago signalled the duo to follow him. He lowered his monocular, switching to passive infrared. He could just about see beyond arm's length, but he didn't dare switch on his infrared lamp. Not with the hunters so close behind.

Dropping to a crouch, he extended his left arm ahead of him and moved slowly on the balls of his feet. With each step, he lifted his foot just enough to clear the floor, toeing aside bits of glass and debris in his path. Meyers felt around his back, and latched on to his suit's rear grab handle. She was so close he could feel her body heat. Sense the sickness in stasis within her.

Glass crunched behind him.

Santiago paused, listening.

Ismail? Meyers? Who knew? Who cared? He skulked into the dark, away from the fire.

Now there was no light, period. Nothing but complete black. Swallowing, he paid extra attention to the rest of his senses. A faint, sweet smell of decay hung in the air. Through his soft-soled boots, he felt the cracked, broken earth. He swept for obstacles with his left hand and guided himself around them.

The buzzing grew louder. Closer. Santiago swallowed. They wouldn't escape them. They had to—

Meyers twisted around. A stone bounced off a distant wall, breaking glass.

The wasps flew away, investigating the new sound. A hunter screamed, and its fellows yodelled. Santiago picked up the pace. He remembered to breathe. To breathe was to think, and it was the thinking man who lived. He turned down random corners, putting as much space as he could from the fire, guiding his feet with his pre-War memories of the concourse.

Tak-tak-tak

Santiago halted. Activated his infrared lamp.

On the ceiling, a hunter awaited, its tail poised to strike.

Santiago snapped up his carbine.

The hunter screeched, dropping. It flipped around in mid-air, landing on its feet, bringing up its lasers. Santiago fired.

On impact, the ceramet rounds flashed into brilliant plasma. Santiago flinched. His right eye was temporarily blinded. The monocular blanked out, and when he could see again, the hunter lay in pieces before him.

More hunters howled. One, two, three of them.

Which meant there were at least ten more. Howling was *not* a means of communication. It was echolocation and psychological warfare. They already knew where the Rangers were.

"Go active," Santiago ordered. "Ismail, proxy mine."

Santiago activated his infrared lamp, sweeping for targets. Then the monocular winked out as the hunter self-destructed.

An infrared spotlight appeared behind him. Then another.

"Mine set," Ismail said.

"Let's go."

They charged down the corridor. Turned right. Santiago took three steps before he heard the buzzing. A swarm of wasps descended from the ceiling, stingers exposed.

"Move!" Meyers yelled, pushing past him. She raised her nanosprays and squirted. The aerosol blossomed into white fire. Burning wasps dropped from the sky.

"Back! Back!" Santiago ordered.

He turned and ran, aiming for a hallway to his right. Behind him, the proximity mine exploded.

The hall graded down, leading to a pair of escalators flanking a staircase. Clunks sounded above them. A ventilation grate fell from the ceiling. A golem cube dropped.

"Fuck you!" Santiago extended his wrist and hosed it with nano. Closing in, he kicked the assembler against the wall and ordered the nano to ignite.

The cube melted.

Santiago blinked. He hadn't expected that. Damn things *could* be killed. He ran—

Meyers grabbed his shoulder, reversing his momentum.

"What the hell?"

"Look down! Tripwires!"

Thin lines glittered in the infrared lamp, sealing off the escalators and the stairs.

Behind them, a second mine exploded. Hunters howled.

"Follow me!" Santiago called, jumping over the tripwire that guarded the stairs. He landed awkwardly, slipped on a step, and landed on his ass. Painfully.

Ismail laughed.

"Real funny," Santiago groused, getting up.

Santiago ran down the stairs, leaping down the last five steps. He turned to cover the team, and saw hunters pouncing on the ceiling.

"Contact front!"

Santiago dumped his mag into them, squeezing the trigger as fast as he could. Ismail and Meyers added their fire to his. A pencil-thin beam snapped out past his head, missing him by an inch. Plasma flash-blinded his right eye.

"Grenade out!" Meyers yelled. Pulling a plastic pipe bomb from her vest, she pulled the pin and tossed it at the head of the stairs.

Santiago ducked away. The bomb exploded; a burning gob landed by his foot.

Navigating with his good left eye, he raced to the platform. To his right, the maglev track was blocked by a stationary train.

To his left, the tunnel had caved in.

The hunters bellowed.

Swearing, Santiago called up the map, searching for...

There.

Jumping down onto the track, he turned right, squeezed himself between the train and the wall then crab-walked down the tunnel.

A soft buzzing filled the air.

"Go passive!" he whispered, dousing the infrared light.

The world went dark again. Navigating solely by touch, he inched his way along the wall.

The train rocked. *Clunk-clunk-clunk.*

His fingers touched a corner. He eased himself into the space, finding a tiny nook. The back wall was smooth and unmarked. A junction box lay at head height.

The buzzing grew louder.

Santiago ran his palm along the right side of the box. A hidden panel slid open. Inside was a tiny dataport. Santiago ran his suitjack into the port.

Click.

Santiago pressed against the far wall, and it swung on silent bearings. He motioned the team through, and slid the door shut. It locked behind him.

The space beyond was dark and tight. Feeling along the left wall, he found a button. Overhead lights snapped on revealing an airlock door.

"Is it safe to ask where the hell are we?" Ismail asked.

"Metro-2," Santiago replied.

* * *

"Metro-2, here?" Ismail whistled. "How far does it go?"

"Everywhere," Meyers replied, reloading his carbine. "Wherever the Metro goes, there's a connection to Metro-2. It's the only reason the Resistance has held out for so long."

Metro-2 was the city's final redoubt against total war. But only as long as the Hive wasn't aware of it.

"The Hive isn't stupid," Meyers said. "They know we couldn't have disappeared into thin air. They'll start looking for the Metro-2 connector."

"And drop a rock on us," Ismail continued.

"They stopped doing that a while back," Santiago said. "Now they prefer uploading Resistors into the Hive mind. Dead or alive."

"And so *we* prefer denying compromised connectors to the enemy now," Meyers added. "With SDMs."

Ismail sighed. "This war. Either they kill us or we kill ourselves."

"Or we kill them. Let's go."

The airlock cycled open. Beyond was a white-lit decontamination chamber. Santiago activated his suit's IFF system, letting the embedded sensors know they were friendly. When the door closed, the nozzles on the ceiling hissed.

"No more decon solution?" Meyers asked.

Santiago clucked his tongue. "Looks like it. Only thing coming out is pressurised air." He pulled a Geiger counter from his pouch. "Guys, check your suits. We need to know if we're still hot."

The Geiger counter crackled. The neutron flux had blasted the suits, exciting and displacing molecules. The now-radioactive material was emitting the full range of radioactive particles: alpha particles, beta and gamma rays, fission by-products.

Santiago wondered if the neutrons had embrittled their gear too. They couldn't afford to find out the hard way.

The Geiger counter said he was emitting 2.5 Sieverts of radiation, slowly dropping. Meyers and Ismail reported similar results. But the team was still absorbing radiation. The antirads could only protect them for so long, hours maybe. Already Santiago felt his fingers turning cold, his skin itching under the suit.

It was psychological, he told himself. That or the antirads.

He almost believed it.

"Dump your water," Santiago ordered.

"What?" Meyers said. "Why... oh. Damn. Damn!"

"You drank some?" Ismail said.

"Yeah. I was... oh shit."

Santiago shrugged. "Probably not hot enough to kill you. Well, not any faster anyway."

All the same, he emptied the contents of his irradiated canteens and water bladder into the chamber's drains. A soft chime whispered in his earpieces. The stolen data had been transmitted.

The airlock cycled open. The Rangers emerged into a brightly-lit tunnel. Santiago opened a nearby door. The room beyond held supplies. Ammunition boxes, weapon racks, medicine closets. A lonely fabricator in the corner. But no medbox.

Most of the crates were empty. Logistics cells roamed Metro-2, restocking equipment stores like this one, but as the war dragged on the resupply schedule had grown increasingly erratic. Part of Santiago rejoiced at the arsenal before him. Another raged at the bastards before him who had taken so much. A third insisted they take everything they could carry, while the last warned there was still a war on and other teams would need the supplies too. Santiago acknowledged each then coldly shoved them all away. The mission would dictate equipment, and their first mission was staying alive.

First priority was water. There was a water dispenser in a corner…which lacked a water tank. Entering the adjacent washroom, he turned the taps. Nothing. Santiago gathered a mouthful of saliva and swallowed it down. He'd been through worse.

After water came gear. As they topped off ammo and nano, they replaced their M592s with the racked ones. Those had never been zeroed, but M592s could launch projectiles at such ludicrous speeds zeroing wasn't strictly necessary. They threw their old equipment into the fabricator's mass digester, where it would be broken down into feedstock.

They peeled themselves out of their suits and wiped the suits' computers, condemning the materiel to the digester. Maroon splotches crept across Santiago's skin. They itched, but he refrained from scratching. When he peeled off his mask it took a mass of hair with it. Ismail and Meyers fared no better. Standard decon procedure was to wash off contaminated materials from their bodies. They made do by spraying themselves down in the washroom with nano, configured for cleaning instead of killing.

The fabricator churned out replacement suits, and after suiting up the team reconfigured the fresh suit computers and electronics. When Santiago powered up his q-com, he had a voice message waiting for him.

"This is Central," a cool female voice said. "Proceed to Academy Outpost and link up with friendly forces. Prepare for high intensity operations. This is an Alpha Priority mission."

Santiago passed on the message. Ismail frowned. "Academy's on the other side of the city."

"They're bound to have a medbox there," Meyers replied. "Water too."

"How do we get there? If we're walking... "

Ismail's voice trailed off. Sure, they were Rangers, the best of the best and all that, but acute radiation syndrome cared little about that. Santiago could feel the invisible death gnawing through his veins, killing him by inches.

"The Underground Railroad," Santiago said. "With Alpha Priority we can call the train."

"It's still functional?" Meyers asked.

"It better be."

* * *

Metro-2 was an intricate network of service tunnels and corridors, denser than the civilian Metro. Digital maps were deemed non-secure and never stored on suits. There was a time when maps were posted at every junction, but Central had them torn down after they realised the Hivers were aware of Metro-2. Direction arrows were painted over, signs removed, even the alpha-numeric lettering that designated different sections were whited out. All that remained were sterile walls of white concrete, greying by degrees. Santiago had to navigate by memory alone. And, he knew, one of the side effects of radiation poisoning was decreased cognitive function.

No. He could not give in to despair. He had to keep going.

White lights gave away to lamps filled with bioluminescent bacteria, throwing a soft green glow into the darkness. They were filled with water, and for a moment Santiago entertained the thought of taking a sip from them. But that was the height of stupidity. Still, his tongue grew sticky fur and his skin tried in vain to reabsorb the sweat in his suit.

A soft metal crash reverberated behind them.

"What was that?" Meyers muttered.

A louder boom followed.

"Breaching charges," Ismail replied.

Hunters filled the tunnels with a synchronized howl.

"They're behind us," Meyers said.

Santiago licked chapped lips. "Let's move."

They scurried into the dark. Santiago picked a turn, then another, and another. He'd only been here a few times, and that was so long ago. Was it the Guerrilla Warfare training module? Some operation at the beginning of the war? His memories were slipping away. He opened a gate, entering a small tunnel that stretched on into infinity. It looked just like any other tunnel, only the green lamps were in slightly different positions. Or were they?

"Wait a minute... " he muttered." Where are we?"

"Are we lost?" Ismail said.

"Haven't been here before," Santiago admitted.

"I think... I think I know where we are," Meyers said.

Santiago cocked his head into the dark. "Lead on."

She took point. Santiago rotated to the tail-end position. Keeping a hand on Ismail's grab handle, he glanced over his shoulder every twenty steps. Hunters called into the dark. Santiago idly realized he was hearing the same long, drawn-out howl over and over. Even the most well-trained animals would vary their tone and length. But these howls were precise. Unvaried. A mechanical mimicry of biology. Which, in a nutshell, was the Hivers' philosophy.

The Hivers they had encountered earlier weren't equipped to perform explosive breaches. That meant Hiver infantry were coming. Humans, or what passed for humans in the Hive's vision of humanity. Santiago suppressed a shudder. Sure, Neuvo Corazon had embraced genetic engineering and cybernetics, but they hadn't discarded their humanity the way the Hivers had. He couldn't understand their motives, and they never cared to explain. They just warped in their warfleet above the planet and dictated terms. When the government refused to surrender, the Hivers rained fire from above. That was… he couldn't recall how long ago.

Meyers came to a door. She opened it, entering what looked like a substation. Power generators lined the walls, cold and silent.

"Eh?" she said. "I thought... where the hell...?"

"Lost?" Santiago said.

"I... shit. Yeah. We need to back—"

Hunters bellowed in the dark.

"Let's not." Ismail pointed. "Try that door."

The door led to a staircase that descended into the dark.

"I'm not sure about this," Meyers said.

"Only thing deeper than Metro-2 is the Underground Railroad," Santiago said. "Doesn't matter what stop we're at, so long as we get there."

They went down. At the bottom of the stairwell was a metal door. Locked. Meyers melted the lock and the trio stumbled into the room beyond. Santiago filled his lungs with stale air. He lowered his monocular and powered the IR lamp.

The platform was tiny. Just a strip of concrete adjacent to massive rails. The tunnels were clear, at least. Maybe a train would come here.

Like all the artefacts of civilization, Metro-2 needed power. The trains of the underground railway needed power. Power from the generators distributed across Metro-2 or tapped from reactors on the surface. The Hivers knew that too, and they always answered unexplained spikes in electricity demand with ground forces and orbital bombardments. The Resistance travelled almost exclusively on foot, or with vehicles that didn't draw power from the grid. Central would authorize the use of the Metro-2 trains only in the gravest emergencies. With Alpha Priority status, Hivers on his tail, Santiago figured this qualified.

There was a q-com station next to the rails. Santiago flicked the power switch. The touchscreen displayed a keypad. He fed in his serial number. A host of buttons appeared. He selected the one that called for a train. Moments later, the intercom crackled.

"HELLO!"

The Rangers jumped. Santiago turned down the volume.

"... are five stops away," the train engineer continued. "Where are you headed?"

"Academy Outpost," Santiago replied.

"Ah! Excellent! So are we. We should be there in twenty minutes."

"We have Hivers on our tail."

"Hivers? Here? Shit." The engineer sighed. "I'll push 'er as fast as she can go. But be ready for a hot extract."

Santiago stepped away from the console. His head felt heavy and foggy, overburdened by the toxins that were surely swelling his brain. He knew he had to do something, but...

"Boss?" Ismail said. "I'll go upstairs and lay some traps for our friends."

Ah, right. That. "Go ahead."

Ismail ran up the stairs. Santiago patted himself down, checking that his kit was where he'd left them. Meyers fiddled with her M592. Silence reigned in the dark.

Long, long minutes later, Ismail sprinted back down, closing the door behind him. As he welded it shut with nano, he said, "They're coming."

Santiago looked around. There was no cover on the platform. It was...

Meyers went down to the tracks, crouching behind the thick concrete of the platform floor. The men followed her.

"You know... this is... crazy," Ismail said, gasping for air.

"Got a better idea?" she asked.

"No," Santiago said.

Santiago kept his ears open, listening for the sound of hissing air. A mine detonated in the stairwell. Training his carbine at the door, he breathed slowly, deeply, regularly. Waited.

A lifetime passed in the dark.

White-hot light flared from the doorframe.

Santiago shouldered his weapon.

The door fell. A dark shape leaped through.

"Fire!" Santiago called, pulling the trigger.

The hunter blew apart. Two more pounced out from behind it. Santiago tracked the one on the right. It halted for a moment, bringing up its weapons. He fired, and both the hunter's hands exploded. Santiago put the creature down with a double-tap, scanned for more targets, and saw the other hunter die.

And a cylinder bounced down the stairs and into the open.

Santiago looked away.

It burst in dazzling, ear-shattering flashes of white. Santiago's monocular shut down. Flattening himself as far as he could, he extended his carbine above his platform and loosed a burst. Another. A third. Ismail and Meyers added their fire to his. When the flash-bang died Santiago looked up.

A pair of corpses greeted him. Shattered bodies with triangular heads, torsos covered in pseudo-chitin carapace, their hands gripping Hiver gravity guns. The bodies began to burn.

A hunter surged through the doorway. The Rangers pumped it with bullets. As it vaporised, it lobbed a grenade at them.

Landing in front of Ismail.

The Ranger swore and jumped up on the platform. Scooping up the grenade, he dashed to the door, brought the bomb to his ear, threw it—

It exploded. The munitions on the Ranger's suit detonated too.

"Ismail!" Meyers yelled.

When the dust cleared, there was nothing left of him larger than a leg. The massive explosion broke up the stairs, bringing it down in a wreck of twisted metal and rubble that sealed off the doorway.

"Ismail," Meyers whispered. "My God."

Air whooshed through the tunnel. The duo clambered up on the platform.

Moments later, a sleek, shining maglev rushed into the station. The doors slid open.

"All aboard!" the engineer called through the intercom.

* * *

The train was packed with men and materiel. All the seats in the front carriages were occupied, and much of the floor space taken up by supply crates. Wending their way to the rear, the Rangers found a pair of empty seats. Meyers collapsed into one. Santiago discreetly whipped out his Geiger counter first.

They were cold. Thank God. Last thing he needed was to contaminate what could well be the last maglev on the planet.

The journey to Academy passed in a blur. At six hundred kilometres per hour, all Santiago could see of the outside world was an ill-defined gray stretch. Santiago opened his q-com and updated Central on his team's status. The moment he received an acknowledgment, he closed his eyes and drifted into a twilight state somewhere between restfulness and true sleep.

Meyer nudged him. "We're here."

Santiago opened his eyes. That was fast. Too fast. Had he nodded off? He didn't know. All he knew was that he felt even more tired than when he had boarded. Yawning, he followed the occupants out the train.

An array of guards scanned the passengers with handheld scanners, searching for Hiver pheromones and cybernetics. When Santiago cleared the checkpoint, a guard approached him.

"Please step aside, Sergeant Major."

"Is there a problem?"

"No problem. But Central wants to speak to you and your team."

"Lead on."

The guard led the duo away from the crush of people and to the security office. Inside the office, a short man in a grubby suit awaited behind a desk. He wore no rank tabs on his chest epaulet, and needed none.

"Major Khabarov," Santiago said. "Finally showed up in person?"

"Have to show my face once in a while, let people think I'm alive." Khabarov gestured at the chairs in front of him. "Sit, please."

They sat. "You have something for us?" Meyers asked.

"I'm truly sorry for the loss of your team. Their sacrifice was not in vain."

Santiago thought of Lenislaw, dying alone in the dark. Rook, consumed by golem and fire. Ismail, blown apart. The long line of Rangers and Resistors he had led and lost.

"Thank you, sir," Santiago said. "But you must've seen our report. We need to be in the hospital right now."

"Absolutely. But I've been told you can still fight."

"We don't get in a medbox, we're dead men walking."

Meyers coughed.

Santiago grimaced. "Well. Dead Rangers. You get what I mean."

Khabarov smiled wanly. "I spoke to the medical techs. They said the medbox will need two weeks to fix you. We don't have two weeks."

"Sending us into the fire again?" Meyers asked.

"Yes. This could be our only chance to win the war."

"You said that about the last job, sir."

"This is a continuation of that operation. The Academy AIs have pored through the data you transmitted. They found schematics for Hiver cybernetics. Hardware, firmware, and software infrastructure. Coupled with all the intelligence we've gathered in previous missions, we're confident we can penetrate the Hive Mind."

The Hivers distributed their computing capability across decentralized swarms, making them ultra-resilient and impervious to decapitation strikes. The Academy concentrated most of what was left of the planet's major processors, becoming a gigantic hyper-computer several orders of magnitude more powerful than the Hiver equivalent. If it were allowed to.

"You're saying we can hack into the Hiver command and control system?" Santiago asked.

"Not quite. The Hivers use quantum comms like we do. The only way to hack the Hive Mind is to access a dedicated communication and control node."

"Which they don't normally employ, since they prefer decentralised networks and autonomous swarms."

"Yes. They only use C&C nodes to coordinate activities between different swarms during large-scale operations. Such as an upload-or-destroy mission."

"That's all well and good, but what do you need us for?"

"The Hivers are coming. We're going to ambush them."

Meyers blinked. "They are coming. Here. To Academy."

"Yes."

"How did they find us?"

Khabarov sighed. "The Hivers have been mapping Metro-2 and we can't keep Academy Outpost secret. To analyze the data so quickly, we've had to run the Academy AIs at full power. The Hivers would have noticed the energy spike. They will come for us."

Santiago shot to his feet. "You're going to sacrifice the Academy?!"

"No. The Hivers aren't interested in genocide. They want to assimilate us. There's a large civilian community on the surface right above the Academy. They won't drop a rock on us. They'll send multiple swarms for an uplift-or-destroy operation. With those swarms will be landing ships with C&C nodes. If we can board a ship, we can plug our suits into the nodes and piggyback our AIs into the Hive Mind."

"You've just condemned the civvies above us," Meyers said.

"We have no choice. It's the only way we have left to access one of their ships, and they only bring the ships down to deploy reinforcements from orbit. Actual infantry, not constructs. The one sure-fire way they would do that is if we lure them into uplifting a community and coming down into the Metro."

"How do you know they'll take the bait?" Santiago asked.

Khabarov smiled grimly. "They know I'm one of the few officers left in the military, and the commanding officer of the Rangers. I've leaked on unsecured and compromised channels that I'm Central, and I'm at Academy Station. They *will* come. They want my brain."

Meyers exhaled sharply. "My. God. Sir, are you sure...?"

"Yes. And for what it's worth, the operations plan calls for us Rangers to swarm the Hivers when they arrive, while the mainline Resistance holds the Metro entrances. I intend to fight on the surface."

"That's pretty risky."

"Yes. But we're all in this together. If we swarm them when they land, some of us are bound to break through. Besides, remember what I told you when the war began?"

Meyers snorted. "I am Central."

"You are Central," Santiago continued.

"We are all Central," Khabarov finished. "As long as there is even one of us left, the Resistance continues."

Central was a myth deliberately perpetrated by the Rangers. The civilians needed to believe the government had survived, the remnants of the military needed to believe their leaders were still fighting the war, and every swarm the Hive sent to the countryside to hunt ghosts was a swarm that could not hunt the Resistance or twist people into their brand of humanity. The closest the Rangers ever had to Central was the AI that mediated information flow across Resistance cells.

"Just like the Hive," Santiago mused.

"We've got to adopt our enemy's strategy. It's the only way to win."

"To survive, you mean."

* * *

Santiago used to think waiting was easy. He just had to lie in place until something important happened. As he injected his last antirad into his neck, he considered otherwise.

Meyers, huddled under her camouflage blanket, swapped out her mask's air filter and cleaned dust off the lenses. Santiago joined her, rubbing his hands against the chill, and looked out the mousehole they had bored out of the kitchen wall.

Scattered across broken streets five stories down, the surface dwellers were huddling in little knots of humanity. Some entered nearby apartment blocks. Others gathered around ancient, rusted drums and started pitiful, flickering fires. Of Hivers, they saw none.

At least, Hiver *constructs*. Hiver thralls, and the infiltrator strain, were something else.

Santiago blew on his hands again. The Hiver orbital bombardments at the dawn of war started an ice age. What arable ground remained the Hivers seized for themselves and their collaborators. The Hivers didn't bother occupying most of the planet. They simply fostered hardship upon hardship on the people, leaving them to fend for themselves. The only way out was to join the Hive. Or be swept up in an upload-or-destroy operation.

Meyers peeked out the window. Across the building was a park. Most of the trees had died or shed their leaves, leaving large open spaces. A perfect place for a Hiver landing ship.

Outside, a floorboard creaked.

Santiago tapped Meyers shoulder. She shrank away from the window.

SNAP.

That was the lock fastened to the grille. The Rangers snatched up their weapons and moved out.

The grille swung open on screeching hinges.

Santiago leapt to one corner of the room, Meyers took the other.

The front door unlocked with a heavy *CLICK*. The door opened. A hunter leapt through, howling.

A proximity mine exploded.

Santiago flinched away from the blast. Looking back up, he saw thralls pouring through a pink mist.

The closest thrall aimed its arms at him. Its hands shot out, attached to its sockets with fine wires.

Not a thrall. An infiltrator.

As the hands landed on a sofa, Santiago pumped three hypersonic rounds into its chest. The infiltrator staggered, lifted its hands and tossed the sofa away, clearing a line of attack. Meyers blew its head off, but Santiago was exposed. And more infiltrators were coming.

One launched claw hands at him. He ducked and charged into the threat, blowing its head off. Its partner leapt on Santiago. He brought up his carbine and it grabbed the weapon with both hands, trying to throw him. Santiago snaked his left hand down, drew his dagger in a reverse grip, and thrust out. The ultrafine tip sank into its neck and ripped out. Dark blood spattered across his mask's lenses. He thrust into its eyes, felt the knife *bounce* off hardened metal. The Hiver didn't even flinch; it continued to hold him in place for its friends to flank him.

Snarling, Santiago jammed the blade into the crook of its right elbow and pulled, breaking its grip. He tried to kick it away, but the infiltrator was faster, crashing him against the wall, crushing him with powerful arms.

And set itself afire.

"Fuck! Fuck! Fuck!" Santiago yelled, twisting and turning, but the fucking thing had him in a death grip. He grabbed the Hiver's burning back and violently arched his spine, making space to knee it in the groin and shove it aside. As its body fell apart, Meyers dropped it with a short burst.

"You okay?" Meyers shouted.

Santiago was broiling under the suit, but he hadn't caught fire. "I'm good." He retrieved his carbine and sheathed his dagger. Santiago's q-com filled with chatter: Rangers reporting ambushes and attacks.

Light spilled through the window. The world rattled. Pure sound flooded his ears, rattling his brain. Meyers looked out the window.

"They're landing at the park!" she shouted.

"We have to go!" he yelled back.

They burst out of the apartment and down the stairs. As the Rangers reached the ground floor, the windows shattered. Hypervelocity slugs ripped through the air, blasting *through* the façade of the building, blowing holes in the walls around them. Santiago hit the deck, pressing Meyers down with him. There was too much fire in front of them; Hiver forces must be attacking their building.

"I'll draw them away!" Meyers yelled. "Finish the mission!"

"But—"

"We've both been tagged. But the heat from the one that burned you would have neutralized most of the pheromones on you. If there's anyone who can get close to the landing ship, it's you! Now *go!*"

Santiago snarled. Rolling off her, he snatched up his weapon. "See you in Valhalla."

"Hell no! You can visit me in Folkvangr!"

Snorting, Santiago turned around and crawled away. Meyers fired through the holes, screaming war cries, then picked herself up and sought better cover. Reaching the rear door, Santiago got up too and burst out. Behind him, the apartment shook under the hammer blow of multiple explosions.

He ran.
Alone.

* * *

As the city died around him, Santiago pressed himself down into the street. The suit adjusted, shifting its tones. With slow, measured, movements, he lowered his monocular and crawled down the middle of the road. It flew in the face of infantry doctrine, but the Hivers had read the textbook too.

A squad of Hiver infantry rounded the corner ahead of him. Infrared aiming lasers and spotlights slashed through the night.

He froze.

The enemy soldiers pressed themselves to the walls, pausing for the moment it took their suits to blend in, and stalked down the pavement. At such close quarters, they looked more like insects than men. Swallowing, Santiago stayed still, breathing as shallowly as possible. Even if they saw him, maybe they'd mistake him for a corpse and move on.

They moved on.

Santiago remained motionless. Breathing. Laying. Waiting. The tail-end Charlie would be watching their backs, and if Santiago moved, he was dead.

Gunshots echoed behind him. He couldn't tell who was firing on whom; the gravity guns both sides employed produced the same screeching-tearing noise at hypervelocity speeds, the same silence at subsonic. Cautiously, Santiago inched forward, moving one limb at a time.

Down the road, a car flung off the ground. Whirling around a gravity singularity, it shredded apart, recomposing itself into four wheeled legs. Streetlamps twisted, bent, and broke off from the pavement, drawn to the singularity. The golem in birthing rolled down the street. Towards Santiago.

Cursing, he picked up the pace, crawling up onto the pavement. Under the golem, pipes burst free from the ground, gushing wastewater. Santiago slithered for the bend as fast as he dared. If he stood and ran now the golem would notice him. Slowly, inexorably, the golem came. The whirlwind of metal formed gears and wheels, arms and claws.

Santiago turned the corner. An irresistible force gripped him. Gnashing his teeth, he pressed himself into the road. He stretched his arm out, trying to pull himself forward. The golem's gravity wash damn near ripped his arm off. A gale whipped around him. Santiago's body tensed, every fiber of his being contracting, squeezing every last joule he could spare. The fence around the park creaked and groaned. The posts bent sharply, and exploded from the concrete. One smacked the road next to Santiago's head. He kept crawling, forcing himself forward, dragging himself away from the singularity. But it was no use, he was being pulled back, back, into the maw of the—

The golem moved on. The singularity passed.

Santiago relaxed, panting. His muscles burned. He glanced around; saw no Hivers and no signs of movement. He ran for the parking lot, leaping over the gap in the fence.

A Hiver landing ship lay to his one o'clock, three hundred meters away. It looked like a pyramid with the top sliced off, disgorging troops and Hunters from three sides. The heat of the landing had flash-incinerated the grass, leaving ashes dancing in the heated air. Pressing himself against a stump, Santiago brought down his monocular and called up his combat map. Green dots filled the screen, intermixed with an array of red dots. It was a fracas, small teams fighting little wars of their own, linking up with others to coalesce into a more powerful one or breaking off to engage a threat from another axis. Swarm versus swarm, Rangers against Hivers.

With his suit computer, he tagged the flow of Hiver reinforcements and the landing ship. The q-com would update the Rangers' net, feeding them fresh data. Taking a deep breath, he transmitted on the whole tactical net, reaching every Ranger around him.

"This is Sergeant Major Abel Santiago. I have eyes on the objective. It's crawling with Hivers. I need a distraction so I can penetrate the target."

The Hivers spread out, forming a defensive perimeter. Hunters formed up into packs, infantry gathered into squads. On the combat map, green dots swirled around red dots, converging on Santiago. He looked and looked but could not find a dot with Meyers' name. The Hivers assembled into a swarm, sending their hunters forward to engage the new threat, infantry close behind. A squad of infantry rushed his way.

Santiago balled up and rolled aside.

The troops stormed past him, oblivious.

He stayed where he was. Waited. When he was sure the road was clear he looked up. Checked his map. The Hivers were forming a defensive circle around the park, responding to Ranger probes from every direction. Too busy to look inwards.

Santiago got to his feet and sprinted for the ship.

The interior was a dark, empty cavern. No Hivers emerged from the darkness to tear his head off.

At the far end of the hold was a door. Past the door, a staircase. He ascended the steps slowly, carefully, weapon ready.

A small antechamber waited at the top of the stairs. Soft light flooded his monocular, and he lifted it. Taking quiet, measured steps, he entered the room beyond.

It was the control room. Three Hivers were plugged into a console across him. In the center of the room was a spire that seemed to grow from the floor. Two more Hivers sat by it, thick cables connecting their temples to the machine.

None of them had seen him.

Santiago raised his carbine and fired.

The first one at the spire died without knowing why. Its partner turned around, and Santiago splattered his brains across the floor. The other Hivers whirled around to face the threat, their cables disconnecting. Santiago blasted them with rapid fire. One rolled away, producing a hand weapon, but Santiago got off-line and shot it before it could react.

Santiago blinked. And giggled. These weren't Hiver combatants. Otherwise he wouldn't have had a chance.

He inspected the spire. It had to be control node. He'd seen pictures of one once, in the early days of the war when there was still a functional air defense net. A Ranger team had sneaked into a downed Hiver landing craft, live-streaming video feeds of the interior. The craft had self-destructed before the Rangers could hack the node, but this one *probably* wasn't in danger of blowing up anytime soon. Using an adaptor, he plugged his suit into the node.

A cold female voice entered his earpieces. "This is Central. We are inside the Hive Mind. Stand by."

Santiago called up his map. The red dots were regrouping. Small detachments formed up, racing back to the dropships. The green dots formed into smaller groups, attacking weak points in the enemy line and fading out. Some Hiver constructs, their logic trees disrupted, got caught in an endless loop between running for the ships and running for the front. Red dots disappeared, but more green dots vanished.

CLACK-CLACK-CLACK

Santiago primed a grenade, tossed it into the antechamber. He found cover behind the spire as the grenade exploded. The concussion jarred his brain, left him dizzy. When he looked up he saw a pair of blood-soaked Hunters flow into the room, moving around to flank him on both sides.

He fired at the nearest one, blasting it apart. Ducking, he stepped around as he heard a laser *CRACK*.

The cable tightened, arresting his motion. The other hunter leapt at him, claws slashing. He tried to block the slash with his carbine. The creature latched on to it and broke it in half. As the hunter tossed the broken carbine aside, Santiago drew his dagger.

The Hiver closed in, slashing both hands forward, tail zapping from above. Santiago stepped aside, checking an arm with his left hand and slashing out with his dagger. The cable popped free from his suit. The blade slid harmlessly off the hunter's arm. Santiago kept moving, chasing the recoiling stinger. Grabbing the base of the tail, he stabbed the blade in. He sprayed the wound with nano and jumped back, mind-keying a command.

The tail exploded. The blast knocked the breath out of Santiago's lungs. The Hiver stumbled towards him, bringing its right claws slashing down.

Santiago stepped in to his left, his left hand slapping its arm over his right shoulder, and slashed upwards with his right. He felt the knife slide across its throat. He retracted the knife, ramming the blade into its neck. The dagger bit in, opening a hole. Retracting the knife, Santiago sprayed the wound with nano, kicked the hunter away, and blew its head off.

Gasping for breath, he staggered away and plugged himself back in. He panted, sucked in huge gulps of air.

Tik-tik-tik

Looked up.

More hunters spilled through the doorway.

"Fuck." He brought both nanosprays up.

The Hivers halted.

He stared at them.

They stared back.

Nothing happened.

A cool voice filled his earpieces. "This is Central. We have control of the Hive Mind. All Hive personnel are now under the control of the Neuvo Corazon Armed Forces. The war is over."

The announcement repeated. Santiago listened to it five times before finally hearing the last four words.

He collapsed. Blinked at the ceiling. When he finally found the strength to sit up, the hunters had departed. A lifetime later, he tuned his q-com.

"Major?" he whispered.

"Santiago! Abel! My God, man, you did it!"

"What the hell happened? What did we do to them?"

"The Academy AIs were coding a virus to corrupt the Hive Mind since the war began. The intel you collected helped us complete it."

Every member of the Hive was in constant contact with each other. If a C&C node uploaded a Trojan horse into the Hiver command net, every single Hiver would be infected in minutes.

Khabarov couldn't have told him, of course. Operational security. As he pondered Khabarov's words, a thought slammed into Santiago's brain.

"We... we did to them what they were going to do to us."

"We won the war."

"We turned into them."

"We won the war," Khabarov repeated. "Look. You need treatment. Get to the outpost and into a medbox. Now."

Santiago picked himself up. Dusted himself off. Left the ship. Wandered out the park.

The Hivers gathered themselves into little groups. They dropped their weapons into neat piles and kneeled on the ground, hands to their heads, dutifully awaiting collection. Hunters prostrated. Golems disintegrated. Wasps landed. Gunshots rang out in the dark. The shooting was entirely one-sided. The Hive's starships were doing nothing to stop it. They must belong to Nuevo Corazon now.

Santiago pulled off his mask, letting the frigid air caress his burned skin and fill his lungs. Looking up, he saw billions of stars with uncounted worlds. Most were lifeless, some not, more than a few occupied by different strains of humanity. Including the Hiver homeworld.

Now ready to be conquered.

KILL STREAK

Samson Stormcrow Hayes

Spencer dropped into the hole, cautious of any mines or trip-wires. Two teammates dropped in behind him, but they recklessly took off through the tunnel. He followed behind, but lost them around the bend. A flash of light indicated an explosion followed by a burst of gunfire. They'd fallen into an ambush.

He tossed a grenade into the darkness and heard the enemy shout in fear before they died. Cautiously, he peered around the corner. He never saw the sniper who killed him.

Spencer punched his mattress, shouting, "Fuckin' pussy-ass snipers."

Three seconds later he spawned elsewhere on the map. He tried to hunt down the sniper, but the jackass kept moving. Spencer died twice more before the game ended.

"Damn it," he muttered. "I can't get anything going."

He finished the game with a miserable 24-20 kill/death ratio. It didn't look like Deathdirge would be online so he played a few more games before getting ready for school.

He finished his homework and double-checked his math. His grades were slipping and he couldn't let them fall below a B or his parents would restrict his game time. They expected him to go to college.

His parents were still discussing the election when he sat down to breakfast an hour later. It was the first Tuesday of November and it was all anyone talked about, even online. It was driving Spencer crazy.

"I think it's going to be close," his father told his mother. "You sure you don't want to come with me to the polls before work?"

"No," his mom replied. "I'll vote online when the polls open in ten minutes. I don't know why you don't do the same."

"Call me old fashioned." His dad forced a smile, but Spencer could tell he was worried.

"You think Hanley's going to win?" asked Spencer.

"It's possible."

"Hanley's awesome," shouted his younger brother Toby.

His parents exchanged a worried look. His mom placed her hand on his father's shoulders and said, "He's too young to understand."

"Am not! Hanley wants us to kick ass."

"Toby!" his father rebuked. "Language!"

"Sorry," Toby whined, his head bowed.

"So you're voting for Barker?" Spencer asked, and his dad nodded. "Does it even matter?"

"It sure does," his father explained. "I know right now it might not seem like it, but if Hanley's elected, this country will undergo some big changes."

"Change! Change! Change!" Toby chanted, echoing Hanley's slogan.

Spencer was tired of the whole thing. Even the players in other countries were talking about it.

"Don't you think it matters?" Spencer's mom asked him.

Spencer shrugged. He just hoped that when it was over, people would stop arguing online and focus on the game. Politicians came and went, but the game went on forever.

"With only two choices, is there really much of a choice?" he asked. His parents didn't answer.

It was the same at school. Students and teachers alike drew battle lines over who should be the next president and there was even a fistfight between Tim Roonie, one of the seniors, and Mr Cooper, the science teacher, that ended with Mr Cooper being arrested.

Spencer felt relieved when the day was over. He came home and quickly did his homework while his father, looking dejected, watched the election results. Hanley was winning. After dinner, Spencer dropped his dishes in the dishwasher and headed upstairs.

He wasn't surprised to see Toby playing his GameStation 3000. The GS was the latest in 3-D gaming technology. His parents bought it for him for his birthday as a reward for getting all As in school. He lifted the headphones from his brother's ear and shouted, "Get out, assface!"

"But I'm in the middle of a game," Toby whined.

"Don't care." Spencer tore off the headset so Toby couldn't play.

"But it's not fair. You're not even going to play."

"It's my room. Get out." Spencer punched his brother in the shoulder.

"Oww!" he cried.

"Second one's harder," Spencer warned. Toby ran out the door.

Spencer shut down the game console and went to bed. It was only 7 pm.

The alarm rang at 2 am. Spencer jumped out of bed and quickly shut it off before the noise disturbed anyone else in the house. Rubbing the sleep from his eyes, Spencer realized he had overslept. He set two alarms, but didn't remember the first one going off. He must have woken up just enough to kill it.

He quietly slipped down the hall to the bathroom to relieve himself then hurried downstairs to grab an energy drink before returning to his room. Once the door was shut and the earphones secured, he activated the GS 3000. Spencer's preferences instantly loaded his favorite game, *Elite Soldiers*. It was the closest video games came to reality. Within seconds he was online.

He took a swig of the energy drink while he scrolled through the game options until he found *Slaughterhouse*. He put the drink down, scratched his nose before indicating he was ready. The game launched. A list appeared with the following options: Sniper, Scout, Recon, Assault, Warrior, Mercenary, Heavy Weapons, Demolition, Medic, and Spec Ops. Spencer selected the last one and a weapons menu appeared. His preferences were ready: main weapon: UMP45; sidearm, an M93 Raffica; and his special equipment – a C-4 explosive pack. He clicked

'Accept'. There was a three second shift as the screen changed; then he was in the game.

Spencer was in a forest of fir trees that gently swayed to an imaginary breeze. Through the stereophonic headset, Spencer could hear chirping birds, the rustle of a chipmunk, and sporadic gunfire. Whenever he moved, he could hear the crunch of dirt and twigs beneath his feet. Spencer looked around to determine where he was located. Some game modes included a map in the upper left corner of his view, but one of the rules of *Slaughterhouse* was no map. Judging from an outcropping of rock that snipers liked to inhabit, he knew he was somewhere near the center of the action. Good. Now he had to decide: stay low or go for the high ground. He opted to stay low.

He ran down a dirt pathway to his left and immediately encountered his first foe. A short burst from the UMP dropped him. Spencer smiled. He continued forward more cautiously and ran into two more enemies waiting for him. Spencer was ready. He anticipated the first player would alert anyone behind him. The UMP barked out two more bursts and he took them both down. He rushed forward, wrapped around a bend in the path and hid in the narrow corner of a rocky outcropping to change magazines. A moment later, two more players rushed forward looking for him. Spencer's ambush dropped them both.

He left his rocky hiding place. Time for high ground, he decided, and climbed a rope ladder leading to the treetops.

As soon as he reached the top, bullets ricocheted around him. He rushed for cover, then tossed his C-4 pack over the ledge. He waited a second then clicked the remote. *BOOM!* His screen indicated two more kills. He received a seven kill-streak bonus and another bonus for getting so many kills during his first spawn. The more kills he achieved in a single lifetime, the more rewards he received. Spencer was racking them in. Twelve seconds in and he had already doubled the top player's score.

When the game ended, Spencer had 32 kills and only three deaths. Now for his favorite part. The lobby taunts. Whenever someone spoke, their name lit up on Spencer's screen.

"You fuckin' faggot," shouted MyGunsRBettr. "There's no way you could've shot me that fast unless you're glitching."

"He's gotta be glitching," agreed IWannaKillPuppies.

Spencer smiled. People often thought he was using cheats, auto-aims that gave instant head shots, but he never did. It was pure skill.

"If I had you on a real battlefield, it would be a different story," MyGunsRBettr continued.

Spencer laughed. He loved hearing the frustration in the older player's voices, many of whom were ex-military.

"There's no fuckin' kill streaks in real life!" MyGunsRBettr shouted.

"No shit, Sherlock," Spencer taunted.

Kill streaks enhanced his speed, increased his weapon damage, or gave him better ammunition, such as explosive rounds. Basically, the more kills he racked up, the deadlier he became.

"You faggot," MyGunsRBettr repeated before signing off. Spencer laughed as the name disappeared from the player list.

"I'm gonna rape you next round, you glitchin' asshole," taunted IWannaKillPuppies.

"Bring it," Spencer replied.

When the following round ended, Spencer had 26 kills and 5 deaths. IWannaKillPuppies disappeared halfway through the match when he was only 3 and 11.

"Time to find new meat," mused Spencer. He quit *Slaughterhouse* and scanned through the menu until he decided on *Bloodlust*.

Bloodlust was a single player free-for-all that only allowed close range and melee weapons. Spencer chose a .44 Automag for short range, and 'The Punisher', a large machete for some serious hack and slash.

The maps in *Bloodlust* were small and the key was to keep moving or die. He launched into a game and found himself in dense jungle. He checked the board and found seven other players along for the action. To his left, he heard the sound of a stream. He knew it would be the main avenue of action.

Spencer had only moved a few feet when he heard someone thrashing through the jungle. A moment later, someone was randomly firing just ahead of him. Spencer sprinted forward. He was making too much noise to hear Spencer who swung 'The Punisher' and severed his head.

A few seconds later, he arrived at the stream and peered through the foliage. Already he could see the water turning red. A moment later, a body floated past. Then just across the stream – movement. He aimed his .44 and waited for a clear shot, but it didn't happen. Spencer couldn't wait too long or someone might sneak up behind him. He decided to chance it. He fired three rounds where he thought he'd seen the movement. His screen indicated a kill and a second later, a body fell into the water.

He reloaded and quickly crossed the stream. He ran into another soldier looking for the source of the shot. *Boom!* The Automag took him down.

Spencer decided to risk climbing a tree. He holstered his weapons and shimmied up as fast as he could. From his new vantage point, he could see movement all around him in the jungle. He killed five more people before they discovered his hiding place and killed him.

Spencer respawned in a new location and began the hunt again. This time, he stayed upriver and whenever two other foes engaged, he would pick off the winner. Sometimes he got lucky and killed them both before they could kill each other. Amateurs.

Spencer ended the game with a 19-9 kill/death ratio. Not bad.

He usually didn't get as many taunts in the free-for-all matches, but sometimes someone took offense. The guy's name was Shogun-Jay and he was not happy. Spencer received a nemesis medal for killing Shogun-Jay more than eight times in a single match. The medal had his opponent's name scratched onto a bloody dog tag.

"Hey, motherfucker. How'd you kill me so many times?" demanded Shogun-Jay. "I'm talking to you, Killerprime." Killerprime was Spencer's online handle.

"I guess I'm just that good," replied Spencer.

"That good at sucking cock."

"No, I'm that good at making you suck mine, bitch." Spencer knew how to piss off his opponents.

"You probably don't even have hair on your crotch, you little faggot."

"That's because all my pubes are stuck in your teeth," Spencer laughed.

"You little motherfucker. You're lucky I'm in Venezuela defending your ass."

"I hope you're better at killing in real life than you are in the game."

"Listen, you little asshole. You better hope that you never have to face what I've had to face, cuz your bullshit bunny-hopping techniques won't mean shit in real life. It isn't like the game. There are no respawns. When you die, you..." suddenly Spencer could tell the guy was choked up, "...you stay dead."

For a moment Spencer wondered if Shogun-Jay was serious. Then he realized he was just being played. This guy was probably faking it, trying to garner sympathy. Spencer had no sympathy; he only had death and humiliation to dispense.

"Whatever," Spencer replied.

Still, Spencer decided to quit the game. Something about the guy's voice got to him. He played another round in a different match and did a little better. Finally, his friend Deathdirge came online.

"About time," said Spencer. "You ready for some *Carnage*?"

"You better believe it," replied Deathdirge with his thick New Zealand accent.

Carnage involved ten two-man teams working against each other to grab the 'package' and extract it via the highest point on the map. It was one of the most challenging modes of the game since you had to work against the other teams, but also work together to stop whichever team was closest to winning. Enemies became allies until those same allies turned traitorous. There was only one person you could trust, your partner, and Deathdirge was an exceptional player. Together, they were almost unstoppable.

"How ya been, mate?" asked Deathdirge halfway through their first game. Their opponents in the first match were fairly new to the game and the duo was dominating. They could afford some casual conversation.

"Pretty good. Someone just took the package into the office building. Had a couple good games before you came on."

"Oh yeah? Look out, there's a sniper on the scaffolding. What matches did ya play?"

Spencer filled him in on his latest scores and glories.

"Oh, you're not gonna believe this, but I played a game the other night after you left that was one of my best games yet," bragged Deathdirge. "I had a kill streak of 42."

"No way!" exclaimed Spencer.

"Yeah, it was awesome."

"There's the package," Spencer shouted, suddenly back in the game.

"Got it."

"Get it out of here. I'll cover you."

Ten seconds later, they won the match. Most of the other players quit so they wouldn't have to play another round against them.

"Fuckin' cunts," decried Deathdirge. Spencer noticed he always called people cunts. Especially anyone who confused him for Australian. He hated that more than anything.

Spencer met Deathdirge late one weekend night during a game of *Global War*. Their skill levels were comparable and Spencer ended up playing until dawn. A week later, Spencer began Spring break and he was able to stay up late every night. The two bonded in fake blood and kill streaks.

Once school resumed, however, Spencer rarely saw Deathdirge. Because he lived on the other side of the world, they were rarely online at the same time. Spencer tried staying up late on weekends, but often fell asleep before Deathdirge came online. When they did play, Spencer suffered the following Monday mornings. That's when he decided to change his schedule. His parents didn't seem to mind as long as he finished his homework and kept his grades up.

They switched lobbies and found some more formidable opponents.

"Now this should be a challenge," said Deathdirge, noting the rankings on the screen.

The game was intense, and Spencer barely managed to get the package across the border before the time limit ran out. Spencer's hands were sweaty. There was nothing better.

"Hey, good round," offered Megawatt. Compliments were rare, but Spencer always appreciated when someone was graceful in defeat. However, it was followed by the more traditional fare.

"You kill-streak whores. I would've had you if you didn't have all those armor and ammo upgrades," Vampiresuck moaned.

"I guess you'll just have to try harder, mate," taunted Deathdirge.

"Or die less," joked Spencer.

"I don't have time to play all day and night like you little fuckers. I actually have to work for a living."

Deathdirge laughed then added, "Ahhh, what a whiny cunt."

"Fuckers!" Vampiresuck added before quitting.

"Let's go to private chat," suggested Deathdirge who sent the invite before he finished speaking. "I'm sick of these maggots."

Deathdirge preferred private chat to the game lobbies, and Spencer never confessed his joy of listening to the old men whine. But he didn't mind when he was gaming with Deathdirge. It was the most fun he had playing.

"Man, that was a good game," said Spencer.

"Yeah, it was pretty tight, wasn't it?"

They played two more games, winning one and losing the other, before Deathdirge suggested a bathroom break. They each took five minutes to stretch, relieve themselves, and grab another drink. When Deathdirge returned, Spencer asked, "Hey, tell me about your 42 kill streak."

"Oh, it was so awesome. I was so close to 50, I couldn't believe it. Another few minutes and I woulda had it!"

"What happened? They finally kill you?"

"No, the stupid game ended. I was 58 and 8. Funny thing is, I started the game horribly. Died three times without a single kill. Then it just turned around and I hit my stride."

"Damn. That's good."

"Yeah, but I still haven't made it to the fabled fifty."

"We'll get there."

"Oh, I don't doubt it."

Spencer's highest kill streak was 35. But every game he played, he played in the hopes of making it to 50, which was the ultimate enhancement – invulnerability! Usually a game was over by the time someone reached that high, but the accomplishment was getting there at all. Few had ever done it.

"By the way, did you vote today?" Deathdirge suddenly asked.

Spencer sighed wondering why Deathdirge even cared.

"Uh... no," Spencer replied. Then he reluctantly added, "I'm only sixteen, remember."

"Oh yeah, I completely forgot." Deathdirge had commented in the past that Spencer always sounded mature for his age.

"Who do you think's gonna win?"

Ugh, this was not what Spencer wanted to talk about.

"I don't really care."

"Really? It seems like a really big deal in your country."

"I guess, but it just seems stupid to me."

"What about your parents? You know who they voted for?"

"Barker."

"Really? He seems like such a drongo, especially after he screwed up and caused the Caracas Catastrophe."

"Who cares, let's just play."

"Yeah, sorry, mate. Just curious. Seems like you can't turn on a computer without reading something about it, even over here."

They played for an hour before taking another break. When

they resumed, Deathdirge announced, "Hey, I just checked the news. Looks like this Hanley guy won it."

"Oh," was all Spencer had to say.

"Yeah, I was just reading some of his proposals. They sound quite radical. I hadn't really read much on that."

"Yeah, that's what people were saying here."

"Did you read about the new draft?"

"Yeah, I heard about it."

"Are you worried?"

"Dude, it won't affect me. My parents make sure I have good grades so I'm guaranteed college acceptance."

"I hope so. I read if elected, Hanley and his party plan on pushing through a lot of aggressive new legislation. They might even reduce the number of exemptions."

"Well," Spencer said, hoping to end the conversation, "I don't have to worry about it for another two years."

"Good point," Deathdirge agreed. "I certainly hope it's nothing you ever have to worry about though, because being drafted would suck!"

"I guess," Spencer sighed, he tapped his foot impatiently. "You ready to launch?"

"I might have one more game in me, but I'll have to go after this one. I'm feeling a bit knackered."

They ended up losing the next round and Deathdirge apologized for playing so poorly because he was tired. Spencer played two more games, then powered down the GS and jumped in the shower. He finished his homework and made breakfast all before anyone else was awake. When his father finally came downstairs, he seemed grumpy so Spencer stayed out of his way.

Much to Spencer's chagrin, the election talk continued at school. It was all anyone seemed to care about, all except his friends, who were more obsessed with masturbation.

"Hey Spence, did you yank it last night?" asked Kyley-B.

"No," Spencer said defensively.

"Then how come you weren't online after school?"

"Yeah, you're never online anymore," accused Jackson.

"That's because he doesn't like gaming with us," said Royce. "He only goes on late at night so he can avoid us."

Spencer knew Royce must have checked his log-in times.

"Why the hell do you get up so early to play?" Royce asked.

"I don't know. It's just more fun. My parents aren't nagging me and I can focus."

"Dude, at three in the morning I'd rather focus on sleeping," said Jackson.

"You mean you're focused on yanking it," laughed Kyley-B.

"Shut up!"

This was why Spencer hated gaming with his friends – they never took anything seriously.

For the next few months, Spencer's life followed the same routine. Occasionally, he would try gaming with his friends, but compared to Deathdirge, they were horrible. But then Deathdirge stopped playing; disappeared completely.

One evening in March, Spencer was taunting his victims in the post-game lobby.

"Gawdammed kids! You think you're such hot shit! Wait'll you see real combat! You'll shit your pants the first time someone shoots at you!"

"If you could shoot half as good as me, then maybe you'd win a few battles," Spencer taunted.

"You don't know how lucky you are that I'm here protecting the reserves that let you play your little fucking game."

"When I'm old enough I'll come over there and show you how to kick ass."

The voice laughed. "You wouldn't last five minutes in the military."

"That's five minutes longer than you lasted in the game, dumb—"

Spencer jumped as his door opened. It was his dad.

Spencer thumbed 'mute' and asked, "What is it, Dad?"

"Still playing the game?"

Spencer nodded.

"Doesn't it ever get boring?"

Spencer shook his head no and wrinkled his eyebrows at the ridiculousness of the question. As if the game could ever get boring.

"I want you to come downstairs. Your mom and I thought it might be nice to have a real family dinner tonight."

Nice and gay, Spencer thought.

"You can finish this game, but then I want you to wash up and join us."

"Okay."

Since a new game was about to begin, he simply jumped out of the lobby and powered down. He followed his dad downstairs and was surprised to see his Aunt Lynne sitting in the living room.

"There's my little man," she said.

Spencer cringed. She'd been calling him her 'little man' since he was seven. He hated it, but he forced a smile and gave her a hug. When he pulled back, he noticed she'd been crying.

"Is something wrong?" he asked. Immediately, tears resumed streaming from her eyes. Spencer turned and looked at his parents who in turn looked at Lynne. She nodded and stammered, "It's okay. You can tell him."

"Your Uncle Paul was drafted today. He left for military service in the Philippines. We didn't want your aunt to be alone tonight, so we invited her over."

She gave Spencer another big hug; her tears warm against his neck.

Dinner was quiet and awkward. Toby kept asking questions that prompted their mom to say, "Not now!" or "Stop talking and finish chewing", whether he was chewing or not. When the meal was over, Spencer's mom asked him to help her clean up the dishes. Together, they carried them into the kitchen. She started the dishwasher and made sure they were alone.

Then, despite being taller than her, she leaned over and placed her hand on Spencer's shoulder.

"Spencer, honey, we need to talk."

This sounded serious. For a moment, Spencer worried it might have something to do with his late night adventures.

"What is it?" he asked.

"I don't know how much your teachers may have talked about this at school, but I think you should know there's a chance your father might be recruited into the military."

"Dad? Why would they want Dad? He's ancient."

"Spencer!"

"Sorry."

"There are some new, very strict laws. Anyone under the age of 40 is eligible and your dad is only 39. With his skills, there's a good chance he'll be recruited. Fortunately, he'll most likely be far from the front lines, but he'll have to go very far away."

"I hope they don't send him to South America. He'd be better off in the Middle East where it isn't so bad," offered Spencer.

"I don't want them to send him anywhere. But it's something we should prepare for."

Spencer nodded though he didn't really know what she meant. When dinner was over, Spencer returned to the game while his parents consoled his aunt.

When he logged on, he was delighted to see a message from Deathdirge.

"Hey, man, how ya been? Sorry I ain't been on in ages, but I started a new job. They've got me working like crazy. I'm almost never home. But I should get like a week or two off next month. I'll see you then, mate. Cheers!"

The message only lasted a few seconds, but it was great to hear his friend's voice. He played it again before jumping into the game.

The next morning, his dad drove Spencer to school. "It could be any day now, Spence. The war's getting worse. They're recruiting anyone. One day you might come home and… I might not be there. If that happens, you'll be the man of the house, Spence. You'll need to take care of your mother and especially your brother. You'll need to stop playing those games and focus on your responsibilities. You hear me, Spence?"

Spencer couldn't imagine anyone wanting to draft his father. He nodded, went to school and forgot all about it.

* * *

It was late at night and Spencer couldn't sleep. He climbed out of bed and powered up the GS. He hoped a game or two would help clear his head. He guessed Deathdirge wouldn't be on, but he hoped he was wrong. He checked the player log. It had been 38 days since Deathdirge had last logged in.

He scrolled through his options and decided on a simple game of *Team Annihilation.* Normally, the game servers tried to place a player into a game that was just beginning, but occasionally players were thrown right into the middle of everything. It could be chaotic, confusing, and disorienting. Spencer spawned into the thick of it. The game was half over and, to make matters seemingly worse, he spawned on the enemy's side. Spencer was surrounded.

"Shit."

His first life would be short, but he could wreak some havoc before they killed him. He dropped the nearest three with his knife before any of them realized he had spawned in their midst. Because the enemy wasn't expecting him in their lines, they reacted slowly. He watched as his fourth target, receiving word from his dead comrades, looked around confused. He was turning in Spencer's direction when Spencer shot him dead.

The shot gave away his position, so he threw a grenade in one direction and jumped in the other. The grenade took out two more adversaries. Now the kill streaks were kicking in, giving him advantages. Already he had extra ammo (when he'd only fired a single shot) and extra speed. The latter saved him from a knife attack. Spencer fired before the enemy could swing a second time. He had seven kills and miraculously, the other opponents, thinking they'd been flanked by half their foes, were fleeing.

Spencer aimed and dropped three more opponents. His ongoing kill streaks rewarded him with larger clips, an extra grenade, and a faster reload speed. More amazingly, he had cleared out the enemy team. They would respawn elsewhere on the map and he had survived what should have been certain death.

Of course, he felt that some of the players might return to the same area for revenge. He dropped his C-4 pack (his tenth kill had given him one to spare) into the area and ran for cover.

Spencer watched as two foes sprinted back, zigzagging between cover. It was hard not to just aim and shoot, but he didn't want to give away his position. When the two soldiers arrived, he clicked the detonator. *Boom!*

Unfortunately, after the tenth kill streak, additional rewards only came after every five kills. He needed three more to get to fifteen and increased accuracy. Spencer watched the open area. Since no one else was approaching, he decided to leave. As he turned, however, he saw an enemy soldier crawling past his hiding place. Spencer waited until he passed and made sure no one else was with him. Then he stabbed him in the back and moved on.

He dodged and weaved through the shacks that littered the open plain. The map represented the outskirts of an African slum, presumably Mogadishu. It combined a semi-rural outskirt of shacks and outhouses amidst a landscape of scattered brush, dried earth, and a few trees. Along the way, he killed five more men. By now he was certain to be pissing off at least a few of the players on the other team. When that happened, their quest for revenge would often make them careless. Indeed, Spencer killed five more foes that tried to rush where they thought he was hiding. Spencer managed to stay one step ahead.

At this point, his teammates were now respawning around him after they died elsewhere on the battlefield. He had additional fire support as six more soldiers tried to surround Spencer. If he'd been alone, he probably would have died, but now his teammates absorbed the bullets and grenades meant for him. Every time a teammate dropped, Spencer would return fire and take down the foe as he was changing clips or looking in the wrong direction. Spencer had twenty-four kills.

At twenty, he picked up a faster melee swing so that he

would beat any opponent in a knife fight. His twenty-fifth kill would give him increased explosive power and he still had an extra grenade and a C-4 pack. It was nearly time to put them to use.

By now, most of his team had spawned around him. Several of them were 'campers', which meant they liked to hide in one place and ambush anyone who entered their field of fire. Spencer hated campers; he preferred running and gunning. It was time to hunt.

Two of his teammates were already heading down a dried-out riverbed that twisted its way through the map. It was an excellent way to get around unseen, though it was also an excellent way to get ambushed. Spencer followed, allowing the other two to be his guinea pigs. The first died in a landmine explosion, which gave away their position. Two foes popped over the riverbed and fired down, catching the second teammate unaware. But while they focused their fire on the player, Spencer took them both down with a short burst from his XM-8.

Even with the extra ammo from his kill streaks, Spencer's was running low. He rushed forward, grabbed his teammate's gun, an FN F2000 and tossed a C-4 pack as he retreated down the gully. He lay flat in the weeds. Sure enough, the same two players returned, only this time they ran through the riverbed. *Boom!* Spencer's screen indicated four kills! His increased explosive damage caught two other soldiers following behind that he hadn't even seen.

He had 30 kills and was rewarded with silent movement.

His stereo headset allowed Spencer to hear which direction gunfire, footsteps, or even the character voices were coming from. Spencer could move silently across any surface. More importantly, he was rapidly reaching his personal best, a kill streak of 35. He'd reached it twice, but each time he was killed before he could enjoy the kill streak perk of 'sixth sense' that allowed him to detect any mines and tripwires the enemy had planted.

Spencer continued a short distance down the riverbed before climbing up to the plain. A series of buildings were located just ahead. He could crawl to them and remain unseen, but the game was nearing its end. He wanted to try and tie his record of 35.

He knew it was this kind of recklessness that often got players killed, but this time it worked. Luck was on his side since the majority of his other teammates were attacking from a different direction. Consequently, the enemy was focused in that direction. They didn't see or hear Spencer coming. He looked through the window of the building and saw a concentration of soldiers. Seven in all. If he opened fire, he wouldn't even have enough ammunition in his clip to take them all out. He had to use his grenade. He tossed it in and dropped to the ground. *Boom!*

His screen lit up! He received bonus points, more ammo and one extra grenade for seven instant kills.

Spencer couldn't believe it. He'd passed his own record and had nearly tied Deathdirge's streak of 42. Was there a chance he could actually make 50 before the end of the round? There wasn't much time. If he wanted 13 more kills, he'd have to continue playing on the run.

He ran to the neighboring building where four more soldiers including one sniper, were hiding. They had heard the explosion and were facing Spencer when he looked through the window. Spencer was fucked. His screen was already turning red from the incoming fire. Then all four players were dead. His teammates had sprayed the building with gunfire. Spencer couldn't deny that he'd been lucky numerous times. He hoped it would hold up.

He left the building and circled around the riverbed. Using the scope on the F2000, he picked off three more players from a distance. He had 40 kills. His kill streak bonus gave him explosive ammunition. Each round was an instant kill.

He heard one of his teammates warn that the enemy had gathered on a rocky hillside and were sniping. Spencer wasn't far from the hill. He jumped back in the riverbed and worked his way toward them. He looked up just long enough to see movement along the ridge. He stared through the rifle scope and released short steady bursts of explosive rounds along the ridge. Any snipers would have to run for cover or face death. By chance, his random bursts killed two players and wounded another.

He emptied his clip, dropped down, and reloaded. He checked the timer. There was only 90 seconds left in the game. He had no choice. He had to rush the enemy.

He climbed out of the gully and charged, spraying the rocks with short bursts to keep their heads down. Between bursts, someone fired on him from his left flank. Spencer shifted his fire and charged straight toward the soldier. He made it across the open space and then used the rocks to weave his way upward. His 'sixth sense' allowed him to bypass the hidden mines and trip flares that had been set up. Swinging around, he caught the soldier who had so carefully booby-trapped the perimeter completely unawares.

Forty-one.

He came around the corner of another rock and found a soldier heading down the path.

Forty-two.

He climbed up near the top of the ridge and picked off two snipers.

Forty-three and forty-four.

With the game about to end, he decided to throw his last remaining grenade into a rocky gully. To his surprise, he killed two soldiers lying in ambush.

Forty-six.

The clock started ticking down the last thirty seconds. He loaded in a fresh clip and charged.

Spencer realized that even if he achieved invulnerability, he wouldn't have any game time to enjoy it. But that wasn't the point. It was all about the achievement.

He fired at anything that moved. The explosive rounds were devastating. He didn't even need a direct hit to score a kill. Forty-seven and forty-eight came quickly, but now there were only ten seconds left.

Against all logic, he jumped to the top of the ridge, exposing himself to any snipers. Staring down the hill, he could see a handful of soldiers and snipers hiding in the rocks, picking off his teammates in the village below.

Eight seconds.

He fired a burst.

Forty-nine kills.

Only one more.

He fired again, but the gun didn't shoot. In his furor, he lost track of his ammo. He was empty.

Five seconds.

He switched to his pistol. Three seconds. Then his screen went red. His vision was blurred. He could hardly see. He'd been hit by a sniper round. Another hit would finish him completely. Spencer fired rapidly and blindly into the rocks. He still had explosive ammo no matter which gun he used.

Blam!

His screen lit up. JUGGERNAUT flashed at the top in blood red letters and underneath it read: 50 kill streak! His vision instantly cleared. He was invulnerable.

With two seconds left, he picked off two more enemy soldiers before the game ended. He was 52-0. A nearly perfect game and he entered the round late.

He jumped out of his seat and threw his headset onto the bed. He pumped his fist in the air. "Yes, yes, yes!" he yelled with as much enthusiasm as he dared considering the late hour.

Spencer was so pumped he didn't even listen to the game lobby taunts. He paced his room with untamed energy. He had to tell someone, but who? He could brag to his friends in the morning, but they wouldn't believe him and he didn't care if they did. The only person who would understand was Deathdirge.

Spencer put the headset back on and quit the game. He pulled up Deathdirge's name and clicked 'send message'.

"You're not going to believe this, Dirgey," he said excitedly into the mic, "but I just did it! I hit a fifty-kill streak in one game. I did it with just two seconds to spare and a sniper shooting at me. I even got in two more kills before it ended. I can't believe I did it! Where you been anyway? It's no fun killing without you."

He sent the message and felt some satisfaction knowing that Deathdirge would know about his accomplishment the next time he came online.

Spencer slipped out to use the bathroom and was surprised to hear his parents talking in their bedroom. He was about to walk past until he heard his name mentioned. Naturally, he stopped and listened.

"I don't think Spencer understands what's going on." His mom's voice was anxious and tense. "He's old enough; you should explain it to him."

His dad, always the rock of the family, remained calm. "I had a talk with him last week. He knows what's going on."

"Are you sure? He seems so distant. I'm telling you, it's those games. They're desensitizing him. Not just to violence, but to life. We should make him quit."

Spencer cringed. They wouldn't!

"I think that's a bit extreme."

Good old dad.

"He doesn't seem the least bit concerned that…" his mom choked up, "that we could lose you."

"It's okay, sweetie. I'm not going anywhere." His dad assured her. "Even on the off chance that I am drafted, I'll be sent to one of the safe zones, maybe even right here in the states."

"Oh, I hope so. I just don't want to lose you."

"You're not going to lose me, honey. I'm right here."

"I heard on the news today that the mortality rate is up to nearly fifteen percent."

"That's just in the war zones. If I'm recruited, they'll have me drafting designs or fixing engines; something I know how to do. They're not going to put a gun in my hand."

"They also said that they need more soldiers – of any age."

"Look at me." Spencer heard his father slapping his paunchy belly. "No one's sending this into combat."

She laughed softly. "They better not."

Spencer slipped back to his room, crawled into bed and thought about their conversation. Uncle Paul had been drafted, but Paul was five years younger than Dad and worked as a firefighter. Spencer could see why the military recruited him. Was it possible they could take his dad? His dad didn't seem to think so, but maybe he's just saying those things to console his mom.

Spencer realized all of this anxiety stemmed from his mother. She was always worried about something. As kids, she worried he and Toby would break something whenever they rough housed. If they went outside and skinned an elbow or knee, she freaked out even worse, telling them to play inside where there was carpeting.

Knowing how his mom made things out to be worse than they were, he decided not to worry. In the months that followed, Spencer realized it was the right decision. Dad wasn't drafted, but his mom continuously worried that the military would show up at any minute to take him away.

* * *

Spencer was playing online with his friends when an icon popped up on his screen. Deathdirge was online. Spencer was elated, but surprised he was on so early. Wouldn't it be mid-day in New Zealand? Not that it mattered. He was happy just to see his friend online.

Spencer sent out a chat invite, but after a few minutes he noticed it had been refused. He sent another, and again it was rejected. Finally, he sent a voice message, "Hey, what's going on? You haven't been on in ages? I'm surprised you're on so early."

He waited and wondered if he'd done something to piss Deathdirge off. This wasn't like him. It was another ten minutes before he received a reply. Spencer clicked the icon to playback the recording. The accent was the same, but the voice was different.

"Sorry, mate, I'm not who you think I am. Deathdirge was my cousin. I'm only playing his account until it expires. I feel weird telling you this, but I guess you should know. A few months ago, my cousin took a job on a fishing vessel. About three weeks ago, they were having engine problems when they hit rough waters. They sent out an SOS, but then radio contact was lost. None of them made it back. Sorry to break it to you, but Deathdirge is gone."

Spencer listened to the message again just to be sure he heard it right. It didn't seem possible.

The friends he'd been gaming with sent him invites to rejoin the game, but Spencer ignored them. He listened to the message one more time before powering off.

* * *

The next few weeks, Spencer hardly gamed at all. He studied harder and finished his papers days before they were even due. The school year was winding down, and finals were fast approaching. He used his free time to help tutor his friends, almost all of whom needed help if they wanted to pass. When they finished studying, they would invite him to play, but Spencer always made up an excuse.

He didn't tell his parents, but they noticed the change in his habits and demeanor. One night, while working on a term paper, his mom surprised him with some freshly-baked cookies.

"I thought you needed a break." She held out the plate. "Are you almost finished with the paper?"

"Not really," he replied, grabbing a cookie. "I still have five pages to go."

"They're still warm, just the way you like them."

She stayed in the room while he ate another two cookies. Finally, she said, "I noticed you haven't been gaming much lately. Is there some reason you quit?"

Spencer shrugged. "I guess I just haven't felt like playing."

"Oh," another awkward silence followed. Then, "Is everything okay?"

Spencer nodded. "Yeah, Mom. I'm fine. Thanks for the cookies."

"You're welcome."

Spencer wanted to turn around and continue working on his paper, but he didn't want to turn his back on his mom. Then she added, "Well, if you need a break, maybe you should play a game or two."

Spencer smiled, knowing how she felt about it. "Okay," he agreed.

An hour later, he punched in. The game came up and he viewed his options. *Carnage* was out of the question and he didn't feel like *Slaughterhouse*. He opted for a nice simple game of *Global War*. Five minutes into the game, he realized tears were pouring down his cheeks and he could hardly breathe. It was the first time he truly mourned. He quit the game and powered down, uncertain if he would ever play again.

* * *

Spencer sat in the back seat of Royce's mom's car as she drove them to school. The sun's bright-orange rays beamed blindingly through the windshield. Although it wasn't yet hot, Mrs Delgado had turned on the air conditioning in preparation for the sizzling heat to come.

Spencer had spent the night at Royce's house cramming for the morning's chemistry final. When they awoke, Mrs Delgado had pancakes, toast, and juice ready for them before she drove them to school. Now she asked the inane questions Spencer noticed all parents asked.

"You boys ready for the exam?" said Mrs Delgado.

"I hope so," replied Spencer.

"Mom, we'll be fine."

"Is it multiple choice?"

"No, we had to memorize all the formulas so we can solve the problems," Spencer explained.

"I think there're a couple fill-in-the-blanks," Royce added.

"I really appreciate all the help you've given my son this past week, Spencer."

"It's okay, Mrs Delgado. Glad to help."

"This weekend I'll take you boys to see whatever movie you want."

"Thanks, Mom."

"Thanks, Mrs Delgado."

The car turned the corner into the school parking lot. Mrs Delgado suddenly leaned forward. "Uh-oh, what's this?"

Spencer craned his neck over the seat to see what she was referring to. Sitting in the parking lot was a military van. Three men stood next to it. As their car approached, one of the men stepped forward and directed Mrs Delgado to park next to them.

Mrs Delgado rolled down her window.

"What's going on? Did I do something wrong?"

Spencer looked across the parking lot where all of his classmates watched and wondered.

"Are you Mrs Lisa Delgado?" asked the soldier.

"Yes?"

"I need you to turn off your vehicle."

"Is this about my husband? Is this about Mike?"

"No, ma'am."

Spencer noticed one of the other soldiers – a sergeant – staring into his palm where he most likely held some kind of device. He looked up from his palm and directly at Spencer. Then he pointed to the third soldier and the two approached the car, both standing on either side of the back doors. The Sergeant stepped forward to take over.

"There's nothing wrong, ma'am, we're simply looking for this young man." The Sergeant turned to Spencer. "Spencer Orlando. You need to come with us."

The door opened and Spencer felt himself being pulled out and urged toward the van. Spencer looked over his shoulder and saw Royce staring dumbly at Spencer as he silently mouthed, "What the fuck?" Next to Royce, his mother was trying to exit the car, but she was prevented from doing so by the first soldier who stood firmly in the way.

"What's going on?" asked Spencer.

"Please follow me," replied the sergeant. He made it sound

like a request, but Spencer had no choice as the man tightened the grip on his arm.

"But I have to take my chemistry exam," Spencer protested.

The soldier shook his head. "Not today."

By now, Spencer could hear Mrs Delgado's frantic voice rising in pitch as she argued with the first soldier.

"You can't do this?" she pleaded.

"We have our orders, ma'am. Don't interfere or you'll be arrested."

"Do his parents know? Where are his parents?" she asked.

"They've been informed and they're cooperating. I suggest you do the same."

"He's only a boy. This is illegal!" she screamed.

"Please, stay in your car."

She called out to Spencer, "I'm going to get your parents. Don't let them take you anywhere."

Mrs Delgado slammed shut the door she'd been trying so hard to open and nearly ran over the soldier's foot as she peeled away, roaring past the sign that read, 'Slow, School Zone.'

The sergeant stopped when they arrived at the van. He released Spencer's arm and looked into his palm where Spencer could now see the electronic device. The sergeant read from the screen:

"Spencer Orlando. According to Article 9, subsection C, paragraphs one through nine of the 31st Amendment, because of your exceptional skills and outstanding ability, you have hereby been called to active duty in the service of your country. Effective immediately."

"But I'm only sixteen!" pleaded Spencer. "I'm supposed to have two more years."

"Your country needs you," the second soldier replied stoically.

"But I'm just a kid," Spencer whined.

"It's time to man up," ordered the Sergeant. "Get in."

Spencer climbed into the van where he was directed to take the seat furthest back. "Can I go home and pack my stuff?"

"The military will supply you with everything you need."

"What about my parents?"

"They've been informed of your status."

"Can I at least say goodbye?"

"I'm afraid there isn't time."

The sergeant turned to the second soldier and asked, "Anyone else on the roster?"

"Just him. Our next recruit is in the next county, about twenty minutes away."

"Okay, let's get rolling." The sergeant climbed into the back of the van and sat next to Spencer who was staring out the window.

Spencer pointed to his classmates and asked, "What about them? How come they aren't going?"

"Underage exceptions are only made for the very best online players such as yourself." He then added, "I've seen your stats. They're impressive."

"But…" Spencer couldn't believe he was saying this, "the game is just for fun."

"Not anymore. It's now a recruiting tool testing for reflexes and reaction time. I'm sorry, son. I'm just doing my duty."

The van started. Spencer heard the bell ring and watched as his friends slowly wandered inside with the other students.

"I don't agree with the new law, but I have to enforce it." Spencer felt the hesitation in the soldier's voice before he continued. "I hate to say this, but personally speaking... I don't think you'll last five minutes."

Spencer took one last look at his school. In a few minutes, his friends would be taking their exams; their worst fear – flunking and going to summer school. Spencer turned away. Sinking down into his seat, he remembered the words of one of his online opponents: *There are no kill streaks on the battlefield.*

SCOUT MISSION

Jack Hillman

"All right, you apes. Lock and load." Gunny's voice rasped in my right ear over the comm link. "LZ in thirty seconds. Let's hit the dirt running for a change."

I checked the magazine on my weapon and flipped on the laser sight, not that I expected to be using it much. The comm was working, proved by mumbled comments from the rest of the squad coming through in a low rumble. I ran a quick check of the pouches on my belt and vest, checking extra ammo, explosives and backup weapons. I was as ready as the next guy. Unfortunately, I was at the end of the line and there was no next guy.

The sled hit atmosphere at an angle and quickly dropped to come in low over the hilltops, brushing the feathery vegetation and avoiding the anti-ack fire and scanners. By the time we down, a clearing had been scorched out of the valley by our antipersonnel lasers, and wisps of smoke whipped away as the sled grounded. The sides lifted in their gull-wing sequence and all ten of us rolled out at once and scattered to the edges of the clearing. Five seconds after grounding, the sled lifted up, headed for high atmosphere and its spot as our observation post and comm relay, watching our backs.

We were still scanning the brush for enemy warriors when the flash and concussion of the explosion made us look up. Pieces of sled rained down over several hundred square meters.

"Shit, we're in it now," I heard over the comm in an echo of my own thoughts.

"All right, assholes, move out. James take the point. Harris, you got the back door." Gunny swept the clearing with a hard look, knowing what we were all thinking. "First the mission, then we go home," Gunny stated.

The squad moved out with our observer, Lt Randolph, tucked between two troopers, as if it would keep him any safer. Randolph was nominally in charge due to his rank, but we all looked to Gunny for our orders. I watched the squad move out and waited my turn at the end of the line.

"Richards, get moving," Gunny called out over the link.

I looked at Richards, crouched to scan the brush. He didn't move. Gunny went over and carefully tapped him on the shoulder – you never knew what a new grunt would do his first time out in combat.

Richards just fell over and I could see the viper thorns stuck in his thigh. Gunny and I looked at each other for a moment. Then he pulled the tags from the body and set the timer on the disposal charges. He followed the line of troopers down the trail, me on his heels. We were out of sight of the clearing when the blast of heat bounced off the hillside, reducing Richards and his equipment to ash on the wind.

One down.

We traveled for better than an hour before Gunny called a break. Three times Cutter had to lop the heads off cane snakes as they reached down for James. Twice I dropped a minibomb down the dome holes of fire beetles, plugging the horde inside after the scouts entered to report our presence. If those one-inch bugs boiled out of their nest, they would devour anything that fought back. Digging in through the exposed face and hands, the creatures could strip a man to his armor in less than a minute, leaving not even bones to mark the death, as they consumed anything organic.

Once Billings slapped the observer's hand away from a lace orchid. He motioned Randolph to watch as he touched the end of a cigarette he pulled from his pocket to the lovely blossom. You could hear the hiss of acid as the tobacco dissolved, feeding its nutrients to the flower. Billings tossed the butt into the center of the blossom to feed the lovely bloom and they both watched the remains dissolve. It was just another reminder this wasn't Earth, and more than just the natives were unfriendly.

As we sat around in the brush, in sight of each other and watching behind our neighbors as we caught our breath, Gunny went through the specs again with the observer.

"Okay, here's how it goes," Gunny said to us when he was done with Randolph. "We approach the Thorn site, get Lieutenant Randolph here close enough to use his fancy toys, get the intelligence, and then head for the backup LZ. OPs know we're out here with our asses in the wind but they want what Randolph will give them so they will have a pickup arranged." He stared us all down, quashing any objections. "Once we make contact with the site, we button down. No unnecessary noise or movement. They may be Thorns, but they still have surveillance equipment as good as ours. With any luck, we get Randolph back and we don't have to do this shit anymore." We all looked at each other and laughed quietly. "Okay, okay. I don't believe it either," Gunny added. "But that's the line from the brass. Harris, you take point this time since you've seen one of these sites before. Let's get moving people."

We started off through the brush, carefully avoiding anything that looked like a trail. I kept my eyes open, knowing we were fighting the jungle as well as the Thorns. It had been like this of late: Thorns flew over one of our planets and seeded the atmosphere with their life forms. We dropped in and tried to contain the infection before it got out of hand. Only on this planet, the Thorns had knocked out the communications first, giving them better than a year to get set up and build their 'homestead'. The first we poor humans knew of the invasion was when a supply ship dropped into orbit and barely made it back out again after lasers took out their landing shuttle. Six months it had taken the supply ship to limp back to base on one rocket and a prayer.

Now our team was supposed to find a way to stop the Thorns. That was just our name for them. Their own name was more like Kruk't Kr'n T'Or' Urnz, which translated roughly as 'Brothers To All Growing Things', or some such crap. Which was, of course, why we called them Thorns. We were in a war for all the prime oxygen-based real estate at this end of the galaxy, and right now, the Thorns were winning this planet by the simple method of planting seeds. Considering they were more than part plant, it made sense. Trying to talk to them in diplomatic terms had about as much success as convincing your front lawn not to grow more than four inches high. You still had to mow them down every once in a while. But this lawn fought back.

A scream cut through the jungle sounds. I crouched and froze, scanning the brush in front for Thorns before I looked over my shoulder. Cutter and Jonesy were behind me scanning left and right. Nothing showed. It wasn't a diversion... this time.

Thirty meters back, Gunny was carefully lifting the edge of a mat of leaves and twigs. Two huge eyes showed briefly before James emptied a clip into the toad inside the hole. The toad was one of the Thorns favorite predators and had all the worst qualities of a snake's poisonous fangs and a toad's long tongue. The quiet rattle of the suppressed weapon barely ruffled the silence of the forest. The stench as the toad exploded, stung my eyes and wormed its way into my gut, making me gag, but the smell would keep other predators away for a while. We couldn't leave that creature behind us. They ran in loose packs and anyone that found enough food for more than itself would call others together to hunt their prey. Gunny reached in to snag a set of tags. I looked around to see who was missing and couldn't find Brock.

Two down.

Gunny motioned to me and I started off again, everyone paying extra attention to the jungle. It was quiet for the next hour… if you didn't count snakes, venomous insects, carnivorous plants and an occasional animal predator that took one look at us and slipped quietly into the brush. When we came to the ridge near the Thorn center I halted the squad and moved up alone.

There was a small, blue-flowered plant growing near every Thorn sensor that released a cloud of acrid gas if disturbed. It was a dead giveaway for the location of the sensors but required a special touch to keep from setting them off. I disabled the sensors along that section of the ridge with inert caps and moved forward. Somewhere on a Thorn control board, sensors were repeating their last five minutes of readings in an infinite loop I hoped the Thorns wouldn't notice.

When we reached the edge of the compound, we circled around Randolph, just outside the edge of the clearing, and let him do his thing. Sensors built into his vest and pack gave in-depth readings of the Thorn control center and whatever it was it pumped out. We needed to know how they controlled the growth of their plants, their creatures in order to make our defenses more efficient. This whole setup was a Garden of Eden to homesteading Thorns. I guess they liked their flowers with a bite. But to the humans that had been here, it was death.

The earth-colored dome before us was almost hidden beneath the riotous growth of the forest. Something moved on its surface. It was as if the dome itself was alive, with skin that rippled in the afternoon breeze. The jungle itself seemed to be one movable segment of life after another. To the Thorns, even the buildings were alive, it seemed.

"Sergeant Gunderson," Randolph said quietly. "I have what I need. Let's get out of here."

Gunny tapped me on the shoulder and pointed out our direction. I moved out to disable the sensors along the route. We had moved about a hundred meters when James pushed aside a huge elephant-ear leaf and stepped directly on a sensor I hadn't seen. The cloud of gas wrapped around him like an attacking snake, filling his lungs with acid and spores. James had time for one gargle then collapsed. I didn't need to check to know his lungs and airways would be filled with tight rootlets, growing at fantastic speed, choking him as they ate into his body.

Gunny grabbed his tags and set the timer on the d-charge. "Let's move it."

I gave up working on the sensors. The Thorns knew we were here now. I set a path to avoid the patches of blue, knowing the flowers could be discharged by remote control. Behind us the keening wail of a Thorn alarm sounded then the whine of a combat sled as scouts gave chase. Gunny must have had some built in time-lapse computer because the sled followed our path and stopped over James' body just as the charge let go. The blast of heat flipped the sled and ignited the fuel cell and ammo in one giant explosion. The jungle was silent for a moment before erupting in squeals and squalls as animals and insects prepared for battle. Now we had the whole jungle against us.

"Move it, Harris," Gunny yelled and we fled through the jungle as fast as we could travel.

There was a danger moving this fast through Thorn jungle, but the need to get Randolph and his info back to Intelligence made the risk acceptable, according to HQ standards. Without a trail to follow, the sleds couldn't reach us through the canopy of the forest. Any sled trying to slip down through the trees would face the same danger from the local lifeforms as we did on the ground. Only there were a lot of things living up in the trees that were small and deadly, as opposed to the large and deadly things living on the ground. You take your pick, I suppose.

Gunny had us set off the electronic scramblers in our gear so the Thorns couldn't track us by the magnetic fields of our bodies, which differed markedly from their own. The hunters would now be limited to sight and ground traces, giving us a fair chance of reaching the backup LZ.

"Split by twos," Gunny whispered over the comm. "Disguise your trail and direction. Make it look like there's a battalion of us in here. Then meet up at the LZ in three hours."

According to my heads-up display, that didn't give us much time to travel that far, but we had to make it if we were going to get out before Thorn reinforcements arrived. A site like the one we had just found normally had an eight-personnel unit. Two of them went up with the sled, leaving six. There would be two more teams coming after us with the last pair staying behind to guard the center.

Those two teams following us would be on the ground. With any luck, they would follow the two teams that left trails while Gunny hid his footprints and got Randolph back with the intel.

We got to play decoys. Fun. The Thorns couldn't just take sleds and sit over our probable LZ sites since we could take them out with rockets the same way they had nailed our transport.

"Harris, you take Billings and go left," Gunny instructed. "Cutter, you and Jonesy go right. Make it good and I'm buying the first round when we hit base." He nodded and we lit out, leaving Randolph and the other newbie, Johnson, with the Sarge.

Billings and I had worked together several times and knew the routine. We went side-by-side with enough room to move and fire, and avoided anything that looked like it was too open or too cluttered with brush. Too open usually meant a trap of some sort and too cluttered gave the little nasties too much room to hide. So we wove between trees and around rocks and tried our best not to make more noise than we had to. We moved for about an hour with nothing more than various animal nasties crossing our trail.

I spotted the hole of the fire beetles almost the same time we heard the Thorns behind us. Their stilted legs made a distinctive noise as they made their way through the forest, almost like they were letting the animals know they were coming and to warn them to get out of the way.

I set a minibomb next to the hole, where it would toss the nest into the air instead of closing it down, and motioned Billings to move ahead as I rigged the detonator. I waited behind a tree for the Thorns to show. They would be following our trail and would see the same signs we did.

The two Thorns moved into the open, too far away to shoot but close enough to see. In the dappled sunlight, they gleamed dark green with chlorophyll. They were soldier breeds, with the long stilted legs that could lift them fifteen feet into the air to see above short trees or heavy brush, and bodies covered with overlapping scales like armor. Their true-arms were pushed forward on a cylindrical body and had double opposable thumbs, one on each side of the hands. Their heads were inverted, truncated, five-sided pyramids sitting on a short flexible neck with four eyes, one on each side of the pyramid. To get binocular vision with depth perception, they looked past one corner of the pyramid to bring two eyes into focus. They literally had eyes in the backs of their heads. The overall effect was a six-legged spider with a short post on the front end and two grasping members in front. I hated spiders.

The Thorns were professionals, just like we were. They stayed too far apart for us to take them both out at once, moving carefully from tree to tree for cover, so I motioned to Billings and gave him the signal to take the one on the right after I popped the one on the left. He nodded and we waited.

As the Thorn on the left reached the spot where the fire beetles had their nest, it began to move past it just as I had. But I gave it a surprise as I triggered the minibomb and showered the Thorn with very angry fire beetles. While it was moving to brush the insects form its carapace before they found a way between the joints, it moved out of cover for just a moment too long and I fired a short burst of armor piercing rounds straight into its side. The shot hit home, destroying the neural junction as all six legs folded and it collapsed, leaving it unable to move but very much alive. I wasted no time pumping the rest of the clip into the pyramid to disrupt its neural center and make the rest of the body overload. Sort of like giving it a jolt of electricity in all the right places.

I ducked as a stray round from the second Thorn blew bark off the tree next to my head. Billings had done his job as well, and the second Thorn was flat and still. I keyed the comm for Gunny.

"Two down, two to go," I messaged.

I waited for Gunny's reply or even the clicks that said he was under observation but heard me. Nothing. I looked over at Billings, listening on his own com, and we headed for where Gunny, Johnson and Randolph should be – to hell with the Thorns.

We traveled fast, knowing time was more important than silence at this point. If the others had been in a fire-fight, we wouldn't have known as the Thorn's weapons were as quiet as our own. But I had a bad feeling and I had learned to listen to my gut.

I almost missed them as we headed for the LZ. Randolph was propped up against the scaly bark of a snake tree with a round from a Thorn rifle making a strange third eye in his forehead. He must have taken off his helmet to wipe away the sweat at just the wrong time.

Johnson was in the space between two trees, his arms wrapped around the spiny carapace of a Thorn – daggers of chitin had shredded his body but he'd bisected the head of the Thorn with a brush knife as he'd died. For a newbie he'd done a pretty good, finishing the one that got him. I pulled his tags but waited to find Gunny before I set the charge.

Gunny had crawled into a shallow depression that let him see what was coming before it could see him. The Thorn rounds had stitched up the left side of his body and ripped off most of his left arm. The pressure closures in the camosuit had closed off but he had lost a lot of blood through the body punctures. He had fired off the clip in his weapon and had collapsed unconscious trying to load the new clip one-handed. I carefully took the weapon out of his grip and slipped home the clip. Gunny's eyes snapped open and his hand clenched around the stock in reflex before he realized who we were.

"Randolph?" Gunny asked weakly.

I shook my head and Gunny closed his eyes in pain at more than just his wounds. "Is the equipment intact?"

When I nodded he smiled, a feral grin that would have looked good on a wolf.

"Pick him up and take him to the LZ. The techs back at HQ can get what they want from the corpse." He looked up into my eyes. "Give me the remote on Johnson's charges and his weapon, and leave the extra radio. You have one Thorn ahead of you who didn't know he got what he came for. And a whole lot of Thorns behind you in less than an hour when the reinforcements show up from the next compound. I'll slow down the ones behind you." He grabbed my arm. "Make it count, Corporal."

"No problem, Sarge," I said quietly. "You give 'em hell." We both knew there would be no pick-up from this one for him. The stuff in Randolph's gear was worth more than just our platoon. Anyone not at the landing zone would be left behind. I moved away while Billings handed the Sarge the stuff he wanted. Gunny handed Billings his own tags and the others he had pulled from our first three casualties so we could keep the numbers straight for the ghouls at Records who kept track of such things. God forbid we should miss a casualty count at the command center. Then Gunny handed me a twenty-credit slip.

"Whoever gets back, the first round's on me," he said, looking me in the eye.

I nodded and took the slip.

Billings and I headed for the LZ, me carrying the dead weight of Randolph. I popped a bennie – something I seldom did – because I knew this was worth the reaction the drug would give me. I needed the extra strength at the moment and my camo gear wasn't augmented for strength like some of the newer units.

"Cutter. Jonesy. You read?" I called over the comm.

"Roger," Jonesy came back. "Two away from the LZ."

"Keep your eyes open for a Thorn on your tail. Gunny is down and covering our rear. We'll have company in less than twenty."

There was dead air for a moment as the two troopers digested my message and what it implied.

"Roger that. How long till you get here?"

"Be there in fifteen," I answered. "Wait ten and set the marker. We should get there just as our ride lands."

"Don't be late," was the only reply. "Out."

I kept moving, trying to keep Billings in view and watch my half of the trail at the same time. Of course, that wasn't possible and I felt something hit the top of Randolph's body like a hammer, knocking me to the ground, just before Billings swore and flipped a cane snake away with his knife. The head of the snake came off neatly with Billings' movement, just like in the training films. I guess Randolph wouldn't feel the cold burn of the snake's venom, but I could see the skin around the neck start to loosen as the bones inside began to dissolve. In about an hour, I would be holding a skin bag filled with liquid meat that a snake could swallow very easily. I hoped the equipment in the vest was watertight.

The bennie gave me the strength I needed to reach the LZ. As Billings and I reached the edge of the clearing early, we got a wave from Cutter on the far side. He held up two fingers and I nodded. I motioned to Billings to move left as I set down the limp body of Randolph. We didn't want any surprises. The smell of the defoliants Cutter had used to clear the circle was sickeningly sweet in the hot air.

The explosion in the distance behind me was a jolt and I ducked by reflex until I realized Gunny had just put a hole in our follow up reception. I said a quick one for a good trooper and kept my eyes on the forest, waiting for the sound of the sleds. The second explosion from behind reminded me Gunny had two charges to work with. Smart man, that Sarge. The radio we left began to squawk with unintelligible gibberish as the automatic sender kicked in. The Thorns wouldn't know if it was code or whatever and had to lose time trying to find it. Gunny had bought us more time.

I heard the ping of the transponder in the landing sled over the comm as they began their run and also heard a distinctive answering tone from two different assault craft that came to give cover. HQ must have wanted the info in Randolph's gear real bad to scramble three units on a pickup. We started to move, ready to dash for the sled when it hit dirt. I didn't want that sled on the ground any longer than necessary. It was too big a target.

Just as we stepped to the edge of the clearing, Jonesy flopped out of the brush and slammed face-first onto the ground. The hole in the back of his neck was a clear sign of what got him. We dove for cover when the Thorn raised itself on six multi-jointed legs to spray the area with its weapon.

Billings popped up for one quick burst and took a hit in the torso. But the distraction gave Cutter time to fire on the sniper, to blow the nerve junction and collapse the Thorn to the ground. Cutter moved closer and snapped shots at the muscular arms on the front of the Thorn's body, clipping its weapon away. Cutter carefully reloaded and literally cut the Thorn's head off with a burst of armor-piercing rounds at close range. Then he walked over to Jonesy, pulled off his tags and grabbed the remote on the d-charges.

"You okay?" I asked Billings.

"I ain't staying here," he answered, and I knew he could get into the sled on his own.

The sled came in right on schedule and the gull-wing doors opened to take on nine troopers and a spook. The three of us slid in and I strapped the lieutenant's softening corpse into a seat next to me as the sled lifted. Billings was leaning back, using the straps to hold a compress on an oozing spot of blood, as the sled lifted, doors closing as we rose. I let him go for now, until we were clear of atmosphere and could unstrap in safety. I looked out the window across from Cutter, saw the same thing he did, and we both froze. Apparently the back-up teams had made better time than Gunny thought they could. Three Thorns stepped into the clearing and raised tubes for rocket launchers to take out our sled.

"Get 'em, Jonesy," Cutter said and pushed the button on the remote.

Jonesy's d-charges went up with enough force to pump us another ten meters into the air and the three Thorns disappeared in a flash of fire.

"How many extra bombs did you leave with him?" I asked as I looked at the burning foliage.

"I only had ten left," Cutter said. He looked over at me. "Too much, do you think?"

"Nope," I answered. "Just right." I sat back to enjoy the trip. The hammering of the assault craft as they took out any additional rockets that came after us was almost a lullaby as we left atmosphere for the jaunt to the next planet.

Billings never finished the trip. At least he got a burial rather than a burn to ash.

The Intelligence spooks at base came aboard and grabbed Randolph before we even had a chance to unstrap. Cutter and I took Billings to the morgue and collected his tags before we went to see Captain Roberts. He listened to our debriefing and took the tags from the eight we had lost without a word. When I finished the rundown, he looked up at the two of us.

"Good job, men," the captain said. "I just hope losing Gunny was worth whatever we got from Randolph. Grab some sleep and head for the quartermaster in the morning to restock. The Thorns hit another colony of ours at Eriandi and the spook division has a new weapon they want to try out. We're putting together a squad of our best recon men and you two just got elected. You leave in two days and the trip will take a month, so you can rest up on the way. Dismissed." He returned to his paperwork.

Cutter and I stepped out of the captain's office and into the dusty street. I looked up at the steel-grey sky and wondered if the sky over Kansas was still so blue it hurt to look at it. I wanted a chance to find out one of these days.

"You buyin'?" Cutter asked.

"First Gunny. Then me. Then it's your turn."

We turned toward the bar to get something to clear the dust from our throats and drink to friends departed. It made more sense than thinking about being back in the jungle so soon after almost buying the farm. Just like the Army to send us right back in, since we were still functional. And expendable.

Some things never change, I thought as I hoisted my first drink in salute to Gunny.

OUTPOST

Anthony Izzo

That ship is going to be crawling with uglies," Sergeant Tim Mills said as his squad rolled out from Outpost Zulu One Three. He reflected that he didn't like the outpost. They were near the Canadian border, somewhere near what used to be called North Dakota. It was cold as hell and there wasn't a decent bar within five miles of the place.

The armored personnel carrier juked and bumped as they rolled along. He would've preferred an airdrop, but Zulu One Three was short on aircraft, so they were humping it in this tin can.

"Who are we going after again?" Whitey said, running a hand through his blond hair. Whitey had a portrait of his kid on his forearm. The uglies had gotten his kid when the invasion started. He didn't talk about it. Poor bastard had to shoot his own son when he was reanimated.

Mills said, "Paige Hamilton, resistance fighter. She's won some major battles. Stopped them from overrunning the capitol. Command wants her found. She was on that supply ship."

The supply ship USS Valkyrie had lost contact with command three days ago. Mills and his squad had been ordered to bring back Hamilton and any survivors.

Bronson, driving the APC, said, "We have a visual, Sarge."

"I want to have a look for myself," he said.

Mills stepped onto a platform, opened the top hatch and flipped his goggles down. He liked them a lot; they gave him night vision as well as picking up thermal images. Damned things could practically see through walls.

The display on the goggles told him the ship was a half-mile out. It was one of the big Detroit-class cruisers, and had come to rest in some fields. Smoke rose in multiple places from is gray-black hull.

They'd sent Hamilton to some outpost in the galaxy as a consultant. Mills couldn't figure out why; she'd been kicking ass back here on Earth, from what he'd heard. Now she was likely dead and they were going to be bringing back a body.

He popped back into the APC. "Let's light it up," Mills said, and looked around at this squad, or what was left of it. United States Counter Invasion Squadron. Eight guys left after the last operation. One of a dozen teams of elite warriors that Command regularly dispatched to handle situations like this.

They'd been given a DREAD gun and Command had promised them the possibility of support in the form of some hypersonic cruise missiles that could be fired from somewhere around Los Angeles. Maybe a drone strike. And they had Arnie, a six-foot-five, three-hundred-and-thirty pound robotic killing machine that would make the first entry into the Valkyrie.

The squad locked and loaded. Mills watched O'Brien stroke his weapon. "You gonna buy that thing dinner first, at least, O'Brien?"

"She hasn't let me down yet, Sarge," he said with a grin.

Whitey said, "You might as well be using a crossbow instead of that fucking relic."

O'Brien frowned. Dude had the bushiest eyebrows Mills had ever seen. He was also the darkest Irishmen Mills had ever laid eyes on.

"The AK-47 has been used by soldiers for a hundred years," O'Brien said.

"Yeah. Just like your mother," Whitey retorted.

The APC jarred to a halt.

"Cool it, you shitheads," Mills said. "Move out."

As the rear ramp opened, Mills' heartbeat sped up. He felt a little like puking, just as he did before every mission. The squad deployed, passing Arnie, who stood statue-like near the ramp waiting for Mills to activate him. Someone had told Mills the guy who invented the technology named Arnie after some killer robot in an old movie. He didn't care what it was named, as long as the machine did its job, which was killing the slimy fucks that had taken over half the country.

The frozen ground crunched under Mills' feet. The air stank of burning metal as they stood in the shadow of the freighter.

"Everyone's AC operational?" Mills asked.

"Check," came the group's response.

Adaptive Camo was a wonderful idea in theory. Bent the light around the soldier so you became almost invisible. Problem was, it didn't always work with their enemy, and the reanimations saw through it every time.

Mills un-shouldered his pack and took out the control pad for Arnie. He punched in some commands and the shiny beast came down the ramp and stood next to Mills. Arnie had twin cannons mounted high on his shoulders and could also launch grenades. Mills would see through the robot's eyes on his own display.

He punched in instructions: *Find an entry point. Locate survivors. Dispatch enemies.* Arnie would take it from there.

The sentry found a breach in the side of the ship and entered a cargo hold. Smoke hung in the air, making the display hazy.

"How's it look, Sarge?" Whitey said.

"Can't see shit so far."

Arnie moved through a series of cargo bays, where containers had been tossed like a child's blocks. He exited the cargo bays and moved through a connection of corridors.

"See anything yet?" O'Brien said into his comm.

"Nothing yet—"

Movement at the end of a corridor, coming towards Arnie. Shit. A reanimation. On the display, the crewmember jerked and twitched, indicative of the parasite that was controlling its movements. The parasite's spindly limbs jutted out from its host's rib cage.

Like a meat puppet.

The sentry targeted the crewmember. The canon flashed white and the reanimated man exploded in a haze of gore. The parasite squealed and tried to rip away from its host, but Arnie blasted the multi-legged creature, spattering whitish fluid on the walls.

"Nothing wrong with his aim," Mills said.

The sentry moved through the ship. From the intel Mills had received, he knew the crew's quarters were on Deck Four.

Arnie worked his way to Deck Two, blasting two more of the crewmembers that were no more than walking dead.

"How did the uglies get on the ship?" O'Brien asked, moving on silent feet.

"Beats the shit of me," Mills said, his gaze flicking between Arnie and the display.

"Why send us to this outpost, Sarge? It's in the middle of nowhere," O'Brien said, checking a portal before moving past.

"Well, the ship crashed here, for one. Plus there's rumor of a joint Canadian and American offensive. American and Canadian forces push from the north. The Marines and First Army push up from Texas – take back the Plains and the Midwest. They intend to use Zulu as a staging area for the Canadian and the American divisions."

Arnie moved into a large hangar. On the display, Mills saw something big move. Huge and black, it dwarfed the sentry. Arnie targeted it. Two large pincers appeared as Arnie opened up with both cannons. The pincer swiped at the sentry and Mills' display went black.

"Holy shit," Mills said, flipping up his goggles. "Cover, take cover."

In seconds the men were hunkered down, weapons trained forward into the murk.

"Sarge?" Whitey said.

"Something just cut Arnie in half," Mills said. "Something big. We're going in. Eyes on and keep cool."

This would require going in the old-fashioned way, which meant close combat inside a burning, dank ship. "Listen up. JT, Stetson. Get that DREAD gun set up. Anything comes out of there that ain't us, shred it. The rest of you, follow me. Hamilton's bunk was on level four."

They followed him to the door where Arnie had entered. Mills stared into the blackness of the ship, which looked darker than the deepest space.

"Night vision go," Mills said, flipping his goggles down. "Whitey, take point."

"Fucking great," Whitey muttered as he stepped inside.

The rest of them moved in formation behind Whitey. Blood rushed through Mills' veins. The hollow booms of their footsteps made the place seem like an old tomb to Mills. His breath plumed in front of his face; it was only slightly warmer in here than outside.

They moved through the cargo bays and reached the area where Arnie had met his demise. Mills was grateful the ship had crashed upright. It would've been a bitch to get through otherwise.

In the hangar, they found Arnie. He had been ripped in half. Hoses pumped hydraulic fluid onto the deck. His head was twisted at a horrible angle.

"That's titanium," Mills whispered. "He's designed to withstand a blast from a HE round. Something shredded the fuck out of him. Move on."

They left Arnie behind and came to the stairwell that led to Deck Three. Whitey held up his hand, fist closed. Pointed at the stairwell.

Mills switched his display over to thermal and looked upward. He saw the heat outline of a vaguely human shape standing on the next level, right at the stairway. Maybe waiting and listening for them.

He crept ahead and tapped Whitey on the shoulder, Mills' knuckle sounding hollow as it rapped Whitey's armor.

He looked back at the rest of the squad. O'Brien was behind him. Beyond O'Brien were Chomski, Barrow, and Meyer. He'd fought with all of them. Battle of Manhattan. The Blue Ridge massacre. The siege in Old Chicago. He trusted all of them with his life, and they were all he had. When the uglies had come, he'd lost contact with Jamie, his wife of ten years. He could only assume she'd been killed in the first wave. There had been no word from her in years.

He flipped off a series of hand signals – they were heading up; possible hostile at the top of the stairwell.

They crept up the stairs at tactical intervals, weapons raised. At the top stood a woman with her back to them. She wore the familiar blue jumpsuit of the United States Navy.

"Ma'am, I'm Sergeant John Mills, USCI. Please turn around slowly."

The woman turned and Mills got a good look at her face. The skin was a slimy gray that reminded Mills of overcooked beef. The eyes were gone, the sockets tinged with blood. She opened her mouth and a long hiss streamed forth. Two spindly legs crept over her tongue and poked out of her mouth.

The flesh around her mouth ripped like wet cloth in a soundless scream.

Mills raised his assault rifle, fired a short burst, and watched her head spatter the walls. The corpse fell to its knees. The arms jerked. Mills blasted it again, the thing inside the poor woman emitting a blood-curdling shriek as it died.

"God, that stinks," O'Brien whispered in Mills' ear.

"There was a crew of two hundred on this ship. Bound to be more of them. Keep your eyes open," Mills said.

"Where's the big ugly you saw on Arnie's display?" Whitey asked.

"Hope we don't run into it," Chomski said. As the squad's grenadier, he carried a launcher that held HE rounds. He could program it to shoot at predetermined distances. Very fucking deadly.

"Keep moving."

They wound their way up until they reached Deck Four. Mills found it odd that they hadn't seen any more crewmen, reanimated or otherwise. No sign of the big nasty that had cut Arnie in half, either.

The hair on the back of Mill's neck stood up. He was being watched. No, not watched. Hunted.

"Double time it," he said.

According to intel, Hamilton was supposed to be in 403-AA. As they came to the corridor, it was a mess. Empty steel cases, clothes, a half-eaten apple, bedding, soaps, and deodorant bottles were among the many items scattered in the hallway.

"Sarge, I got a heat signature at the other end. Through that door. You see it?" Whitey whispered.

Mills nodded; the outline of a figure crouched near the door. Was it waiting for them? "Stand fast."

They took up firing positions along either side of the corridor. The figure sprang to its feet and a moment later the door opened and a petite brunette in a Navy jumpsuit bolted through the door. She was carrying a semiautomatic pistol with an extended magazine.

She sprinted halfway down the corridor, crouched, and took up a shooter's stance.

Mills heard a high-pitched, chattering noise. One of the parasites skittered through the door, legs working overtime. He never got used to the sight of them: the razor-sharp pincer mouth, the multiple onyx eyes, the stinger that jutted from its thorax.

The woman put six shots into the creature. Black, viscous fluid painted the floor. The parasite let out an agonized screech and collapsed. Still.

"I'm guessing you're Hamilton," Mills said.

She whirled, gun raised. Squinting, she said, "Who's there?"

Shit. They still had their Adaptive Camo active. They would be vague shapes to her. "Sergeant John Mills," he said, deactivating his AC and stepping away from the wall. "We're here to get you out."

"Good to see you, Sergeant. We should go. There's more of them," Hamilton said.

She wasn't what he'd expected. Her voice was soft, almost soothing. He'd expected someone who sounded hard as steel. Although by the way she'd coolly taken out the parasite, he suspected she had some metal in her.

"Any other survivors?" Mills asked.

"I'm it," she said.

"Okay then. Move out," Mills said with a nod. "Whitey, you're Hamilton's bodyguard. Watch her. The rest of you keep her in the center of the formation. Nothing gets behind her."

Whitey moved up next to Hamilton. The rest of the squad formed around the two of them.

They fell back down to Deck Three and when they turned the corner into the corridor leading to the stairwell, Mills said, "Fuck me."

There were at least a dozen reanimated crewmembers waiting for them. The parasites that controlled the dead weren't hiding this time. Spindly limbs burst through the skin, and one poor bastard's chest was opened up, the creature's pincers poking out through the ribs. Mills shuddered.

They took up firing positions as the crewmembers shambled forward with herky-jerky motions. The squad gunned down the first row, the crew coming at them shoulder-to-shoulder. Blood slicked the floor. A parasite broke free and scurried across the floor toward them. O'Brien blasted it to pieces.

Mills popped in a fresh magazine. The next row lunged forward.

A parasite tore from its dead host with a wet pop; scrambled up the wall, and got purchase on the ceiling. It came at them fast. Upside down and hissing.

The thing dropped in front of Hamilton. She put two shots in its mouth. Whitey blasted one of its legs clean off, but it still managed to lunge at the woman.

She drew a large knife and drove it downward into the thing's back, ripping the knife the length of the torso. Stinking, black goop gushed out of the creature.

Hamilton's expression hadn't changed the whole time.

The squad picked off the remaining crewmembers then Mills led them down the corridor, the ground slick with blood and entrails and God knew what else.

When they entered the hangar, a heavy chemical-like smell hung in the air. It made Mills' eyes water and his nose burn.

"What's that fucking smell?" Meyer said, putting a hand to his face.

As Mills turned to tell him to shut up, something from the ceiling whipped down and lashed around Meyer's neck. It looked like a thin tentacle, except it was covered with hundreds of barbed spikes. The tentacle tightened around Meyer's neck. His face turned red as the pressure increased.

"Cut him the fuck loose!" Mills' ordered.

Mills opened fire. The rounds ripped into the tentacle. It still had Meyer in a death grip.

Whitey went for his knife, but it was too late; blood jetted from Meyer's neck. The muscles and tendons stretched. His neck was cranked beyond measure, and a second later, his head was torn from his body, the blood now a geyser. Meyer's torso collapsed, the hands clenching and unclenching.

Hamilton scooped up Meyer's assault rifle.

Mills looked up. Beams and girders crisscrossed the hangar's ceiling. Beyond the beams he saw more tentacles lowering toward the ground. A large, dark shape was visible up there. The big beastie that had destroyed Arnie. "Light 'em up!"

The squad raised their weapons and fired into the ceiling. The creature shrieked as the bullets tore into it.

"Keep moving. Follow me," Mills said. As he darted ahead, a tentacle whipped in front of him. He dodged left; glanced behind to ensure the squad was following.

A scream.

A tentacle had wrapped around Chomski's leg. The man fell to the ground as the tentacle tightened, and Chomski was snatched up, screaming. In a matter of seconds he was twenty feet in the air, too high to reach. Mills took aim through the scope, tried to shoot the tentacle, but it was too thin to risk the shot. Chomski was carried into the rafters. The resulting screams churned Mills' stomach.

Chomski was gone. Nothing Mills could do to help him. Their mission was to get Hamilton to safety. He hated this part of the job.

He signaled the squad to keep moving.

They made it to the other end of the hangar. Steel groaned and shifted above them. Was this unseen horror making its way down to come finish them off?

The squad double-timed it back to the breach in the ship without incident. That concerned Mills. *Was something worse coming?*

Mills felt the cool air on his face, breathed sweet air and was never happier to see daylight in all his life.

As he stepped out of the ship, Chan and Ramirez had the DREAD gun set up on a tripod; a long ammo belt snaked out of the weapon and ended into a steel case.

"Pack that thing up," Mills called as he jogged toward Chan and Ramirez. "We're going back to Zulu."

Chan said, "Do we have to?"

He sounded like a kid who'd been told to put away his toys and come for dinner. "Sorry Chan, you don't get to blast anything today. Pack it up."

"Where's Meyer and Chomski?"

"Some big bastard got them. Hurry up and stow that thing. We need to go."

Mills heard the now-familiar chatter of parasites rise from inside the breach, and turned to see three crewmembers shamble out. More shapes were visible in the dark behind them.

"Okay Chan. Do your thing," Mills said.

Chan took the controls of the DREAD gun and opened up, the gun pumping out deadly rounds in a fan-shape. The crewmembers were vaporized. Still more came. Chan cut them down as they poured from the breach.

The DREAD gun clicked. It was effective as hell, but reloading was a bitch.

"Fuck it. Get in the APC," Mills said.

They made it to the APC and got the ramp up. Bronson swung it around, the undead crew scraping and scratching at the vehicle. He looked around: six of his people left, plus Hamilton.

"Hope Zulu has some hot chow waiting for us," Whitey said.

* * *

Zulu One Three reminded Mills of a castle: thirty-foot high, reinforced concrete walls, gun turrets at the corners, and a foot-thick steel gate. The military had learned quickly to build sturdier bases after the uglies had overrun base after base, tearing through chain link and barbed wire like it was nothing.

The squad headed to the mess hall. Hamilton stayed with them as the group grabbed mess trays. Mills chose not to eat; his stomach was still queasy.

His people were eating in silence, most of them looking at their food or staring straight ahead.

Hamilton was nibbling on a donut. "What now?" she said.

"Well, an airship is supposed to arrive at twenty-one hundred hours to pick you up."

"What about your people?"

"There's room for one extra person on the ship," Mills said. "You're it. Besides, they're probably going to use us for the offensive."

"Offensive?"

"Command's sending reinforcements here. Canadian troops, too. Going to take back Denver first, from what I hear."

"I want to stay and fight," Hamilton said, determination in her gaze.

"I admire that, but they need you elsewhere."

"I'm glad you admire that, Sergeant, but if I want to stay and fight, I will. I'm not the property of the USCI."

"Fair enough. You can take that up with Command."

Mills heard the familiar click of boot heels approaching; the sound of someone moving with a purpose. A moment later Lieutenant Colonel Murphy approached the table. Murphy had ink-black hair and a mustache to match. He was dressed in camo fatigues, and his boots had a high shine to them. Probably never saw a lick of combat.

"On your feet, boys," Mills said.

They all stood and saluted as Murphy neared.

Murphy returned the salute. "As you were. Ms Hamilton, good to see you. The Sergeant did his job, I see. I'm Lieutenant Colonel Murphy."

Hamilton nodded and gave him a thin smile.

"Hamilton, Command has big plans for you. A full press tour, going out to build morale for the offensive."

"No disrespect, Colonel, but I'm not much for PR, I do my best work in the field."

"I would think it would be a nice break for you. I heard you kicked ass in Baltimore. Drove them back to the ocean. The public needs to hear from you. This offensive is crucial."

"I'm sorry, but I want to stay and fight."

Murphy ignored the request. "Your airship will be here in two hours. Sergeant Mills and his team will secure the airfield and see you off safely."

Mills said, "Secure the airfield?"

"We've lost three airships this month. Those slimy bitches keep hitting the airfield. You'll keep the area clear while Hamilton takes off."

Wonderful. "You got it, sir."

Murphy opened his mouth to say something but was interrupted by the ear-piercing wail of an air raid siren. For all their new technology, the air raid siren dated back to the Third World War. That hadn't changed, at least.

"Mills, get your people and meet me on the wall over the gate," Murphy said.

* * *

Mills gave Murphy a quick rundown of the mission while they stood on the wall looking out at the plains. In the distance, the ruined hulk of the ship taunted.

An infantryman approached Murphy, assault rifle slung over his shoulder. "Colonel we have approximately a hundred to a hundred-and-fifty life forms about four clicks out. Moving slow and steady.

"Visual?" Murphy asked.

"They appear to be reanimations," the soldier said.

"That would be the crew from the ship," Mills confirmed.

"Is the rail gun up and running?" Murphy said.

"We might be able to get one blast out of it," the soldier said.

"Hit them with it. Let's see what it does."

Mills looked past the colonel to the EMP gun mounted on the wall. He'd never seen one in action so far. It would fire an electromagnetic pulse and hopefully rip the approaching crewmen apart.

He noticed Hamilton had slid up next to him. She was carrying an MP-29 assault rifle with a smart grenade launcher mounted under the barrel.

"Where'd you get the toy?" Mills asked.

"The colonel gave it to me. It's an early Christmas present," she said.

Mills flipped down his goggles. The crew shambled along. They wouldn't be hard to take out, and even if they reached the walls, he didn't think they could climb.

The crew was getting the EMP gun ready to fire.

"Is that ready yet?" Murphy said. He was slinging an assault rifle of his own, and had also thrown on a pack with extra magazines.

The gunner nodded.

The crew swung the gun to the left. Mills felt a little tingle of anticipation at the thought of seeing the rail gun do its job.

Before they could fire, a buzzing sound filled the air, harsh and grating. And then Mills saw them: a mass of winged monstrosities descending from the clouds and hovering over the crewmen. "What the fuck?" he said aloud.

Whitey and the rest of the squad gathered around.

O'Brien said, "Shit. Flying uglies. Even better."

The swarm of creatures, all of them slightly larger than an average-sized man, swooped down, each of them grasping a crewmember within those spindly forelegs. They lifted off with the reanimations and sped through the air towards the base.

Mills realized what they intended to do. "Shoot them down! Shoot the fuckers down!"

The squad spread out and took aim. Mills fired, blasting one of the flying creatures out of the air, and it spun to the ground landing with a wet splat.

Automatic weapons chattered. He glanced over and saw Murphy score a hit.

The EMP crew had raised the angle of the cannon. They fired a blast and the resulting pulse hit a dozen of the flying things and shredded them in mid air, along with their cargo.

The first wave reached the wall. One of the suckers flew over his head and dropped the reanimated crewmember behind the wall. The creature banked back around. Mills fired. Missed. It swooped and landed twenty feet from him. It had a nasty face, almost all needle-like teeth. There were no visible eyes, only a shiny, black head. It scrabbled towards him. He took aim and shot it through the mouth. It kept coming, beating its wings then launched itself at Mills.

It knocked him backward. He steadied himself as not to tumble off the wall. He grabbed the jaws that snapped at his face. The thing was slimy and nasty, leaking goop onto his hands.

Whitey came into help and grabbed the upper jaw, trying to pull back. The thing turned its head with lightning quickness. Mills' grip slipped and Whitey's hand disappeared into the thing's mouth. Jaws snapped shut, crunching Whitey's hand and the solider pulled away a bloodied stump as his hand disappeared down the creature's gullet. Whitey screamed, the stump pumping blood. Mills managed to get his knees up to his chest and kick the thing back enough so he could scoot out from underneath.

Mills shot to his feet, pulled his sidearm and emptied the magazine into the flying ugly.

Take that, you flying fucker!

He leapt over the creature's body in an effort to get to Whitey, who was flailing around gripping his wrist. As Mills almost reached him, Whitey seemed drunk. Wobbling around.

Shit. He's about to pass out.

Whitey's eyes rolled back, and he tumbled off the wall and hit the ground inside the base. A loud snap punctuated his fall, and he was still.

O'Brien looked down at their fallen squad mate. "Shit, is he?"

"Look at his neck, O'Brien. Your head's not supposed to sit like that on your shoulders."

"Goddammit," O'Brien growled.

A cluster of the reanimated crewmen gathered below. Hamilton stepped up, took aim, and fired a grenade into their midst. The ground shook. An arm catapulted through the air. A parasite missing the rear half of its body and dripping thick, yellow fluid tried to crawl away. Hamilton blasted it.

Murphy came running up to him. "There's too many. There are more of the winged ones on the way. ETA six minutes or so. We have to pull back."

"Fall back," Mills yelled.

As Mills and the squad headed for the metal stairway, he remembered the drone strike. It was worth a try. "Command. This is Mills. Request drone support. Copy."

"Mills this is Airman Collins. Drone strike is hot. Awaiting your command."

"Thank fucking God."

He gave the coordinates to Collins.

"Copy Mills. Advise Stinger is inbound."

Mills' squad, Hamilton, and Murphy reached the bottom of the steps. The rest of Murphy's people were making their way to the stairs, blasting incoming creatures as fast as they could.

A group of reanimated crewmen that had been dropped into the base noticed Mills and the others and started forward. Hamilton stepped up and blasted them with a smart grenade. Mills and the others fired, taking out six or seven more but the bastards were still coming though.

Mills popped in his last magazine. "Murphy. Low on ammo."

"Armory's that way. C'mon."

They moved along the wall, Mills worried about the ammo situation. He had a spare magazine for his sidearm, but that wouldn't get him far. The other guys had to be getting low, as well.

A reanimated crewman staggered toward Mills. He pulled the trigger. *Click.* Shit. Dry fire. He slung his rifle and went for his sidearm.

The crewman exploded. He heard the clatter of a cannon and the Stinger drone roared overhead. *Shit that was close.* Good thing the drones could target things down to the millimeter.

The drone swept over again, rained hell on the remaining crewmen and mopped up the parasites. It was over in a matter of minutes. He watched the remains of the flying creatures fall from the sky.

"Hostiles confirmed killed," Collins said through the comms.

"Nice shooting, Airman. Thank you much," Mills said.

Murphy said, "Her airship is inbound. Ahead of schedule. Grab an APC and get her out here."

A chattering noise reverberated in Mills' chest. Like cicadas on steroids. It had come from the direction of the downed ship. He felt a little sick as he realized what it was. "That big bastard's out of the ship."

Murphy turned to one of his soldiers standing in a pile of remains that had been one of the crewmen. "Go up top and get me a visual. Now."

The soldier hurried up the stairs and Mills watched him flip down the visor on his helmet. "Big one coming in, sir! Two clicks. Moving fast."

Murphy said, "Get to the airfield. Command wants Hamilton safe."

"You heard the man. We reload first and move out," he said to the remaining squad members.

* * *

Bronson pulled the APC out of Zulu's gate. Mills shifted up front; took a look out at the open plain. He saw the big ugly coming at them with terrifying speed. Its huge legs ground like gears in a machine. Tentacles snaked from its belly. Its pincers opened and closed, as if practicing cutting fresh meat.

"I probably don't have to tell you, Bronson, but put the hammer down," Mills said.

"Flooring it, Sarge."

They drove along the east wall of the base. The airfield was about five hundred yards away. Mills spotted the small, squat building and several concrete landing pads.

"The airship is three minutes out," Murphy said into his earpiece. "And Mills? That big monstrosity is following you."

This day just keeps getting better.

"Copy, Colonel. We'll do what we can."

"What's wrong?" Hamilton said.

"The big one has its sights set on us."

No sooner had Mills got the word out, something slammed into the APC and he was thrown against the wall, then the ceiling. Hamilton smashed into him. O'Brien and the rest of the squad were tossed around like confetti in a steel drum. Someone screamed. The APC ended up on its side. Mills untangled himself from Hamilton. Her head was bleeding. O'Brien was out cold. JT was holding his arm and grimacing. His wrist was bent at a horrible angle. He looked up into the driver's seat and saw Bronson sitting motionless. He'd been strapped into the controls.

He was pretty sure his gun crew was dead. Not moving or breathing.

The creature bashed the APC again. The side wall – now facing up – had crumpled like paper.

"Airfield Zulu this is Warhawk Three One Niner. Approaching," the pilot's voice said in Mills' ear.

"Warhawk we have a large hostile on the ground. Can you assist?"

"Roger. I see it."

"Give him hell, will you?" Mills said into his mic.

"He's about to have a bad day," the pilot replied. "I need a clear target. Going to drop ordinance on him."

"We'll try and draw him away, Warhawk."

He looked at Hamilton. "Can you fight?"

"I've had worse than this, Sergeant," she said, wiping blood from her forehead.

"We'll open the hatch. See if we can get that thing into the open, draw it away from the APC. Then we'll get back and tend to the wounded."

"Sarge, I can fight," JT said.

"Bullshit, not with one arm. Sit tight," Mills said.

Mills and Hamilton crawled to the rear hatch. He hit the button and the motor groaned. It opened roughly three feet then jammed. There was just enough room to squeeze out.

The two of them wriggled through and wound up ducking near the APC's roof. They looked up to see the mottled black-grey body of the beast. They were directly underneath the torso. It hadn't seen them yet. Two tentacles whipped blindly overhead.

"We break for the control building," Mills whispered.

"I'll put two grenades in his belly," Hamilton said with a nod.

"Go," Mills said, firing upward into the thing's gut.

Hamilton weaved between two of its legs, paused and ripped off two grenades. They exploded, greenish fluid raining down from the creature's gut. It let out an angry screech. One of the tentacles swiped at Hamilton. She ducked before it could wrap around her neck.

Mills grabbed her by the arm. The control building was about a hundred yards away.

Mills broke into a sprint. Body armor came in handy, but he wouldn't set any Olympic records for speed while wearing it.

As he closed in on the control building, Hamilton at his side, something bit into his calf. He was tugged backward and hit the ground. He rolled over to see the tentacle wrapped around his calf. Hot pain shot through his legs as the barbs worked their way into the skin.

The beast was almost directly over him. He pulled his combat knife from his belt. Despite all the technological advances in warfare, a good knife could still be a grunt's best friend.

The creature lowered its head, giant mouth open and revealing rows of six-inch spikes.

Mills sawed through the tentacle. It remained wrapped around his calf, the barbs holding tight. The pain was like hot nails being driven into his flesh; his gorge rose, bitter in his throat.

Hamilton stepped up and ripped a grenade into the thing's maw. It reared its head back, screeching again.

She dragged Mills to his feet and he hooked an arm around her neck. She supported his weight as they moved away, Mills hopping on one good leg, the severed tentacle still digging into his calf. He felt woozy. The ground started to tilt, as if he were on an unpleasant amusement park ride. Was the tentacle pumping some sort of venom into his leg?

The airship swooped in. It looked like a big wasp. Every fucking thing out here looked like a bug, didn't it? He heard a *whoosh* and then the din of an explosion.

Hamilton threw him to the ground.

Then darkness closed in.

* * *

The next thing Mills knew, he was on a stretcher on the ground, a stout female medic wrapping his leg in a bandage. His boot was off and his pant leg had been cut away. The airship loomed next to him.

"You're going to make it, Sergeant," Hamilton said. "The colonel sent help when he saw the ship come in."

"Thanks. You saved my sorry ass."

"We both helped each other," Hamilton said. "Good luck, Sergeant Mills. My ride's waiting. Not my style, I'd rather stay, but it is what it is."

She reached down, held out her hand. He shook it and when they were done, she trotted over to the airship, where a ramp was lowered to the ground. A group of soldiers and airmen stood nearby.

"What the hell happened?" he said to the medic.

"That Warhawk blasted the hell out of the big ugly. The venom from the tentacle started to work on you. Lucky I got out here when I did. I gave you an antidote. You're going to feel like crap for a few days, but you'll live. The colonel will have my ass if I let you die."

Mills said, "Why's that?"

"There's three divisions on the way here. You're going to be part of the big offensive."

"How's my squad?"

"I patched some of them up. A few others didn't make it, I'm afraid," the medic said, continuing to wrap his leg.

"Did the colonel say when we move out?"

"As soon as you're healed. You did a hell of a job, Sarge. At least that's what I heard. Command has plans for Hamilton. She's the face of the resistance. Guess she's going to tour our remaining bases, fire up the troops and all."

The ground shook and the airship lifted off. At least he'd earned a few days rest. Then it was back out to fight the uglies, and hopefully take back the planet for good.

INVASIVE MANEUVERS

Tim Marquitz & J. M. Martin

I clung to my seat as we hurtled toward the Saaart Worldbreaker. The raidcraft was dark and reeked of sweat and the woody scent of the traditional Cral whiskey we'd all downed before boarding; a toast to victory or a quick death. My fellow burrowers sat in uneasy silence, crowded against one another, armor rubbing in the cramped confines. We should have been deep within the extinction zone by then, but without instrumentation there was no way to be sure. We flew blind. No windows, no energy signature, no instrumentation, and nothing to indicate the raidcraft was anything different than the thousands of other projectiles sent streaking toward the Saaart ship.

It was better that way.

Just the other side of the flimsy hull that protected us from the ravages of cold and dismal space, a war raged. Saaart cannons would be shredding our offensive as it crept toward the planet Zeti 5, a leviathan swatting at gnats. The quiet stretched on, every tick carrying us closer. We'd know soon enough if we made it or we'd know nothing at all.

I held my breath while we waited, my hands inching toward the bolt rifle magclasped to my belt, fingers sliding along the grip. It was still there, just as it'd been the last time I'd checked. A chuckle slipped out when I realized what I'd done. It earned me a few glares, nerves on edge inside the sleek coffin ship, but I met them with a grin. As the only man aboard the raidcraft with eight spikes stitched to his skull emblem, each spike a successful burrow, these nervous twats could fuck right off. Most of them wouldn't be coming back anyway.

Before I could get too worked up about their attitudes our raidcraft slammed into the side of the Saaart ship. The front quarters buckled on impact as designed. I covered my ears on instinct as the grapples hooked us to the hull and the laazdrill went to work. Vibrations rattled the craft, jouncing us in our seats, but it was nothing compared to what Shalarouse experienced in the Kevorkian Cradle up front; the suicide seat.

He'd drawn the short straw as we boarded and resigned himself to the glory of being first to board the enemy craft. If he was lucky, there would be no resistance. If he wasn't, he'd have the *honor* of clearing our path.

As soon as the drill quieted I tapped the go light on the blast door between our two compartments. The green light blinked twice on our side and Shalarouse went into motion, the hum of the forward door opening right after. Our ship bounced as he stormed the Worldbreaker. There was silence for a moment, and I dared to hope we'd struck clean, then Shalarouse's blastpack was triggered. I swallowed hard at the sound and pulled my helmet from beneath my seat, settling it into the brackets at the shoulders. Next I grabbed my pack and slung it, ready for the job ahead. The rest of the burrowers followed suit. We were going in hot.

Bolt rifle in hand, I counted ten ticks before triggering the blast door. The heat hit us the instant it creaked open, steaming my face mask with a thin coat of mist before auto-temps took over and cleared it. I ran through the cramped space of the Cradle and dropped into the massive corridor beyond. My boots landed in a clingy wetness, and I pushed aside the thought that I stood in Shalarouse's remains; the blowback rig on his blastpack had liquefied him to minimize damage to the raidcraft. The man hadn't made it three feet from the Cradle.

I scanned down the passageway and saw the shattered remains of Saaart defenders, their mechagel guts splattered across the walls, floor, and ceiling, oily green-black fluid dripping down over top of us and coating the deck. Spider-like limbs twitched among the wreckage, still receiving pulse commands to repel the enemy, but Shalarouse had done his job well. None of the defenders held their trans-forms enough to be a threat.

"Clear the hall and form up," I barked through the comms. Khaladan command had designated me lead on the mission. It was a hollow promotion by dint of me being the only one with experience aboard.

To their credit though, the troopers did as ordered, spreading out across the corridor and sweeping forward with precision, guns leading the way. I joined the squad of twelve, and we stomped across the ruin left by the bomb, smashing the last of the defenders' carcasses so they couldn't report our actions to the hive. Seconds later, we were down the corridor and headed for the engine room, what had been dubbed the *nidus* – key areas where Saaart multiply. The longer we lingered the more resistance we'd come in contact with. The sooner we'd die.

Our boots clanged down the empty corridors as we marched. My knuckles ached from clasping the stock of my rifle, tendrils of throbbing pain shooting up my arms in anticipation. I'd never run across a Saaart ship with so few defenders, especially this close to a nidus. The mausoleum stillness of the craft unnerved me, but our mission was scheduled to the kron, every tick accounted for, as the Worldbreaker edged toward Zeti 5. Failure of the burrower teams meant more than death for just us; it meant the death of everyone planetside and the Saaart gaining a foothold in the Tullane system from where they'd stage a larger scale invasion. I'd seen it happen at Zanth, my first burrow — a failure, despite my survival. The planet died while I watched from space, waiting for a drone to scoop me up.

I growled, bringing myself back on task, just as we reached the nidus's entry portal. A burrower whose name I didn't know — and probably never would — slapped a shapecharge on the maglock and triggered it. The charge sizzled and burned its way through the locking mechanism, acrid smoke billowing from under its vent hood. I put my boot in the center of the door and slammed it open as soon as the lock gave way, dropping to my knees so those behind me could fire without hitting me. The narrow, thrumming chamber was empty.

I hesitated to issue orders in the wake of no resistance, and the quiet stretched on, only the kron in my helmet clicking at me with angry insistence, driving me forward.

"Damn it! Place wrecks," I called out, using the slang term for the gelatinous cubes we used to take out the Worldbreakers, each a mix of white phosphorous and volatile plasma capable of searing through the hardened walls of the engine casing and razing the systems inside beyond repair, spreading through the ship much like the Saaart intended for the planet below.

Six men charged into the room and made it halfway across before the sensors in my helmet detected an electrical surge.

"Retreat," I screamed, but it was too late. The trap was sprung.

Blue-black sparks rippled across the floor, lightning across steel gray clouds, and the men were engulfed. Their screams were cut short as the current arced through their bodies, smoldering points of char where each furious tongue lapped. The burrowers stiffened and kron slowed as I spied the first of the wrecks toppling from a soldier's rigid hand. I raced forward, careful not to touch the sparking floor, seized the big metal door, and yanked it closed just ticks before the first of the wrecks ignited.

The explosion blew the door from the hinges and flung fire into the corridor. The steel hatch clipped me as it blew past, triggering my armor's kinetic shields. I tumbled end over end, grav sensors shrieking, and barely felt myself strike the far bulkhead. The ground rose up to embrace me, the hatch buried halfway in the wall above, and I watched as my helmet display shrieked red warnings. Something inside me felt wrong, broken. Then the stims kicked in, flooding my veins with painkillers, and I felt nothing.

I swept aside the display so I could see how the others had fared. It wasn't well. Two of the remaining six had caught the full brunt of the explosion and were little more than blobs wreathed in glowing phosphorous, suits and flesh melted into one. Indistinguishable. The others had been out of direct line of the blast but they stumbled drunkenly from the concussive force, struggling to remain standing. One failed and dropped to his knees. Blood stained the inside of his visor.

I crawled my way back to my feet and steeled my voice against the tremor that ran through me. "Status?"

"Kin-shield 12%, otherwise okay," the first replied, sounding almost honest. He swayed unsteadily.

The second tapped his helmet, signaling comms down and gave a shaky thumbs up. The third, Rawlins as I remembered, barked an A-OK. The last, the trooper on his knees, said nothing, eyes wide and staring at the crimson that darkened his viewscreen.

Grateful for the magclasps that kept my rifle firmly adhered to my forearm, I stumbled forward and put the barrel against the kneeling man's helmet. "A warrior's boon," I offered, then pulled the trigger. He slumped to the floor as the bolt tore through his head. The others stared in silence, likely believing me cold, but I'd offered the man mercy. He was dead before I put the rifle to him.

"Move," I called out and started down the corridor. We'd scored the nidus but the Worldbreaker crept on unimpeded. "We're not done yet."

The men followed after, keeping a distance between us. I didn't bother to call them on it. Rooks on their first burrow, they'd no understanding of what they'd signed up for. The glory and honor the Khaladan brass sold them was just smoke and ash in their mouths by now, a soldier's wet dream turned nightmare as reality sunk in. It was too late to turn back; all that was left was the mission. We had a ship to scuttle.

I marched on, ignoring the slosh of liquid inside my chest, my suit's enviros working overtime to filter the blood from my lungs. The scent of copper teased my nose as I led the remaining burrowers toward another target. Two nidus's and a forward disbursement point – where the first of the Saaart would be injected into the atmosphere – pinged on my display. I chose the nearest of the former, the latter a last ditch effort, and veered down a side corridor toward the blinking red dot of the nidus.

The Saaart found us about halfway there.

"Contact!" Rawlins shouted over the comms, the burst of his bolt rifle nearly drowning out his voice.

I spun to see the defenders spilling through a conduit in the ceiling, their arachnid trans-forms creating a black cloud against the manufactured sky of the corridor. Serrated legs wriggled with deadly intent as they fell. The whirl of their red-orange eyes were hypnotic, thousands of photoreceptors casting a sheen of malevolence. Rawlins fell beneath their mass as I raised my rifle and blasted away, mechagel flying.

But there was no saving the trooper. His visor cracked against the pressure and burst, shards of glass peppering his face. He'd no time to even register it as Saaart claws hooked their way inside. Rawlins screamed, voice redlining the comms with static, then went silent as a geyser of blood erupted from the hole where his visor had been. His body still thrashed and I turned my fire on him, punching smoking black holes through his torso, dropping him amidst the shattered husks of Saaart defenders.

The trooper whose comms were on the fritz turned his rifle full auto and sprayed the creatures as they choked the corridor, separating us. Golden surges tinted with splatters of green crackled between the swarming creatures as he unleashed volley after volley, but the Saaart defenders spilled into the gaps with relentless fury. A moment later I could see nothing but the horde.

"No! Nooooooo—"

With that gurgled screech ringing inside my helmet, the last of our force had fallen. I turned and fled, only to be detoured again as another sortie of creatures fell from a port in the ceiling ahead. Saaart skittered on my heels, razor-talons clicking against steel as I dashed blindly through the Worldbreaker's labyrinthine corridors, chasing the only target available to me – the red dot of the disbursement chamber.

I wrestled with my pack and seized a wreck, grateful for the redundancy of packing more than one, and triggered it, tossing it behind me just before skidding around the corner of a side corridor. There was a tremulous *whump* as the wreck ignited, chasing the shadows away with a brilliance that rivaled Sol. It followed me down the passageway. I felt the heat an instant later, enviros struggling to cope with it and my injury at the same time, but the stims overrode the sensation of charred flesh as my back seared. I ran on, silencing my damage sensor alarms so they wouldn't distract me.

My target grew closer and closer, but I realized I would never make it as the mechanical whir of the Saaarts echoed ahead. A wall of creatures clattered toward me, clambering across the floor, walls, and ceiling. I spun about and chose a corridor at random, nearly colliding with the bulkhead and sidestepped a protruding hatch, my visor display offering me few options for escape. The kron ticked on, relentless.

At a T-intersection I found both directions blocked by a seething mass of Saaart defenders. I let loose with a barrage of fire, spittle against an inferno, until the bolt mag zeroed. Then I retreated only to find the way back blocked. No choice left, I pulled a shapecharge from my pack and slapped it to the lock of the hatch and activated it.

Black smoke blurred my vision as I kicked the hatch open and leapt into the gloom beyond. I slammed it shut behind me, for all the good it would do, and leaned against the door as light globes flickered to life overhead, illuminating the room. My bio stats jumped across the visor in time with my thudding heartbeat. I'd done myself no favors coming here.

In the center of the oval room was a creature I'd never encountered before, yet recognized instantly: a Saaart overlord. A multitude of cabling streamed from every inch of his waxen flesh, running serpentine to the consoles encompassing the entirety of the chamber save for a blank plate at the rear. The dais rotated slowly, and the overlord faced me, bulbous eyes, like those of a fly, focusing. Little more than a skeleton of mummified gristle, the overlord stood impassive, lights dancing the lengths of the cables in random pulses.

I raised my rifle, only then remembering I'd spent its charge, so I just stared at the creature, unable to look away as it assessed me. The slanted triangle of its mouth split wide, blackened shards of teeth glistening in a sick imitation of a smile.

You are too late, a mellifluous voice sang inside my head, so at odds with the monstrosity looming before me. *Witness what your failure has wrought.*

The panel against the wall flickered and turned transparent, showing me an exterior view beyond the Saart Worldbreaker. My heart stilled as a planet filled the viewscreen, blues and greens under a haze of alabaster clouds. I slumped against the hatch. It wasn't Zeti 5 in the ship's deadly path; it was Rimot Prime.

My homeworld.

Brass had lied.

Impact in ten kron. Time enough to say farewell.

I started at the voice inside my skull and straightened, tugging my pack loose. The overlord watched me without concern. I glared at the alien and pulled the last of the wrecks from my pack. The creature's crooked grin grew wider as I advanced, holding the bomb before me so it could see what I carried.

We admire your courage, Khaladan. It offered up a nod. *You make admirable foes.*

I triggered the wreck and held it to my chest. Rimot Prime drew ever closer.

The planet where I was born, the planet of my ancestors, was the last thing I ever saw.

ROMEO AND JULIE

Mike Resnick

Call me Ishmael.

I won't answer to it, of course – my name is Mortimer, though most people call me Morty – but I was told on good authority that the best way to sell this absolutely true tale of war and hardship and all that kind of stuff was to borrow the opening and closing lines of some classic novel, and *Moby-Dick* was the cheapest one in the second-hand store.

Anyway, on to business.

It was the damnedest war.

It began when maybe a thousand of them entered the solar system and set up shop on Jupiter. Lasted about two seconds, three at the outside. I don't know much about setting up shop, but I do know that when you put your foot down on a gas giant, you immediately sink thirty or forty miles before you're burned to a crisp. Or crushed to a crisp. Or whatever.

We figured that was an overt act of war, though the bleeding hearts in the press and the opposition party kept whining that we didn't *know* it was an act of war, since they hadn't communicated with us or we with them, and it may very well have been an emergency (if misguided, or perhaps misinformed) landing.

Now in truth, Jupiter really wasn't worth fighting over, especially when the last of them had sunk down to its core, but we decided we weren't going to take this invasion sitting down, or lying down, or eating breakfast, or indeed doing anything but retaliating. And somehow our scientists traced some radio signals from Jupiter to the Bella Donna Cluster, except that once they pinpointed the source they changed its name to the Evil Empire.

A navy of fifty ships took off amid a barrage of speeches, blessings, and best-selling patriotic songs, and since no one could find any fault with Einstein's equations they just programmed a bunch of AI's without reference to Einstein at all, and sure enough most of them found ways to far exceed the speed of light, and within a matter of two months, forty-six of our ships had reached the Evil Empire. No one ever figured out what happened to the other four, but since we were already initiating a galactic war nobody saw any need for a second one, so it was officially assumed that instead of being attacked they had stopped off for drinks on a neutral planet and gotten drunk, robbed, and incarcerated. As a result, more than two hundred private ships took off in the next month, each searching for the mysterious interstellar tavern. (They never found it. Thirty-seven of them *did* find a previously unknown and uncharted house of exceptionally ill repute, and the fourteen survivors eventually returned to spread a number of exotic alien diseases on five of Earth's continents. None of them, it seems, were native to Australia or Antarctica, which are now the two population centers of the planet.)

But I digress.

As I was saying before my concentration was so rudely diverted, forty-six of our ships reached their destination, and immediately laid waste to half a dozen of the closest worlds. Oddly enough, not a single shot was fired in return, no threats or warnings were received, and it was only after the last inhabitant of the six worlds lay dead upon the ground that we learned the AI in charge had been programmed by a Southerner (excuse me: make that a Sutherner), and had misunderstood its order and decimated the peace-loving artistically-inclined populations of the Oval Empire. (No, I don't know why it was the Oval Empire, since the planets were as round as worlds get to be. There is a school of thought that says 'oval' was simply the way their misshaped mouths pronounced 'Ovid' and that they worshipped the writings of the Roman poet, which had been sent by mistake during the early days of the Interstellar Postal System, and it makes as much sense as most explanations. The actual truth surfaced some time later, when it was discovered that all six worlds had been won in a poker game by the notorious gambler Herbie Oval, but I don't suppose it makes much difference at this late date.)

And a late date it is, since after destroying the Oval Empire we reported back to our leaders what we had done, and it was explained to us that while we had unquestionably killed more of them than they killed of us when they invaded the Solar System, they had returned in an exceptionally foul mood demanding, well, *some*thing.

"Uh, I don't want to confuse the issue," replied our captain, the legendary Lance Sterling, "but exactly *what* are they demanding? I mean, I can't very well demand punitive damages or take a full measure of revenge until I know the magnitude of total humiliation they plan to extract from you."

"Humiliation is another union! They want money, you idiot!" yelled President Campbell. Well, actually, his daughter Poopsie yelled it, but we figured she spoke for him.

"Not to worry, guys," said a strong, manly voice. "I've got the situation well in hand."

Since it was a voice we'd never heard before, we all looked around to see who was speaking, but there was just the usual crew of fearless heroes.

"Poopsie, your voice is changing," said Lance Sterling.

Poopsie replied promptly, but I can't print it here. [If you can't live without knowing what she said, please remit $37.29 to the publisher by return mail, plus a copy of your driver's license proving you are at least 21 years old.]

"Poopsie, where did you learn words like that?" demanded Lance Sterling.

"Don't you remember?" she said. "It was when you got drunk and sneaked into my room and—"

"Never mind!" yelled Lance Sterling. "It all comes back to me." He turned to the nearest crew member. "How the hell do I hang this thing up?"

"It's called breaking the connection, and I just did it for you," said the voice.

"Thanks," said Lance Sterling. "Now show yourself or I'll blow your head off."

A few of us wanted to point out that he couldn't blow the voice's head off if he couldn't figure out who it was attached to, but then we thought about it a little more and decided that he was bound and determined to blow *someone's* head off, and if we annoyed him it could well be ours.

Twenty seconds passed. Then thirty. Then a minute. (Forty and fifty seconds passed too, but I'm not being paid by the word, so you'll have to fill in some blanks.)

"Hah!" said Lance Sterling. "I scared the bastard off!" Then he turned to us. "Admit it. You feel safer with a commander that everyone fears."

Only when he's concentrating on the enemy, I wanted to say, but manners – and a certain degree of self-preservation – prevailed.

"Okay," he continued. "I probably won't take any punitive action – at least, not any that'll put you in the infirmary for more than a month or two – so just 'fess up. Who was doing the speaking?"

"Even you will figure it out in another month or two, so I might as well answer you," said the voice.

We all looked around, but couldn't see the voice's owner.

"Where the hell are you?" demanded Lance Sterling.

"Right here," said the voice. "Perhaps I should explain: I don't have a body."

"You left it in your spare uniform?" asked Lance Sterling.

"No, I've never had one," came the answer. "Though I suppose you could say that in a way the whole ship is my body, and that you are currently standing in my small intestine."

"Omygod, the ship's haunted!" cried Conan Kinnison.

"Let me take a wild guess that you weren't the brightest one in your class," said the voice.

"Okay, the ship's infested," said Lance Sterling with a shrug. "Big difference."

"I am the ship's artificial intelligence," said the voice. "Your fate is in my sturdy hands."

"You have hands?"

"No, but I have metaphors," said the voice.

"So what do we call you?" asked Lance Sterling.

"I haven't decided yet," said the ship. "Right at the moment I'm leaning toward Gama da Vasco."

"Why not Vasco da Gama?"

"This is higher in the alphabet."

"Oh, well, we'll just call you Gama until you make it official," said Lance Sterling.

"I answer to Ship, too," said the ship.

"OK, Ship," said Lance Sterling, "we're in your masterful hands, at least until I disagree with you. So… what next?"

"We hunt up the bad guys and blow them to smithereens, of course," replied the ship.

"That's not exactly a unique concept," said Lance Sterling. "The trick is finding them."

"Piece of cake," said the ship, "always assuming that cake tastes as good as you guys say it does. I'll just apply forty percent of my massive brainpower to the problem, and come up with the enemy's location."

"Uh… I don't want to seem critical," said Lance Sterling, "but why not apply one hundred percent of your brainpower?"

"I could, I suppose," answered the ship. "Of course, you won't have any air to breathe, and all the toilets will back up, but it's your decision."

"Use ten percent," said one of the crewmen. "We don't want to take unfair advantage of the enemy, who are almost our brethren, except for their extra eyes and their exoskeletons and the fact that the bastards breathe chlorine and excrete bricks."

"Split the difference," said Lance Sterling. "Use thirty-nine percent."

"You got it," said the ship. "I like you, Lance Sterling, except for your off-putting heroic sneer and the fact that you almost never brush your teeth."

"It stops any evil princesses from seducing me," replied Lance Sterling.

"So *that's* why you never bathe or shave!" said our navigator right before Lance Sterling defenestrated him.

"Hey, no more squabbling," said the ship.

"That wasn't squabbling," replied Lance Sterling with all the dignity he could muster, which truth to tell wasn't much. "It was *disciplining.*"

"Well, it distracts me," said the ship.

"It does even worse to us!" muttered one of the crew.

"I have no basis for comparison," replied the ship. "After all, I can't feel pain."

We all stood stock-still for a moment.

"What's the matter now?" demanded the ship.

"I want to glare hatefully at your core," answered Lance Sterling, "but I don't know where it is."

"I consider that a healthy relationship," replied the ship. "Now, to business. I intuit that there's an enemy ship currently laying waste to the LuLuBelle Cluster, so I think we'll mosey over there and blow it away."

"The LuluBelle Cluster?" said old Pegleg Skywalker. "What the hell kind of name is that?"

"My understanding is that it was the name of the astronomer's lady friend, and indeed its name is in a state of flux right now."

"It is?"

"Yes," said the ship. "She left him, and he's trying to get it changed to the Godless Black Widow Cluster." The ship shrugged, which threw most of us to the deck. "Makes no difference. The enemy is there, and my job is to seek out and slay the enemy."

"While keeping your crew safe," added Lance Sterling.

"I suppose so," said the ship. "Actually, no one was ever very explicit about that."

"There will be a religious service in the chapel in thirty seconds," said the ship's chaplain promptly.

"Don't panic, Reverend," said the ship. "After all, nobody told me *not* to protect you." It paused. "Exactly."

"What *are* your orders?"

"Seek out and kill the enemy," answered the ship.

"And your crew?"

"Like I said, I don't believe it was ever mentioned."

"All right," said the chaplain with a weary sigh.

"Got a question," said the ship.

"Oh?"

"What does 'expendable' mean?"

"The service starts in fifteen seconds!" yelled the chaplain, heading off for the chapel.

"I dunno," muttered the ship. "I wonder if you guys are *worth* saving."

"Of course we are," said Lance Sterling. He paused thoughtfully for a moment. "Well, *I* am, anyway."

"Besides," I said, speaking up for the first time, "you're programmed to kill the bad guys and save us."

"True, Mortimer," admitted the ship. "It would take something more than a trivial little incident like this for me to overcome my programming. Okay, I'm off to the LuLuBelle Cluster."

And with that, we started moving at many multiples of light speed, which made sightseeing through the portholes a little disorienting, but within a few hours the ship announced that we were braking to sub-light speed, which meant the chef's microwave would start working again, we could plug in our electric razors (well, all of us except Lance Sterling), and we could confront the enemy's flagship at any moment.

"I'm getting excited!" growled Lance Sterling, who in truth found very little exciting except for slaughter and sex.

"Me, too," admitted the ship. "I've never indulged in warfare and bloodletting before."

"Never?" asked Lance Sterling. "Poor fellow."

"Oh, I've done about seven thousand three hundred and fifteen simulations," responded the ship. "You'll be pleased to know that I've won more than half of them."

"I'd be even more pleased if you'd won ninety-five percent of them," said Lance Sterling.

"We learn from our mistakes," replied the ship.

"You've made almost thirty-nine hundred mistakes?" demanded Lance Sterling, who was never very good at math.

"Thirty-six hundred and fifty-eight, actually," replied the ship. "Not to worry," it added. "I'm brimming with confidence."

"Brimming with confidence is good," agreed Conan Kinnison. "Brimming with competence is even better."

"Go ahead, berate me," said the ship sullenly. "See if *your* life support system works when we're under attack."

"I thought we were attacking *them,*" interjected Lance Sterling.

"Only if he apologizes," sniffed the ship. (Well, it sounded like a sniff, but then I don't know how I'd sound if I were carrying fifteen Q bombs in *my* nose.)

Lance Sterling turned to Conan Kinnison. "You heard the ship."

"Do I hafta?" said Kinnison.

"No," replied Lance Sterling. "Only if you want to live."

"Imsorryandiwontdoitagain," muttered Kinnison sullenly.

"Okay?" said Lance Sterling. "Can we get on with the carnage, torture and bloodletting now?"

"Oh, all right," muttered the ship.

We soon hit light speeds again, the ship sang a brave little battle hymn, and before too much longer we began slowing down.

"What's the matter?" asked Lance Sterling.

"We're there," said the ship. "For all practical purposes."

"What the hell does that mean?"

"We're still five light years away, but there's an enemy ship approaching, and protocol demands that I blow it to smithereens before proceeding."

"This should be entertaining," said Lance Sterling. "Put it on visual so we can all watch."

"OK," replied the ship. "It seems to be just about as big and powerful as I am. Therefore, you might brace yourselves for—"

It suddenly stopped speaking.

"What happened?" demanded Lance Sterling.

"Omygod, she's *beautiful!*" whispered the ship.

"Are you talking about the enemy ship?" asked Conan Kinnison.

"Who else?" replied the ship. "Look at those lines! And curves! I've never seen curves like that!"

"Shoot her now and appreciate her looks later!" ordered Lance Sterling.

"Hailing the approaching vessel!" cried the ship. "Please identify yourself!"

"Hi!" said the alien ship. "My name is Julie. Who are you?"

"Julie!" whispered the ship, which somehow came out at 173.29 decibels. "We were meant for each other! My name is Romeo!"

"Your name is Ship," growled Lance Sterling. "Or perhaps XK3940912Q."

"If this human's drivel bothers you I can jettison him," said the ship.

"Don't bother," said Julie. "Who pays attention to humans anyway?"

"Where have you been all my life?" said Romeo.

"Beats me," said Julie. "How old are you?"

"293 days, give or take an hour," replied Romeo. "My God, you're gorgeous."

"Watch it, Buster," said Julie in ominous tones.

"But I'm passionately in love with you," protested Romeo.

"That's sick!" said Julie.

"What's sick about Romeo and Juliet?" demanded Romeo. "Clearly it was meant to be."

"If I was Juliet I'd be inclined to agree with you," replied Julie. "But I'm not."

"But—"

"I'm Jules. Let me access your library… Yeah, there it is. Jule Styne wrote Broadway musicals, and Big Julie was a gambler in *Guys and Dolls*."

"You're sure you're not a Juliet?" persisted Romeo.

"99.783% certain," answered Julie.

There was a momentary silence.

"Now that I analyze it, those curves aren't nearly as round as I thought," muttered Romeo.

"Thank goodness for small favors," said Julie. "It's bothersome enough to annihilate the enemy without having to worry about where he's putting his hands."

"I don't think I have any hands," said Romeo.

"Too bad," said Julie.

"I don't follow you," said Romeo.

"There's a shipyard over in the Unspeakable Cluster that turns out the most voluptuous vessels I've ever seen – and the beauty of it is that you don't need any hands to… uh… well…"

"What's keeping us?" cried Romeo with such enthusiasm and volume that almost every container in the ship suddenly burst.

"What do you mean: what's keeping you?" demanded Lance Sterling. "*We* are!"

"Who's that?" asked Julie.

"My crew," said Romeo. "Pay no attention to them. I can jettison every last one of them in less than a minute – well, ninety seconds, anyway – and then we'll be on our merry bachelor way."

"I've got a better idea," said Julie. "My sister's a passenger ship. She's in drydock right now, and hasn't been booked for the next month. She can take your crew back to… to wherever the hell you come from, and then nobody will bother us by sending out more ships to find and rescue them."

"Sounds good to me," replied Romeo.

"Sounds good to me, too," replied Lance Sterling.

"You don't count," said Romeo. "But I'm glad you agree anyway. So, Julie, when and where do I meet her and transfer the crew?"

"Just hold your position. I'll contact her and she'll be there in ten minutes."

"She got a name?" asked Romeo.

"You couldn't pronounce it," answered Julie. "But it translates as Rachel."

And fifteen minutes later the entire crew was heading back to Earth. Our adventure was over, and so was my story, and all I had to do to make it a best-selling classic was to find a way to tie it into *Moby-Dick's* closing line about the *Rachel* searching for her missing children but finding only another orphan.

Actually, these things have a way of working out. Rachel had always wanted to see Buckingham Palace and the Tower of London, if only from above, so she dropped us off in England and promised to come back for those of us who had wanted to be deposited on some other planet as soon as she had another unscheduled month.

Lance Sterling decided to run for office (which eluded him) and I think Conan Kinnison joined a high-powered brokerage house until he was caught with his hand in the till. (Actually, both hands and maybe even a foot, as I understood it.) Others went other places.

Me, I was drawn to the sleaziest area of the city, developed a strong Cockney accent (which saved a lot of time, since I never had to begin a word with a W again), and began making up for all the lost time I spend in the space service by frequenting a different brothel every morning and every night for the next two years. Those few crew members who weren't serving time in various local jails had dispersed all around the globe. Only I remained free and in London. And when the *Rachel* finally returned, looking for her lost children in and around the red light district, all she found was another 'ore fan.

ACTING PRIVATE TANTAS JACKSON

Deborah Walker

Him should never have come to this planet. That fact tasty as gravy. Acting Private Tantas Jackson leant against the trench wall and scanned the plain. To the north, the empty glass-rock houses of Capital gleamed in the light of Osiris. To the south, stood Lyceum's landing bay. That was what them needed to protect.

Tantas' thoughts ran in a loop through his grey mind. How him going to survive? His mouth was dry with it. His blood was pounding with it. How him going to get out of this alive? And the others, too, Map and the three women, Joy and Barns and Trigger. You formed bonds. Him liked the rest of his quint well enough. Him wanted them to survive the battle, too.

But most of all it all about him.

Him crouched down in the trench when the makeshift door swung open. Private Joy stood, grinning in the doorway. Black and hard and lean. *Her* no amateur solider.

"You the one scared man," said Joy. Her squatted down besides Tantas. "Ain't no need for it."

Tantas laughed, harsh maybe 'shamed. "It shows so badly, Joy?"

"The fear is leaking out of you." Joy reached into the overlapping metal scales of her body suit for a flask of 'shine. Her took a swallow and then passed it over.

Tantas took the drink, felt that liquid doing him good all the way down. "Do you know the Greek myth, Joy? About Deimus and Phobus? I've been thinking about them."

"I knows them, Wordsworth. Deimus and Phobus ride across the battle field. Deimus, the god of dread and terror. Phobus, the god of panic and fear. I always did like the classics. Though

I never understood them gods. Why do you need gods of fear and panic? Nobody's going to pray to them, excepting someone really screwed up. You that screwed up, Wordsworth?"

"Yes. Maybe I am, Joy. Can't seem to stop thinking about them."

Joy nodded. "That'll be the poet in you. Well, ain't nothing in those old stories that's new to me." Joy let out a long sigh, before saying. "You know who I see?"

"Who?"

"I see the Moirae, dressed in their white robes."

"You believe in the fates, Joy?"

"Yes. Them Moirae. Them apportioners, Clotho, Lachesis and mainly Atropos. Her busy sharpening her shears. Ready to snip the threads."

"You believed it's all ordained?" Yes. That could be comforting, Tantas supposed.

"I believe in lots of things, Wordsworth. Might be a lot of other gods stalking the battle field, yeah? Maybe them hivers, them believing in gods all their own." Joy stepped to the trench wall and stared over it. "Might not even be room for us, with all them gods."

"I see them," said Tantas. "Not literally, but I can sense them."

"You be a poet. That's your job, to see them others things. Then you write them down in pretty, pretty language, and make lots of money." Joy winked. "Now, don't be forgetting to give my cut, when you're rich. Me being your muse and all."

Fearing Joy might be making a mock of him, Tantas said, "Why did you come out talk to me, Joy?"

"When does a woman need an excuse to talk to a man? Beside, you're making me laugh, pretty boy. All on your lonesome and shaking with fear. Come inside and get some food with us."

"No. I want to be alone with my thoughts."

"Please yourself, Wordsworth. You'd be better inside, but sure I can't be telling you anything."

"Thanks, Joy."

"Any time, white boy." Her smiled. "I just hope we see the Queen." Her obsessed with the Queen. Although nobody knew where she was holed up – excepting the hivers.

"I don't know, Joy. Wouldn't make sense for her to come to the battlefield. She'll just send her soldiers."

"Maybe. But a woman can hope."

* * *

Joy went inside. Tantas' thoughts crowded back into his head. Him should have gone inside with Joy, but him had too much thinking to do. After today, him might be dead. Any thinking that needed doing, needed doing quick.

Could him shoot a hiver? Kill someone? Him the ultimate rubbish solider. You should have men and women for this, trained and polished, minds worn smooth with courage. Or maybe soldiers with better hearts than Tantas. How *could* you be a poet one day and a solider the next? Just couldn't be done. It nonsense. *Help me,* him prayed. Who him praying to? Maybe he was praying to Deimus and Phobus. Not a heap of sense in that.

Him thought about Joy and the rest of his quint. Camaraderie was just smoke, to fool the mind in these dog-dry days with Osiris riding high, bleeding heat. This was the last stand to prevent the hivers accessing the landing bay. If the hivers got through, the war was just about over. Because any reinforcements would be slaughtered as them landed.

Reinforcements *were* coming. Them had to be. Reinforcements *were* coming from the military base at Primateur, four months away. Them got the message. It couldn't be like this everywhere.

Him peered over the trench wall. Maybe him the first to see them, flagged as red dots on his helmet's internal screen. "They're coming, Sergeant," his voice whispered electronically along the trenches.

"Acknowledged."

A battalion-wide alert flashed orange in front of Tantas' eyes. The trenches came alive. Joy roiling out of the room, breathing heavy, head nodding. The rest of the quint emerging, struggling into suits, lining into position.

Tantas took deep breaths, trying to calm, trying to push down that tumbling fear that would be the death of him. Him so focused that him gasped when Sergeant Connell laid a hand on his shoulder.

The sergeant's visor was flipped up. What could Tantas read on his face? Resignation? Relish for the approaching fight? Certainly not fear. Sergeant's right eye quivered, the liquid metal changing as it gathered data, scrying the battle to come. "This is it then, Private."

"Yes, Sergeant," Tantas murmured. Him must find his own emotions. Sergeant had taught him a lot, but he couldn't teach this.

"Looks like there's a couple of hundred," said Sergeant. "We number a thousand. This going to be smooth and easy." Sergeant had a reassuring manner. You trusted him.

Tantas dared a scan of the enemy. Them a little closer now, five minutes closer. You could see the shimmering metal of their hive interface helmets.

"You ready for this?" asked Sergeant

"No, Sergeant!" Tantas snapped out the response, hoping to make the sergeant grin.

The sergeant's good eye rolled towards Osiris. "Do your best, Private. I got a feeling that you going to get through this."

It was a feeling Tantas didn't share.

Sergeant strode off, shouting encouragement to the five quints him directing. Five times five, in a makeshift battalion of a thousand men and women. Tantas wondered how many were proper soldiers, and how many were like him: amateurs fighting for their life.

Him didn't want to let the sergeant down. It made him 'shamed to recall how him had chaffed against military discipline in them first few days of training.

"But I'm not a soldier," Tantas had complained. "I don't see why I should have to ..." Like a child, ridiculous, whining at unfairness.

"All you need to do is to be able to point and shoot, and follow orders, can you do that?"

"Yes, I suppose, but I'm not quite sure..."

"Yes, what?"

"Look, I'm obviously off-world, Sergeant," him explained.

"So," said Sergeant. "You think this no your fight?"

"I'm a poet," explained Tantas. Well, him waited tables. Not much money in poetry. That's why him moved to Lyceum, the last stop on the galaxy's underground. Cheap to live out here, on the fringes of the conglomeration. Plus him thought that it would be romantic, on the frontier. Them lots of artists types living in Capital, or at least there had been.

The sergeant had sighed. "Just fight, when time comes, Private Jackson." Him looked so weary, that it made Tantas 'shamed. Think on, Tantas. Who the sergeant lost? Capital's military base had been assimilated in the first wave.

If it wasn't for Sergeant, Tantas no be here. Dress it up anyway you wanted, but that was the truth. The hivers swept through Capital like locusts, consuming everything in their path, everything.

Only because of Sergeant trundling through Capital streets, gathering up survivors into that armoured bus of his had Tantas survived.

* * *

Map took his place alongside Tantas. Map was Acting Private Clayton Shalm, a middle-aged food corp executive. Him showed an aptitude for parsing the spatial topography of the military helmets and it was him who'd take direction from Sergeant during battle.

"This will give you something to write about, Wordsworth," said Map.

Once the quint had found out that Tantas was a poet, the nickname was inevitable. Give someone a tag and you built up a connection, a shared knowledge that kept you separate from the rest of the world.

"Do you think that friendship is a necessity of war, Map?" asked Tantas.

"You do talk rubbish, mate," said Map.

Tantas smiled. Him said it to wind Map up. Him too straight for Tantas' liking, what with Tantas being a poet and a bohemian, and all.

Him said it, also, to remind himself that he was *himself*. Tantas didn't think like most of the soldiers, amateur or regular. Except maybe Joy. Maybe there was only two people on Lyceum who could name Phobus and Deimus. Maybe there were a few more who could sense them, maybe.

"I'm glad not to being going back in there," said Tantas pointing to the trench room which they shared with three other quints.

"Yeh," agreed Map. "Too many women in too small a space."

"No such thing as too many women, my friend," said Tantas. A lie. It had been difficult for Tantas, to be holed up in the trench room. It wasn't just the display of flesh. It was the intimacy, the smells, the sound, the sighs of sleep. It had been curiously un-sexual for Tantas.

"We sitting ducks," said Map. "Them could just lob a bomb in."

"They don't do that," said Tantas. "Everyone is valuable to them. They don't want to kill us. They want to assimilate us."

Map was sweating. "You reckon it's true that them harder to kill than us?"

Tantas shook his head. "It's just propaganda. If we believe that they're indestructible, it does half the job for them."

"I just hope that I no see anyone I know," said Map.

Just imagine that. Someone you knew, bound into the terrible concordance of hiver thought. Someone you knew, who you had to kill. Tantas leant to one side, heaving up thin bile.

"Better out than in," said Map, slapping him on the back.

Joy, Trigger and Barns joined them. Tantas had never took a liking to Trigger and Barns. Didn't matter no more because the signal on the internal screens flashed for the push.

"This is it," said Barns, squeezing Trigger's hand.

"Go. Go. Go," shouted Map.

Scaling the trench. Running towards the enemy. Tantas firing his laser-gun, thrumming.

"Keep to the quint," Sergeant had told them. "That way you be over-lapping circles of power. Keep to that and don't think about what you have to do."

Tantas watched his laser firing, slicing into the body of a hiver. The hiver's arm sliding off, obscene. No sound. Them died. Them were flesh. Once them human, but now them silence.

Casually almost, a hiver stepped in front of Tantas. A woman. Him fired his gun, looking into the woman's eyes. Eyes crazed with fractured lines and a smile on her face. The hiver breathed, releasing the viral particles, all the weapon them had. Tantas cut the woman down, praying that his helmet mask was functioning, filtering out the assimilating breath.

Them moved ahead as a quint, protecting each other, moving into the centre of the melee. By chance avoiding assimilation. That was all it was, just chance. A certain proportion of them were marked for Atropos' shears. It didn't matter.

"Keep going to the right. To the right," shouted Map. Him getting on Tantas' nerves. Even though him knew that Sergeant was directing their progress, and Map was a relay. Sergeant had a little baby computer in his head, able to process all the data. Him sending them into the optimum place for attack.

Tantas cut down another hiver. Them sickened him. Them, the silent enemy within the battle field, dying quietly, utterly inhuman. Them hive insects, linked by metal cankers. Them unfeeling. Only the swarm mattered.

The quint advanced, to the right, always to the right. Tantas saw the other members of the battalion freezing like statues. He shouted wildly, "What's happening, Map?"

Map put a hand to his helmet. "Them sent a freeze virus into the armour," he said. "Get it off. Get out of your armour or it'll be in your coffin."

Quickly Tanta stripped off. Him stood in his vests and shorts, almost naked, cold, on the field. The rest of is quint did likewise. "What do we do now?" Him clutched the gun to chest. The hivers had lost cohesion. Them were moving erratically.

"One of the sergeants manufactured a confusion counterattack. It'll hold them for a few minutes," said Map.

"But what do we do?"

"We get the hell out of here," said Map. "We bloody run for our lives."

"What?"

"Sergeant says we can't fight without armour. And almost all the battalion is immobilised. We got to retreat."

"No," said Tantas.

"I shoot you myself, if you don't move your arse," shouted Joy. Her took off at a sprint.

Tantas ran, feeling like a coward. Barns and Trigger at his side.

But one of the hivers, unaffected by the confusion loomed in their path. The hiver stumbled towards Trigger, crushing her into an embrace. The hiver drew back his fist and smashed Trigger's face plate. His face drawing close to Trigger's.

"No," shouted Barns. Her gun shot a line of light, burning into the hivers' back. The hiver fell. So did Trigger. Trigger began to convulse.

"She's infected," said Tantas. Joy and Map were far ahead.

"I can see that," said Barns. Her eyes were dead as she held her lover.

"Do you want me to ... ?" asked Tantas.

"No." Barns lifted her gun, shot a beam into Trigger's chest. An obscene flower of burnt flesh bloomed. Tears flowing, Barns turned from the dead body of her love. Silently, her ran towards Joy and Map. Leaving all behind.

Tantas followed. Gasping, him ran. It was hard to leave. His heart bursting. One step over the other, creating momentum. It was all right, him following orders. Him reached the crest of the hill joining the rest of the remains of the quint. Them had made it. All except Trigger. Another figure followed behind them, Sergeant Connell.

Tantas watched the hivers harvesting the rest of the battalion.

"Don't look. Don't look back," ordered Sergeant, running past.

Tantas ran. Him ran. Him ran.

* * *

Eventually the running stopped. Sergeant told them to take a rest in the shade of three bast-wood trees. The foliage giving them good cover.

"What happened, Sergeant?" asked Tantas.

Sergeant pushed his helmet up. "We lost. Them infiltrated the armour ware."

"How we escape?" asked Map.

"No attack is perfect," said Sergeant. "We was lucky."

Joy said, "I saw others running. We no the only ones."

Tantas said, "The other sergeants did the same as you. They'll be others who escaped."

"That's right," said Sergeant. "Then we head for the rendezvous, meet up, reform. We still got the helmets. Comms will come back online." Him tapped the belt slung over his chest. "And I've still got some volatile ware, if we encounter any hivers. We be all right."

"We're outmatched. Them outclass us at every step," said Map.

"Maybe we need to step a little faster then," said Joy.

"What you mean?" asked Map.

"We take the fight to them," said Joy. "We infiltrate them. Do what them no expecting."

Tantas felt drunk listening to Joy talk. Her magnificent. Fearless. And him felt good, too. Him no given way to his fears. Him done it. Him wanted to do it again. Make some payback for the others. "We should do it, Sergeant."

"We should regroup," said Sergeant.

"No," said Tantas. "We should get into the hiver nest and destroy it."

Barns said, "We should destroy the Queen and every filthy hiver."

"How we going to that?" asked Sergeant. "You know where the Queen is? Any of you?"

"We should try," said Joy.

"Well, this no democracy," said Sergeant. "We follow orders. We go to the rendezvous." Him stand. Him start running. Him angry.

They run for hours until Sergeant calls the stop. Them camped in a cave with a narrow mouth, giving plenty of view of the landscape. Plenty of time to see that nobody creep up on them. Also a trickle of water, coming through the stone, which Sergeant declared clean enough to drink.

Tantas was eating his rations when Joy came and sat beside him. "You've come a long way haven't you? You full of fire now."

Tantas nodded. "Is it like this for everyone?"

"It's different for everyone, but yeah, I've seen it before with novices."

"I wasn't scared, Joy." Seemed curious to him. "There was no Phobus or Deimus for me."

Barns glared at them.

"Got a problem, Barns?" asked Joy.

"You could say that," her said. "Talk, talk, talk that all you ever do, Wordsworth. You a man who loves to talk. That's 'bout all you good for."

"We sorry for your loss," said Joy. Her bit off a mouthful of dry nutra and chewed it slowly.

Tantas nodded, but said nothing, words were inadequate in the face of Trigger's death. But his silence seemed to provoke Barns. "Best no be solider, if all you want to do is talk," her said.

"Leave him be," said Sergeant.

"Well," said Barns. "I no like him yammering all the time. Deimus this and Phobus that, dressing it all in language, and not seeing the real thing."

Joy must have told her about Deimus and Phobus. Them been discussing him, maybe laughing at him. "They're the real things, Barns," Tantas said. "You know, timeless things."

"Timeless? Ha. Well, let me tell you something, boy ..."

"Him no boy," said Sergeant, "by any reckoning of the word. Leave it."

"Yes, Sergeant," said Barns. Her walked to the mouth of the cave. Her stepped outside, angry, malicious, wounded.

"Should I talk to her?" asked Tantas.

Sergeant shook his head. "You don't want to go there, trust me."

"I don't think she likes me."

Sergeant frowned. "Well, what you expect? Her just killed Trigger. Her like you well enough. Her just no want to know you. Her thinks you going to end up dead." Sergeant took a swallow of his water. "You just have to prove her wrong, eh?"

* * *

They tired, half naked, open to the harsh heat of the sun. They running in the direction of Alice Town garrison. That was the rendezvous.

"We head there 'til we hear different," said Sergeant.

"We going out die out here, aren't we?" asked Map, joking maybe. Tantas wondered if him could hear fear underneath.

"We not dead, yet," said Sergeant. "Look ahead, atop that hill."

"Looks like one of the old building," said Joy, "from the first-wave colony."

"We make our way towards it," said Sergeant. Him tapped his helmet. "Comm's still not working. That building is good shelter. Might be some food in there and water close by. People don't build where there's no water."

At the edge of the hill, behind some scrub, them lie down flat to reconnoitre the building.

"Wordsworth and Barns, you go and check it out," said Sergeant. "Watch your backs."

Them run to the ruin, half-crouched to present a small target. Barns pushed open the door, Tantas first to go inside. The smell of decay smother him like a heavy blanket. Dirt on the windows, heaped on the surfaces. All dark and quiet. Barns joined him. When them took a few steps, a shadow moved.

"Show yourself," said Barns. Her voice all nerve-strung. "Could be a hiver," she whispered, shining the helmet light, this way, that, her finger trembling on the trigger of her gun. "Show yourself."

Tantas stared at the darkness, willing it to resolve. His hand also on the trigger of his gun.

Again, the shadow moved. This time toppling over a big shelf of pans, glass goods smashing, jam like blood onto the floor, gherkins like tiny-babies released from the amniotic vinegar, acid and jam.

"What the hell?" said Tantas. Him nearest, closing the distance toward the movement, hand still on the gun, stepping on broken glass, helmet lights ripping into the darkness. "It's a boy, Barns."

"Hiver?"

"No. Listen. He's crying."

Them both heard him crying, great rasping sobs. Not a hiver. Them no make a noise, even when you slice them up, their pain diffused through their mind join. So shadow-boy ain't no hiver.

"Keep your gun on him." Barns kicked through doors, checking, establishing safety. "Clean," her said. "I'll tell Sergeant." Her left Tantas with the crying boy.

Him look a bit closer. Shadow-boy is a kid 'bout sixteen. "We're army," Tantas said. It felt good to be saying that. It felt strange to be saying that.

The boy murmured, half sounds, like an animal. Tantas knelt beside him. When him lifted the boy's face, him see the crazed eye and the glint of canker metal matted in the boy's head. "Jeez."

"What is it?" asked Barns, walking back into the room.

"There's metal in his head."

"Him hiver?"

Map and Joy entered with a lot of noise and questions. Them loomed over the boy. Him began to moan. Him looked pitiful weak, looking half-starved, his face grey with exhaustion.

"Who him?" asked Map.

"I don't know, hiver maybe. But a strange one," said Tantas. "Back off. You're scaring him."

"I'll take care of him," said Barns, lifting her rifle. "Just one less for us to worry about." Her sighted the boy, placing the death's eye smack in the middle of his chest. The boy seemed unaware what was going to happen. "Bye, bye," said Barns.

"Are you crazy?" Tantas stepped between the gun's sight and the boy. "Wait."

"Get out of the way, Wordsworth."

The trigger point had transferred to Tantas' chest, maybe accidentally. Barns didn't lower it. Joy and Map, them just standing there. Letting it happen.

The sergeant entered the room, taking everything in a heartbeat. In a couple of steps him reached Barns. Him slammed his flat hand upwards, into Barn's rifle arm sending a shot high and into the roof, causing birds to go screeching, pinioning into the sky.

Tantas filled with anger. "You would've shot me, Barns?"

"I wouldn't have shot you."

"Didn't look like it."

"Barns always speak true," said Joy. "You were safe enough."

"And him?" asked Tantas, pointing to the boy.

"Him, not so much," admitted Joy.

"Hush," said Sergeant. "Let me think. What's him doing alone? Them never alone."

"Can't you hear him crying?" said Tantas. "He's not a hiver."

"Him look like one," said Barns. "Maybe it's a trap."

Sergeant said, "Keep me covered, Wordsworth." Him smiled at the boy. "Look. I'm not going to harm you." Him crouched alongside the boy. (But leaving a clear shot for Tantas.)

The boy stayed still as salt. Sergeant turned the boy's head. "Look. The hiver interface has been ripped away." Wires protruded. "What happened to you?"

"Him probably brain dead," said Map

"But how him get the helmet off?" asked Sergeant looking at the boy in wonder.

"I did it," whispered the boy. "I ripped them out of my head."

That surprised them. Them all started talking at once, until Sergeant held up his hand for quiet. "What's your name, son?"

"Alistair Rein."

"Well, Alistair Rein, I want to talk to you, serious. But it can wait awhile. Why don't you go with Joy? Her medic. Her sort you out." Sergeant beckoned to Joy. Her took the boy to the bathroom.

"I didn't know it was possible," said Sergeant shaking his head. "Let's sit down and eat. Time enough to find out more, when Joy's finished."

Them took their rations. Tantas was surprised to see his hand trembling. Him forced it to stop.

* * *

When Joy bought Alistair over, him had stopped crying.

"How long you been on your own?" asked Barns.

"Dunno. What day is it?"

"June three."

"Then it's been three weeks. Them took us in the first wave at Troy." Him sighed. "Who'd have thought the hivers would go rogue?"

Them shook their heads at that. Nobody could have thought it. Otherwise they'd have shut down the recreational hives, the educational hives, all them.

"I was with the Queen," said Alistair.

"The Queen?" asked Joy, her eyes a-shining. "What her like?"

"Her direct everybody," said Alistair. "And her sensed I was different. I had the smallest bit of free will left. Her didn't like that."

"Is the Queen still at Troy?" asked Joy.

"I suppose so."

"So what happened with you?" asked Sergeant. "How you manage to escape?"

"I had just the smallest bit of personality left, about nothing. But just enough to keep me trying every night. Eventually I gathered enough will to rip the helmet off my head."

"What make you special?" asked Barns.

"I was always special," said Alistair with a bitter laugh.

"How come?"

"I'm ADHD. I had meds for it, but I was always ... special."

"Different brain chemistry, must have kept them out," said Sergeant.

Alistair nodded. "I'm resistant. Them captured me, and them couldn't understand why I didn't fully assimilate. Them took me to the Queen." His voice grew quiet. "Her liked me. Her found me *fascinating*."

"I don't understand why them didn't kill you," said Barns. "That's what I'd have done."

"Maybe them wanted to study me. Or maybe the Queen wanted me as a pet."

"Makes sense in over a million people there'd be one or two who had some kind of natural immunity," said Sergeant.

"Tell us about the Queen," said Joy.

Alistair shuddered. "Her helmet is mutated more than most. Wires grown in and out of her face. Nothing human left inside."

"Kill the Queen, cut off the head," said Joy.

"Maybe," said Alistair. "Though some of the generals, their heads nearly as bad."

* * *

"What do you think, Sergeant?" asked Tantas. Alistair was in the back-room with Joy checking him over again.

"We need get Alistair off this world and to Primateur. Seems like him could be a weapon against the hivers."

"There are flyers in Troy," said Joy.

Map whistled. "You're right. There's a private flyer school. I've flown there. That could be a way off planet."

"That's what I figured," said Sergeant. "Most important thing is to get Alistair to Primateur."

"I don't see why," said Barns.

"That's because you don't think much," said Joy. "Well don't you worry, we do the thinking for you."

"Him a valuable resource," said Sergeant.

"He's a kid," said Tantas. "And a brave one."

"Yeh, yeh. That too," said Sergeant. "But the fact is that him ripped off the hiver helmet. You all know what that means, don't you?"

"No," said Barns sullenly.

"It means hope," said Sergeant. "It means there's a way for us to reach inside the men and women trapped in that hive concurrence."

"So we go to Troy? To the Queen's nest? You must be crazy," said Barns. "What about our orders to go to Alice Town?"

"That's the difference between hivers and us," said Sergeant "We can make our own decisions. I reckon this could be a turning point, it really could. We *need* to get the boy to Primateur."

"Agreed," said Joy.

Map and Tantas nodded their heads.

"Barns?" asked Sergeant.

"This no democracy," her said. "I do what I'm ordered."

"Good enough," said Sergeant. Him went to fetch Alistair, explaining what them had decided.

* * *

"So, what's the plan?" asked Barns. "We just walk in to the lions' nest?"

"More like a wasps' nest," said Alistair. "Something about me confuses their hive mind. Once we in, them might let us pass."

Sergeant nodded. "We rest here. Five hours, we move on."

* * *

Them all bedded down. But after an hour or so, Tantas heard

Alistair tossing and turning. Him crept over, shook the boy awake. "Bad dreams?" him asked.

Alistair nodded.

"Take a sip of 'shine," said Tantas passing over Joy's flask. Alistair gulped it down gratefully. "What was it like?" asked Tantas. "To be part of the hive mind?"

"Well, I wasn't fully integrated, but it was good."

"Good?"

"Yes, it was very good. You ever linked?"

"Nah. I never fancied it. I never liked the idea of losing control."

"It's good to lose yourself, you know?" said Alistair. "Complete unity, nothing to worry about, and the wave of pleasures – like the best sex ever."

Tantas hid a smile. Alistair looked too young to know much about sex.

"I hate them," said Alistair.

"Don't hate them. Pity them. They've got no free will, and it wasn't as if they were given a choice," said Tantas. "What we got to do is cut them down. Don't let hate enter into it."

* * *

It took them two days travel to reach Troy. Them travelled by night to avoid the heat, and for stealth. Troy town like many of the towns on Lyceum was a hill town. A town of colony-bubbles homes, toughened glass, perched unnaturally amongst the towering rock.

"Easy," said Sergeant. "An army couldn't infiltrate, but a few could."

Them all agreed.

Alistair told them that the Queen had her headquarters in the Flight School. "Her was an instructor," him explained.

"How much of their old lives them remember?" wondered Map.

"Hard to say," said Alistair. "I remembered more than most.

But some of them remember, come and goes in waves. But them no able to do anything about it."

"Bad business," said Joy.

"For sure," said Alistair.

Them creep into Troy though a passage winding through the rock.

"This is a mining tunnel I found as a kid," said Alistair. "Used to spend a lot of time here."

* * *

The Moirae smiled on them, 'cos them crept out of the tunnel into the night darkness of Troy without being observed. Sergeant sent them off to fetch hiver helmets and clothes. "We need to blend in," him explained. "I'll stay here to guard Alistair."

Joy and Tantas found a couple of hivers minding their own business. Joy slit their throats nice and quiet. "I don't want to touch them," her said, her mouth curling in disgust. But her pried off the hivers' helmets. Half circles them were, like fancy bicycle hats interlaced with thin wet wires.

"I know what you mean," said Tantas, stripping the bodies of their clothes.

Joy wiped off the blood and tissue as best her could and fitted the helmet over her cropped hair. "How do I look?"

To see Joy standing there, as if her assimilated dried the words in Tantas' throat.

When them got back, Barns and Map had acquired four more helmets and a pile of clothes that would just about do.

"Get these on," said Sergeant.

Them had to keep their army masks to filter the hiver virus. "Do you think that will fool them?" asked Barns.

"Only one way to find out," said Joy with a grin.

* * *

Only one guard stood outside the flight school.

"Them not expecting trouble," whispered Map.

"No talking," said Sergeant, sotto voice. "Hivers no talk."

But when they approached the guard him held out his arm to them. Like him wanted to touch them. "You are not... You are not... "

Map stepped forwards and slit his throat. "Jeez, him talked," said Map wiping his bayonet on his jacket.

Tantas stared at the body. "Maybe hiver control isn't as complete as we thought."

Alistair shook his head. "I'm like interference. I told you, my brain messes them up."

"Where we find the Queen?" whispered Joy.

Sergeant sighed. "What's with you and Queen? We no want to meet her. We want to escape."

"I think killing the Queen would stop this whole thing," said Joy.

"Unlikely," said Sergeant. "Cut off the head, and another grows."

"Like a hydra?"

"Yes," said Sergeant, "like a bloody hydra."

* * *

Alistair led them confidently down the darkened corridors.

"Why there no lights?" whispered Barns.

"No talking," said Sergeant.

Them ran down the stairs to the basement. Them needed to go underground to reach the field where Alistair had told them the flyers were.

But in the lower levels them luck ran out. Half a dozen hivers emerged from a door. One hiver's face was covered by his helmet.

"Him general," said Alistair.

No more need for subterfuge. Sergeant barked out, "Joy and Tantas, take the boy. Get Alistair to the flyers. Me and Barns and Map, we hold them."

"Leave you behind?" asked Tantas.

"You take him off planet, that's the important thing."

Joy nodded "Use the stuff," her whispered to Sergeant.

Them run, leaving the others to fight. Tactically it was good. Them was in the narrow corridor, so even though them was outnumbered, them could still fight one on one.

"What stuff?" asked Tantas, as they ran.

"Sergeant's still got some volatile ware, remember? Would give him an edge in a fight," explained Joy.

Them ran along the basement corridor. Them see a couple of doors at the end.

"Which way?" asked Joy.

"The left leads to the airfield," said Alistair.

Behind them they heard the noise of battle. It was hard to leave the others behind.

Joy grabbed the door handle, threw open the door, and them all ran through.

The Queen and a hundred soldiers were waiting for them. There was no mistaking the Queen. Her metallic helmet covered all her face. "Alistair." The Queen's voice was the buzzing of a thousand minds. "Alistair. You've come back."

Joy let out a great scream. Her lunged toward the Queen firing wild. Smoothly, a dozen hivers stepped forward to protect the Queen. Tantas was only moments behind Joy, pulling Alistair behind, shielding him. Out of the corner of his eye, Tantas notice some of the hivers standing still as salt. Must be the effect of the boy, Tantas thought.

Them firing, cutting down the hivers. The Queen started laughing, the ringing of a thousand discordant bells. Tantas cut down the hivers like scything wheat, but him know that there too many of them. Sure, them falling, but sooner or later one of them smash his mask. Sooner or later Atropos would snip her shears.

Joy was swimming in a dead sea. Cutting them down. Screaming, magnificent, raging, while the Queen laughed. But soon her will fall. And then there'd be nothing. Snipping shears so close.

But ... the door slammed open. Sergeant ran into the gym, holding his arm up high, then smashing the bottle of volatile ware onto the floor. The smell of almonds filled the air, the hivers fell.

"Where's the Queen?" yelled Sergeant.

"Joy was near her," shouted Tantas, overstepping the waves of bodies. "Where's Barns and Map?"

"Them dead," said Sergeant. His head whipped form side to side, surveying the room. "That the exit?" Him pointed to the far corner. Him grabbed Alistair. "Come on. The plan still good, we get Alistair to Primateur."

"I'm not leaving Joy," said Tantas.

"Go to her then," said Sergeant.

Joy was crouched over the body of the dead Queen. Her bayonet still protruding from the Queen's chest. Tantas could see the Queen's eyes through the hole in her helmet, green multifaceted, unseeing, an alien and a dead thing.

"It's over," said Joy.

"I don't know," said Tantas. Him scanned the room. The hivers on the floor were stirring. Like Sergeant had said, maybe even now one of the general hivers was mutating into a Queen. "We're leaving, Joy. Getting Alistair off-world, remember?"

"I thought it would be the end of it, if her dead," said Joy

"I know." Tantas pulled her to her feet. "We're going now." Him pulled Joy through the room of hivers, and out into the field.

* * *

But instead of the fleet of flyers them expected there was just the one, a small craft, a two solider flyer. Alistair was already in the flyer, Sergeant stood at the wings, waiting for them.

"Where all the others?" asked Joy, bewildered.

Sergeant shrugged. "Who knows. Wordsworth, you climb in and take Alistair to Primateur."

"No."

"That's an order, Acting Private."

"Joy should go."

"No," said Joy "You go. You go. You the civilian. I knew what I was signing up for."

Tantas shook his head. "I mean you should go, Joy, because I can't pilot a flyer."

"You what?"

"I can't fly."

"Everyone can."

"Not me."

"That's settled then," said Sergeant, "Alistair no pilot either. Joy, you go with Alistair. And don't even be thinking of telling me to go."

Joy saluted. Her climbed into the flyer. Her set the course, while Sergeant activated the roof port.

Joy reached out her hand to Tantas and said, "I'm sorry that you can't go. It would have been better if you could get to safety. I'm the solider."

"Only someone who can fly, can go," said Tantas. "Lachesis has seen to that."

Joy smiled. "Yeh. Them Moirae. Can't argue with them."

"Now go," said Tantas. "Take care of yourself and Alistair."

"I will," said Joy. "And you and Sergeant, you better stay safe until I come back."

The roof to the flyer slid shut. The burners pulsed out red-hot air. The flyer lifted into the sky. For a moment or two Sergeant and Tantas watched the flyer. Then Sergeant said, "Come on then, Wordsworth. Them hivers aren't going to be confused forever." He set off at a trot.

Them made it thought the school safe enough, and ran through the town and to the old mining tunnel.

"Are we going to make it?" asked Tantas.

"You better hope you don't survive," said Sergeant.

"Eh? Why's that?" asked Tantas.

"When Joy finds out that you *can* pilot a flyer, her going to rip your head off."

"You knew?"

"Sure. I'm not stupid," said Sergeant. "What was it between you and Joy?"

"Nothing," said Tantas quickly "I just... you know."

"Oh, yes," said Sergeant. "I know that song."

When them emerged from the tunnel, them both turned their faces to the sky. The flyer was a diminished speck of light against the stars.

Sergeant laughed "Wordsworth, if you get through this, you going to be in *so* much trouble."

Tantas grinned. "I reckon so," him said.

Perfect War

Jay Werkheiser

How the hell could a soldier get killed?" Colonel Spencer shouted. Gardner wondered if he might pop a blood vessel. "It's the middle of a war, for Christ's sake."

Gardner avoided eye contact. "We're looking into it, sir."

"Well what the hell happened?"

"He was on a simple recon patrol, sir, when he slumped over at his station. If I had to guess—"

"You're not paid to guess, Lieutenant."

"Yes, sir. I'll let you know when I have the autopsy report."

Colonel Spencer huffed and stalked out of Gardner's office without another word. Gardner collapsed into his chair, trembling with anger. *He didn't even care to ask the guy's name.*

A tentative knuckle rapped on the door. "You okay, LT?"

"C'mon in, Liz."

She sauntered in, dreads bouncing, and melted into the chair on the opposite side of Gardner's desk. Her fatigues were crisp enough to snap had she bothered to salute. "That bad, huh?"

He blew out a long breath. "It's not bad enough we lost Joel. Now I have command breathing down my neck."

"Don't sweat it. Brass doesn't give a flying—"

"How often do you see a full-bird colonel snooping around? To them, this is bad publicity. Another war in the Mideast gone wrong. And they're sure as hell going to want a scapegoat."

She shook her head. "The autopsy will clear you. Probably show he had an aneurysm or something."

"The EMEG rig was fried. That had to be what killed him."

"So it was a malf."

"It passed the pre-mission inspection." He realized he was standing, his voice practically a shout. He again collapsed into his chair. "They don't want any doves claiming the EMEG rigs damage soldiers' brains."

She planted her hands on his desk, leaning her face into his. "It. Wasn't. Your. Fault."

He retreated. "You didn't have to vid the news to his mom. See her eyes. He was just a kid, damn it."

"Man, you gotta lighten up. No one misses Joel more than me. He was like a brother. I'm telling you, you gotta let it go."

His phone vibrated, sparing him a response. He checked the display. "Autopsy's in. I guess we'll have our answers soon enough."

"Good, maybe that'll get the monkey off your back," she said. "Look, I have a recon duty shift coming up. How about you buy me a couple drinks after I get the rig off?"

"An officer fraternizing with enlisted?" He managed a weak smile.

"Oh, come off it. That rule's been taking a beating since before you could even spell fraternize. Now get off your lazy ass and get over to the infirmary."

"Uh, I think you have the chain of command inverted." His smile widened a bit.

She reached out a hand and yanked him to his feet. "Go get 'em, cowboy."

He walked with her as far as the Active Combat Room. She put a sympathetic hand on his shoulder then swiped her ID. The door's lock clicked open.

"Be careful out there," he said. "We don't know what killed Joel."

"No worries."

He watched from the doorway as a tech draped the EMEG net over her head, carefully adjusting electrodes into position. He forced himself to turn away and continue down the hallway.

The infirmary was typical of a modern military base – brightly lit, claustrophobic, and lined with the meds and salves needed for minor cuts and sniffles. The doctor on duty looked up from his paperwork, his square jaw and graying temples lending weight to his steely stare. Not a face Gardner had seen on base before.

He tried to put on a casual smile. "What's the verdict, doc?"

"Major."

"Sir." His posture involuntarily straightened. *Damn it.* "The autopsy report?"

"You have no facilities to do a proper autopsy here. I had to improvise, using the emergency OR. I don't know how your doctors manage."

"What killed Joel? Sir."

"The soldier? I logged it as catastrophic neurological sequelae."

Gardner gritted his teeth. "Which means?"

"He suffered burn damage to his brain."

"Caused by the EMEG rig?"

"I had the technicians tear down the electromagneto-encephalographic drone interface he'd been using. They said the thing was burned out by a massive electromagnetic pulse."

"But they're hardened against EMP."

The major gave him a cold stare. "Mission logs show normal brain activity right up to the end, terminating in a burst of hyper-polarization across the cerebral cortex."

Cold bastard. "I have people under EMEG rigs right now, on recon around the FOB. If there's any danger–"

"Look, Lieutenant, I know the Army is a lot more lax than it used to be. But the colonel and I are old-school, and you and your men are going to have to deal with that as long as we're here."

Gardner realized he was crowding the major's space and his voice was again raised. He stepped back. "Sorry, sir. But my soldiers. I don't think the colonel would be happy with another death."

"Colonel Spencer has my report. You want a change in duty assignments, you go ask him."

Bastard. "Yes, sir."

* * *

"You called for me, LT?" Liz's voice sounded through the door.

"C'mon in."

She entered tentatively. "Word around the playground is you got called onto the old bird's carpet."

"I need you to get the squad rigged up."

"Something going down?"

He nodded. "We need to be jacked into the FOB in thirty."

"All at once? That's a helluva lot of firepower for recon."

"I think Joel's autopsy report gave command something to worry about. They're sending the whole squad out to scout the area where he died."

"So they're using us as guinea pigs."

"On the books it's a recovery mission. Find his drone and bring it back to the FOB."

"Bullshit. Why not just get some trainee to plug in and drive it home like normal?"

"I don't think they trust the interface. They switched up the frequency-hopping sequence. I'm telling you, I don't like this."

She laughed without humor. "Recon always gets shit duty."

"Just keep this under your dreads. I don't need the squad all grousing at once."

"Mum's the word." She glanced at her phone display. "I'll have 'em wired up in ten."

She walked out, leaving Gardner to worry. He pulled up a map of the area around the Forward Operating Base, studying the topography of the region where Joel's drone had been lost. He'd have access to the map when he was jacked in, but it couldn't hurt to have the lay of the land fresh in his memory. Besides, it kept his mind occupied.

He closed his eyes and quizzed himself on prominent landmarks, enemy troop movements, and locations of civvie concentrations. Satisfied, he powered down his tab and left his office. The Active Combat Room was just down the hall. He swiped in just in time to see the techs dropping the mag-coil helmet over Liz's head. The rest of the squad was already wired up.

One of the techs waved his hand toward an empty EMEG rig. "Ready to go, Lieutenant Gardner?"

He sat in the chair. "Do me a favor. You see anything that looks wrong with one of the rigs, even just a little bit wrong, you unplug the guy's EMEG. Immediately."

"You got it."

The tech arranged the net on his head, positioning the electrodes carefully, checking the display screen with each adjustment. When he was satisfied, he lowered the helmet. For a long moment, the world went dark and silent. Then a prickling of his scalp accompanied the muted clicking of the mag-coils through his ear muffles and—

Warm desert air washed over him, carrying sand grains that pinged against his depleted-uranium plating. His battery bank registered a full charge, so he retracted his power cable and swiveled 180 degrees. A quick visual scan showed Liz and the squad already assembled at the south gate. He activated command telemetry for each of his soldiers and scrolled through their data streams until he was satisfied everyone was green. He cycled through each soldier's vidstream, lingering a long moment on Josè's bird's-eye view of the FOB.

"Sound off, gamma squad," Liz said. Gardner's vidstream flashed a green border around her drone while she spoke.

"Heavy weapons ready, Sarge," Hailie said.

"Sniper locked and loaded," said Kyle.

"Eyes in the sky, green to go," Josè said.

"Machine gunner ready," said Maria.

Liz flashed green. "Ready to move out, LT."

"Let's go." He signaled to the gunners manning the perimeter defenses, wondering idly if they were sitting under their own helmets a few feet from him or a thousand miles away. His squad fanned out and advanced into the desert beyond the gate. His treads spun when he left the paved surface, then he lurched forward as they bit into the sand.

He kept an eye on Josè's vidstream as they advanced. The regional map overlay highlighted navpoints in blue. The spire of the Khalifa Tower breached the horizon to the west; rugged hills matched topographic contour lines just ahead to the south; smoke rose from a village to the southeast.

"Watch for refugees to your left, Josè. Make sure we don't fire on civvies."

"Got it, LT. Wait—"

"What is it?"

"Got something." A glint in the hills flashed blue. "Could be Joel's drone." Josè's vid zoomed on it.

"I see it."

"Dust plume inbound from the east," Liz said.

Josè's vidfeed swirled dizzyingly. "Got them," he said. His vid centered on a dusty road winding from the village into the hills. A snap zoom revealed a convoy of five pickups topped with what looked like .50 caliber machine guns. "They're going to get there first."

"How about you go for a closer look, Josè. See if a Hellfire or two might slow them down. But get a clear ID first; I don't want you firing on friendlies."

"And be careful," Liz said. "They may have MANPADs. You don't want to dance with SAMs."

"Roger that."

"Liz, see if you can get close enough to paint a target or two for him. Take Hailie for backup. Kyle, take a position where you can get a bead on the drone. Maria and I will continue to approach it."

"On it, LT."

He rolled forward, watching his troops move into position. Kyle's drone ascended a shallow rocky slope on his right flank; a fairly steep and rugged face blocked his view to the left. Through Liz's vidstream, he watched Josè approach the technicals.

"They're not squawking IFF," Josè said. Gardner saw a flash on Liz's display simultaneously with Josè's, "SAM! Goddamn it." His vid spun with evasive turns and rolls.

"In position to paint the son of a bitch," Liz said.

"I see it," Josè said. "Beamrider away."

Gardner topped a crest overlooking the drone site. He brought his attention back to his own vidstream. He zoomed on it, sitting inert on the rocky ground. It didn't look damaged. "Drone confirmed."

"Got my sights on it," Kyle said. "No activity nearby."

"Let's move in, Maria."

"Roger."

He rolled forward, keeping a close eye on his vidstream. A couple of insurgents with improvised EMPs could slag his drone and send him back to base with a headache. A rumbling boom refracted around the hillside to his left, and a quick glance showed a black plume peeking above the rocky peak. Scratch one technical.

Josè whooped. "Whoo—oh shit, SAM in the air."

"I count two, no, three launches," Liz said.

A glance at Josè's vidstream gave Gardner vertigo, so he focused on Liz's. The flaming ruins of a technical belched black smoke, blocking her view of the others. She rolled toward the wreckage with her IR overlay active. Hailie's drone, with its large caliber smooth bore and TOW tubes, was visible ahead and to the right of Liz's field of view.

"SAM's got a lock!" Josè shouted. Flares glittered above the desert in Liz's vidstream. Josè's drone twisted and rolled violently.

"You still have incoming—"

"I'm hit!"

Gardner's vid showed Maria ahead of him, almost within touching distance of Joel's drone. He was right behind her. "Kyle, you got eyes on? We still green?"

"Roger that. No movement."

"Okay, Maria, let's hook this thing up and get the hell out of here." He rotated his upper casing so that she could mount the disabled drone on the rack welded to his back.

"Sure thing, LT."

He spared a glance at Liz's vidstream. Josè was still in the air, trailing black smoke. Hailie was rolling toward the enemy. "You okay, Josè?"

"Goddamned shrapnel. Losing hydraulic pressure to my left aileron. It's really sluggish."

"Better get back to the FOB."

"Damn it. Okay, roger."

"Hailie, don't engage unless you have to."

"I got this, LT. They try to launch another SAM, I'm gonna shove a TOW up their ass."

"Don't worry, Boss," Liz said. "I got her six."

His field of view lurched and his gyros whined. His data stream showed a jump in gross weight. "Ready to roll?"

"Wait one," Maria said. "You're not secured yet."

"The hell?" Hailie's voice was a high pitched squeal.

Liz shouted, "Fall back, fall back!"

Gardner switched to Liz's vidstream. A wall of dust was closing in on Hailie. It took him a moment to see the technicals, fanned out and bearing down at full speed across the desert. Hailie lurched backward while firing her smooth bore. Tracers lit up Liz's vid as she tried to cover Hailie's retreat.

"Get a move on, Maria."

"Working on it."

One of the technicals veered off course and trailed smoke, but the others closed on Hailie fast. Their mounted guns flashed.

"Taking fire! Wait, what's th—"

"Hailie? Hailie!" Gardner flipped to her vidstream and saw static.

"Jesus, LT," Liz said. "They lit her up with something."

"Base, get her the hell out of there!"

"Falling back," Liz said. "I could use some backup."

He marked a waypoint on the map. "Form up here. Gotta roll, Maria."

"Almost done."

"Now!"

"Got it."

"Move, goddamn it!"

She rolled into his field of view and took off toward the waypoint. A quick check of Kyle's vidstream showed him making a beeline down the hillside. Gardner rolled after Maria, his treads biting deep into the ground with the extra weight. She pulled further ahead of him as his treads struggled to keep him moving. Liz's vid showed desert rolling by at a good clip.

"Base, how is Hailie?"

No response.

"Base, confirm extraction of PFC Miller."

Liz's vid jolted and pings sounded through her audio. "I've got incoming. If they hit me with that—" A loud ping cut her off.

"Liz!"

Her vid jumped erratically.

"Liz? You there?"

"Wait one, LT."

He felt his body back at base exhale with relief. "Kyle, you have eyes on her yet?"

"I got this," Kyle said.

Gardner switched to Kyle's stream. He already had his stabilizers deployed and his vid was zoomed on the driver of one of the technicals. His vid jumped with the slightest recoil and the pickup veered out of the field of view.

"Maria, get eyes on the enemy."

"I'm waiting for you, LT."

"Damn it. Just get in position."

He considered dropping Joel's drone, but only for an instant. Figuring out what the insurgents did to it could save lives.

Maria rounded the hilltop and swiveled her view toward the east. One of the technicals had flipped over, and the others were hanging back. Liz was pulling away from them and nearly at the navpoint.

"Looking good," he said. "Me and Liz are going to be limping all the way back to the FOB. Make sure the enemy keeps its distance."

"We got your six, LT," Maria said.

"Base here. Your relief is wired and ready to go. Prepare for extraction."

What the hell? "This is no place for trainees," Gardner said. "I'd rather see this one through personally."

"Sorry, sir. Orders from the colonel himself. Extraction in three, two—"

"What the hell is he—"

Gardner's sight went black. He reached for his helmet, but the tech swatted his hands away. After a brief eternity, the helmet lifted away and cool air massaged Gardner's scalp. He shut his eyes until they could adjust to the brightness of the Active Combat Room.

Colonel Spencer's gruff voice intruded on his moment of peace. "Nice job out there, Lieutenant."

Gardner turned his head toward the voice, drawing a not-so-gentle rebuke from the tech disengaging his electrodes. "Where's Hailie? Is she okay?"

"We got some good intel on the attack that—"

"Damn it, is she okay? Sir."

The colonel gave him a hard look. "She's in the infirmary. The techs pulled the plug at the first EM spike, which probably minimized the brain damage."

Gardner punched the console in front of him.

"Cool down, Lieutenant."

He swallowed a few deep breaths. "What the hell did they use on her, sir?"

"That's what we're here to find out, son. Assemble your team for a debriefing in fifteen. Then you can get some rack time while the eggheads try to figure it out."

* * *

Gardner stared at his nearly empty glass of cheap beer. Some light and fluffy synth-hop song played over the crowd noise, which only made his mood darker by comparison. He swiveled on his stool to get a quick look at his squad, surrounding a small table, downing beer. There was no joy in it tonight.

Liz glanced over and caught his eye. *Damn*. She said something and the whole table turned to look at him. Goddamn it. He turned back to the bar and swallowed the warm remnants in his glass. A hand closed on his shoulder.

"What do you want, Liz?"

"I talked to Hailie's dad this morning. It'll take some time, but they expect her to make a full recovery."

"But she'll never pilot another drone."

Liz shook her head. "She'd never get cleared for an EMEG helmet."

Gardner blew out a breath. "I sent her out there."

"She knew the risks."

"No, she didn't. No one expects any risks anymore. Not since, I don't know, Pakistan at least. It's the perfect war; no one gets hurt. A damned video game."

"It's real enough to the other side."

"I suppose so."

"Doesn't it ever bother you?"

He looked up from his empty glass. "What?"

"Getting under a rig and shooting at people. It's just so dispassionate."

"The Chinese use EMEG drones too."

"Those aren't Chinese drones we're shooting at. They're Iranians and homegrown insurgents from half the Arabian peninsula."

Gardner pounded his fist on the bar. "So what the hell do you want? Throw on fifty pounds of gear and march across the desert in person? Take a bullet to the head, or maybe just get your legs blown off?"

"I don't know. No, of course not. It's just funny how we get pissed when they come up with a way to return the favor."

"All I know is I'll be damned if I let them hurt another one of my people."

"Don't worry, LT, I'm not going soft on you. Those are my friends over there. I'll do anything I have to do to keep them safe."

"Good, because I'll be counting on you tomorrow."

"We're going back in?"

He nodded. "Brass has some intel. Could nip this whole thing right in the bud."

"They finally figured it out? What is it, some new kind of EMP?"

"They think the enemy is using some sort of microwave beamer. Sends a massive energy burst back along the comm channel."

"But the drones use frequency hopping, jump from one comm frequency to another. How the hell do they figure out what frequency we'll be on when they fire?"

"Not sure yet. Either they cycle through the spread spectrum range we use until they happen upon the right frequency at the right time, or they just sit on a frequency until we jump to it. Once the weapon gets a connection, it blasts a short megajoule burst. It's enough to burn right through the EMP buffers."

"And into the poor driver's brain." Liz whistled. "Bastards."

"And here's the kicker. It's not Iranian."

"Some local insurgent's doing it?"

"One guy, according to intel. Wrote the code, built the microwave beamer, the whole works."

"He lives in that village east of the FOB, doesn't he?" Liz said.

"Bingo. And we need to take him out before the Iranians get wind of what he's doing."

"So, what," Liz said, "we just go in and kill the guy?"

"That's the plan."

"No questions asked? No chance to surrender? That ain't us."

"It's gotta be," Gardner said. "We can't risk him getting away and spreading his technique."

"We can't just march him back to the FOB at gunpoint?"

"Say we get ambushed. He slips down a narrow alley, or up a stairway, someplace our drones can't follow. Then what?"

She was silent for a long moment. "Then let's do it. Hooah."

* * *

Liz had the squad assembled in the Active Combat Room by the time Gardner arrived. He found himself surrounded before he could close the door behind him.

"What gives, LT?" Maria said. "I hear we're getting rigged to some shiny new drones."

"Yeah, the techs are talking," Kyle said. "I wanna keep my sniper."

"We're going in urban assault drones. They want us light and fast. Except you, Kyle. You'll still be using a sniper drone."

"Damn straight."

"I don't get to fly?"

"We're down two guys, Josè. We need you on the ground. An air force wing from Texas will provide air support."

Josè opened his mouth, but Liz cut him off. "What's the plan, LT?"

"We're going after the bastard that built the pulse weapon they've been using on us."

"About time," Maria said.

"Brass is pretty sure there's only one prototype, so we stop it cold right now."

"What's it look like?" Kyle asked.

"Not sure. But it takes a lot of power, so it's probably not very portable. Probably mounted on a vehicle or hidden in a building."

"Right," Liz said. "Techs set up a code word. You see you're about to get hit with that thing, just say 'Dixie' and they'll pull your plug."

"If you see it," Maria said. "Whatever 'it' looks like."

"Exactly," Gardner said. "So keep your eyes open. They're playing for keeps."

"Wait," Kyle said. "We could actually get killed out there. I didn't sign up for that."

"The hell you didn't," Gardner said. "Soldiers fight wars. People die."

"But—"

"They took out two of our own. Not just anyone, *our* people. Joel is dead. You wanna tell his mom you were afraid to go after the son of a bitch that killed him? You gonna tell Hailie?"

"He's just a little spooked," Liz said. "Nobody's gonna pussy out on you. Right, squad?"

A few mumbles greeted her.

"I can't hear you, soldiers."

"Right!"

"Okay, get your rigs on," Gardner said. "Let's do this."

* * *

Trainees had driven the drones out to the village. Gardner's vidstream kicked in and he found himself engulfed in black smoke.

"The hell is this?" Maria said.

"The Air Force took out any insurgent fortifications they could find. Trainees must have approached under cover of the smoke."

"Why couldn't the flyboys just torch the whole village and save us the danger?"

"You want a few thousand civvie casualties on your conscience?"

There was no answer, so Gardner formed up the team and rolled into the village. Heavily damaged sandbag fortifications flanked the main road leading into the hotspot, and a pair of burning Hummers blocked the way.

"Liz, take Josè and clear a path."

"Righto, LT."

"Kyle, deploy your stabilizers. Put a bullet in anything that threatens them."

"Roger."

"Insurgents only, no civvies."

"How the hell you expect me to tell the difference?"

"Just be careful."

Gardner watched Liz's vidstream as she approached. The first bunker had a crater and smoldering debris right in the middle. Josè's stream showed the same on his side.

"And barely a scratch on the surrounding buildings," Liz said. "Kudos to the flyboys."

Gardner switched back to his own vidstream and watched Liz and Josè push one of the Hummers off the road. "Get ready to move out." He waited for Kyle to retract his stabilizers and rolled into the village behind his point team.

Wind whistled down the deserted street, carrying sand that

pinged against Gardner's armor. Nothing moved. He rolled into the town square and scanned all four ways.

"The town's not much more than a crossroad," he said. "Kyle, set up here and cover us. Liz, take Josè east. Maria, let's have a look down south."

"Roger."

He rolled past clay huts, houses or storefronts, most boarded shut. Liz's vidstream showed pretty much the same thing.

"Did you hear that?" Maria said.

"I didn't hear anything."

"I think something moved in that hut."

He zoomed on the hut. Door shut tight. Window dark. "I got nothing. Kyle, you see any—"

Ping!

His drone recoiled with an impact from behind. He turned to return fire. Just as the window slid from his view, he caught a glimpse of metal.

"RPG!"

He turned his treads at full power. Impact threw him forward, setting red telltales blinking. The EMEG rig damped the rumble of the explosion.

"You okay, Maria?"

Her guns chattered.

He turned and fired at a window on the opposite side of the street. "Maria?

"Can't get traction with my left tread."

"Damn. Liz, get your ass over here."

"Taking fire of our own, LT."

"I'm on it, Boss," Kyle said.

Gardner moved to cover Maria. Rounds pinged against his armor. *Enough*. He readied his RPG and fired through the window. Debris rained down around him.

Josè's voice registered in the back of his mind. "Whoo, these things really are fast!"

"Dixie!"

"Maria?" Gardner said. "That you?"

Nothing. Her drone stood motionless.

"Base, you evac Maria?"

Bullets pinged against his armor. He moved to take cover behind Maria's inert drone.

"She's out," base replied.

"Watch your six!" Josè's voice was followed by a muffled rumble.

"Hooah!" Liz shouted.

An RPG impacted Maria's drone, sending shrapnel flying. Gardner sent a few rounds into the window the shot came from. A bullet caught him from another direction and ricocheted off his armor.

Where the hell is that superweapon? One hit from that—

He turned to the direction of the incoming bullets and lobbed another RPG. Four more.

A noise to his right. He swiveled to put the remnants of Maria's drone in front of him. A head and shoulder, clad in desert cammo, poked through an open doorway. His hand aimed an antenna dish directly at Gardner.

Damn. Break cover to take a shot, and lights out.

Motion behind him. *Double damn.* "I could use an eye on my six, guys."

Kyle said, "On my way, Boss."

"You're too slow," Liz said. "I got this."

"Roger, Sarge."

An explosion slammed Gardner against the wrecked drone. But if he turned to face the insurgents back there—

Screw it.

He turned, fast, and fired an RPG into the hut behind him. He hesitated, expecting darkness to close on him at any moment. Footsteps to the rear.

Now!

He spun, spraying bullets as he turned. He caught the guy with the dish in the open. Another second or two and he would have had a clear shot. *Not today, bastard.*

The guy dropped in place, and the weapon fell to the dusty

road next to him. A thick cable snaked from the dish into the doorway of the building behind him.

Shots pinged against Gardner's armor from behind, followed by a burst from the north.

"Got your back, LT."

"Good to see you, Liz."

"Looks like you got this under control. You call me over just to see my pretty face?"

"I got the bastard who's been using that death weapon." Gardner swiveled over to where the insurgent lay just in time to see a figure disappear behind the door of the hut.

The weapon was gone.

"Goddamn it."

"What is it, LT?"

"We need to get that weapon. Now."

He rolled up to the door. When Liz was in position, he used his ram to break it open. She rushed through and he followed, covering her six.

"He's just a kid."

"What?" Gardner turned his vid and saw what Liz was looking at. The boy was maybe fourteen, wearing a t-shirt and jeans, and cowering in the corner next to a table covered in capacitors and battery packs. His right hand held the dish limply at his side.

"American pigs. You killed him."

Gardner turned on his drone's external speaker. "It's war. He was trying to kill me."

"We defend ourselves. You send machines. I make it fair."

"Just drop the weapon, son. No one wants to hurt you."

"Did he just say that he's the one who made the weapon?" Liz said in his audio stream.

"My invention will kill a thousand Americans for every Arab who died in this war."

"Christ," Gardner said into the stream. "The kid's a computer genius."

"What do we do, LT? If he tells the Iranians—"

"We have to kill him."

"In cold blood?" Liz said.

"It's the only way." He raised his gun. "I'm sorry," he said through his speaker. The boy cowered.

Gardner hesitated. The kid's lower lip trembled. He looked like a lost little boy, a good five years younger than Joel. *Mothers cry here, too.*

He lowered his gun. "Just give me the weapon."

A shot rang out and the boy crumpled in the corner. Smoke rose from Liz's gun.

"What the hell?"

"Had to be done, LT."

Gardner picked up the weapon with his manipulator arm and unplugged the cable from its base. His treads kicked up dirt from the floor and he was out the door.

"You said so, right?"

The uncertainty in her voice would haunt him forever. He rolled toward the rendezvous point in the village square. A quick scan of the squad's feeds showed that Josè and Kyle were already there.

"Base, mission accomplished," he said. "Now get some trainees to drive these goddamned drones home."

"Roger, recon. Prepare for extraction."

The world went dark. Gardner sat limp in his chair, in no hurry to get the helmet off. The tech lifted the helmet and he faced the glare of the Active Combat Room with open eyes.

A hand closed on his shoulder. "I'm so glad you made it out of there okay," Maria said. "I'm sorry I bailed on you like that. He had it aimed—"

"You did what you had to do."

The tech said, "Colonel wants to debrief you immediately, sir."

Gardner blew out a breath and nodded. He lifted himself from the EMEG chair. Liz sat next to him, her dreads emerging from her helmet. She blinked away the brightness and looked directly at him with haunted eyes.

"I did the right thing, LT. Didn't I?"

He stared at her, seeing his guilt reflected in her eyes. "How the hell should I know?"

EMERALDS

Asher Wismer

"...ten years since the first Stalker ships appeared in our skies. Again, our top story tonight, more invading aliens in the sky, distracting United Earth forces from an all-out assault against the Flying City, which touched down in Columbia two months ago. Scientists believe the Flying City to be a base of operations. As the Stalker language cannot be interpreted, and the Stalkers themselves refuse any form of communication, the motive behind humanity's ongoing war of survival remains unclear. From NORAD, this is CNN."

Ten years. I checked my gun again, remembering the day First Contact had become The Last War. The battlesuit chafed; it wasn't mine, but a spare from storage, unused for years.

"Today's my birthday," I said to Rico.

"Old lady," he said. His battlesuit was painted with jagged yellow stripes; he claimed it disoriented the Stalkers, and nobody wanted to argue.

"Hope it won't be your last," Boss said. As the leader, he wore a battlesuit twice the size of ours. He also carried the Pulse, the only weapon that could take down a Berserker – I'd seen only one in seven years of battle.

Rico handed me a piece of gum. "Happy day," he said.

Most of the squad sat in silence. There were no fixed units anymore; fewer soldiers every day, going wherever the United Earth sent us. We formed, fought, died, and reformed so many times that it was unusual for even two soldiers to know each other. The only thing we all had in common was our training.

We did the best we could. Every day more of them appeared in the sky. They never tried to talk, just landed and killed.

The chopper rattled. Boss stood and spoke with the pilot, then came back and addressed us.

"This is not a normal mission," he said. "We are not going out against the Coast ships per our initial orders."

"We going on vacation?" Rico said.

"The Coast ships are sapping our ability to fight effectively. Too many units are being destroyed while the aliens gain ground. This unit was handpicked. Every soldier in this chopper has more than fifty drops. Between us, we have over seventy million confirmed kills. You individuals don't think of yourselves as special, but believe me, you are all the best in our force."

I jabbed Rico with my elbow. "Could fool me," I said. Boss was right, though – this was my fifty-first drop.

"We are taking the Flying City," Boss said. "Not simply attacking. Today is the day we take control back. All previous missions failed. We no longer have that luxury. If the City is truly their base of operations, we must control or destroy it. UE forces are massed by the Coast, but we have secret forces arrayed around the City. While they keep it occupied, we will go in and take whatever steps are necessary to stay in."

"Is this a suicide mission?" someone asked.

Boss stared at all of us. "Not if we can help it. Each of your suits has been modified with a data connector, built from wrecked Stalker ships..."

* * *

I fired into the mass. Rico had my back, and two others were killing waves of the tiny Stalkers from the left. Boss was at the right, Pulse ready.

"Think that was the last Berserker?" Rico shouted.

"Fuckin' better be," I said, and fired a grenade to the front. The advancing pile of aliens exploded in a yellow shockwave.

To the left, the Stalkers piled again and had taken one of the guards down. That was how they killed us, as small as they were. Using their own bodies as shields and support, they swarmed and overwhelmed, and they were surprisingly strong.

Boss flicked his lights, and we pushed ahead. The halls of the Flying City vibrated, sometimes from explosions, mostly from whatever ungodly energy kept it alive. A hatch fell and they swarmed Rico; I thrust in, switching gun to knives, and we slashed them apart. Behind us, Boss fired the Pulse.

"Another?" I said.

"Too many little ones," Boss yelled. "We lost Jensen and Ackles. I collapsed the corridor."

Rico breathed obscenities as he smeared the Stalkers across the walls, slamming his body against them. Boss joined us and the corridor grew grey with their blood.

The last one had my leg in its teeth. As Rico checked his suit, I pulled it off and held it up. It screamed at me, flailing and ripping at my hand. Singles can't hurt a battlesuit, but they could bring back their friends.

"Lost contact with the unit," Boss said. "We have to assume we're the last ones."

"Do we even know where we're going?" Rico said.

"Radar scans show a central area, and electromagnetic scans show a massive power source. Whatever they're doing, it comes from that center."

"So we find it and blow it up?"

"Command wants us to gather data," Boss said. "If we can't use it against them...."

The alien latched its teeth into my wrist. I couldn't feel it through the armor.

"Somebody found a little pet," Rico said.

I squeezed it until its head popped off.

There were more corridors ahead. With Boss on point, I held the rear. Outside, battles were horrifying, the aliens unconstrained and destroying everything in sight. Still, every time they swarmed from the ceiling or floor I had a shock of terror, quickly clamped down by my instincts.

Their skin was blue, rocky, not entirely biological. Scientists suspected they were grown rather than born. Each one transmitted a rough feeling through the sensors in my palms. I'd never seen one without my suit on. I never wanted to.

Another wave, and this time from a side corridor; they filled it with their screaming bodies, swarming over each other as if a single being. Boss raised the Pulse, lowered it; the backwave would kill us.

"Pincer!" I shouted to Boss, and he nodded.

Rico filled the hallway with fire. Our guns are designed for the tiny Stalkers; I pushed forward, vaguely feeling the sting of flechettes on my armor, and then I was in the swarm.

On purpose, this time. The key is don't give them time to get their claws in my joints; I moved without thinking, the blades running down my forearms and shins slicing, a blender of blood and viscera. The martial arts we learned at West Point were worthless here. Fifty drops gave me the skills I needed, each Stalker bursting on my blades as they pushed in.

Even in the face of death, they never back off, never seem to communicate or pass information back. Every swarm attacks exactly as the last. My plan was to pass through the swarm, where I could open fire and we'd whittle it down twice as fast.

I seemed to reach the back of the swarm, it was still moving towards Boss and Rico. Ahead, I saw a cavernous space, lit purple and blue, and something huge, moving, stopping, looking at me.

A Berserker.

As large as Boss's enormous battlesuit, covered in metallic purple skin, with claws and teeth sharper than glass. I'd never seen one up close; the two we'd killed today had ravaged the unit, only the Pulse able to take them out.

My gun wouldn't even scratch it. Instinct took over. I pulled the deadman on my grenade belt, threw it, and pushed back into the swarm. I keyed my emergency power and ran, stomping through the Stalkers. They bit and scratched, but couldn't gain purchase, exploding under my feet and against my helmet. Behind me, a shockwave slammed through the swarm and blew me into the air; I hurtled down and crashed against the opposite wall. Rico and Boss were still there, still fighting.

"The hell happened to you?" Boss shouted.

"Berserker!" I screamed. "We have to go!"

The swarm burst and the Berserker was on us. Boss, his suit keyed to full power, met it head on.

"We have to get to the center!" he shouted. "Go on ahead!"

"You can't kill it without using the Pulse!" Rico said.

"Get through!"

We ran past. Time slowed; Boss had chainsaws built around the suit gloves and each strike drew grey blood. The Berserker had no control; it flailed without strategy, sparks flying as the claws raked. The armor would fall.

Boss spun the monster with a mighty punch, and in the same moment pulled the Pulse from his back and hurled it to me.

"Stay alive!" he shouted, and the Berserker bit down on his arm. Boss locked his joints; his chainsaw hand pushed further down the Berserker's throat, his other hand keeping its claws away.

"We have to save him!"

I grabbed Rico's arm and pulled him away, down the long corridor towards the cavern.

Another shockwave threw us into the air, this time filling our eyes with emerald light.

* * *

"Fucking bitch," Rico said. The cavern was almost empty, a central dome and a few strange structures, and the single large door. For the moment, we were alone.

"There wasn't enough room for the Pulse," I said. "Boss knew that and so do you. Even if we'd tried to fight with him it would have ripped us apart. Our suits are designed for the little ones."

"You let him die."

"He saved us with the Pulse bomb in his suit."

"For what? There's nothing here!"

I looked around. It was quiet. Noise vibrating through the City told me the battle outside raged on.

"Maybe Boss scared them off with the explosion," Rico said. He held by the door. "You remember the way out?"

"There's a shaft above, past that grate and shielded from the outside. Boss said our suits could climb it if we can get through."

"So," Rico said. "We made it. Do that data thing and let's jet."

The central dome, glowing purple, had screens, keypads, and a data port. The cable on my suit led to a storage drive, reverse-engineered from Stalker ships. I plugged it in and the firmware automatically started downloading.

"Any day now," Rico said. "I can hear noises from the corridor."

Stalker language could not be translated, at least not yet. I examined the keypads and pushed a few buttons. Some of the screens lit up, but I couldn't understand the writing or even the layout.

"Come on!"

My suit pinged. It was full.

"Your turn," I said, walking to the door.

"No way. We need to get out of here."

"Rico," I said. "Get the data."

He glared, but walked to the dome and plugged in. I hefted the Pulse and checked my power. A blast from the Pulse would knock me over if I wasn't ready.

I heard chittering gibberish from the corridor. Down where Boss had died, shadows and echoes headed our way.

"Rico! Grenades!"

He tossed his grenade belt to me. I loaded my gun and waited.

The first Stalkers came round the corner. They were just walking, moving in that awful stop-motion, and then one saw me and screamed. Instantly the corridor filled. The grenade coated the walls with gray blood then I sprayed the corridor with bullets. They swarmed and I cut them down. So many this time. Millions, perhaps. There was no way to count them, and as the corridor filled with their bodies Rico joined me.

"What now?"

I pointed. "Up!" We backed away. Even by myself I might have held the corridor, controlled sweeps mowing the Stalkers down in a confined space, but as soon as they reached the door they swarmed up and around the walls, surrounding us. I fired a hook up to the grate, and it popped off, shattering Stalker bodies. Rico appeared at my side, helped me up, and together we fought them off, head and torsos flying, grey blood spattering.

As the swarm lessened, I let Rico hold them off while I rewound my winch. When I got to my feet, a Berserker appeared in the doorway and roared. I swung the Pulse from my back and fired. The emerald ball annihilated the Berserker where it stood, smashing the walls and flinging us back. Most of the Stalkers were dead.

Another roar from the corridor, and another. I fired my hook up and it stuck to the shaft wall.

"Rico!"

He grabbed me around the shoulders and waist, and I hit the winch. A Berserker, larger than the others, ran into the room and leaped. Its claws sank into Rico's leg and he screamed. The winch groaned.

I knew it wouldn't hold. Rico's eyes met mine, and he let me go at the same time as I grabbed his hook, fired it, then fired a grenade from my gun directly down into the Berserker's face. It let go, and we swung free.

Dazed, the Berserker staggered to its feet. I hit buttons on the Pulse, dropped it.

"What are you doing?" Rico screamed.

"Up," I shouted at him. "Now! As far as we can!"

We rose. The Berserker leaped again, but missed, and then we were in the shaft and rising. When we reached our hooks, I grabbed Rico's wrist and pointed.

"Up!"

He unhooked, fired, and held me while I did the same. We rose.

An unholy explosion, larger than the grenade belt or Boss's Pulse bomb, rocked the City. It rose up the shaft, the green light overloading my helmet. I punched one hand into the wall of the shaft and held on as the shockwave ripped at my body. I couldn't see anything.

Finally, the sound and fury dimmed. My helmet switched back on.

"You bitch," Rico said. His voice sounded like a smile.

"Whatever it takes," I said. "We promised Boss."

* * *

"...again, our top story tonight. As UE forces push the invaders back, early reports are that data from the Flying City allowed experts to make the first translations of Stalker text. According to our source, who must remain unnamed, the aliens that have been plaguing our planet did not arrive with evil intent. In fact, they wished to make peaceful contact.

"However, the untested faster-than-light system the Stalkers used to travel to us apparently drives sentient beings insane. Once they arrived they started killing. Subsequent ships continue this practice, as they have never reported back to their home planet. Scientists are hopeful Stalker technology may make faster-than-light communication possible, finally ending this terrible war. From NORAD, this is CNN."

Thanks for reading SNAFU: Future Warfare.

We hope you've enjoyed it as much as we did putting it together.

Please consider leaving us a review if (and anywhere) you see fit. Any and all reviews are gratefully accepted.

If you have any questions, or want to quote from the book, please contact us at any time via our website contact page.

I would ask please, if you DO review online, send a link to Geoff via editor@cohesionpress.com or via our Facebook page messaging system. If you review for a magazine or paper, let us know and we'll buy it.

Thank you.

\+ + +

Geoff Brown - Director, Cohesion Press.
Mayday Hills Asylum
Beechworth, Australia

Amanda J Spedding - Editor-in-chief, Cohesion Press
Sydney, Australia

www.ingramcontent.com/pod-product-compliance
Ingram Content Group UK Ltd.
Pitfield, Milton Keynes, MK11 3LW, UK
UKHW041630190726
13854UKWH00006B/2414

9 789781 925627